THOSE WHO GO
BY NIGHT

THOSE WHO GO
BY NIGHT

A NOVEL

Andrew Gaddes

CROOKED
LANE

NEW YORK

Published in the United States by Crooked Lane Books, an imprint of The Quick Brown Fox & Company LLC.

Crooked Lane Books and its logo are trademarks of The Quick Brown Fox & Company LLC.

Library of Congress Catalog-in-Publication data available upon request.

ISBN (hardcover): 978-1-68331-840-8
ISBN (ePub): 978-1-68331-841-5
ISBN (ePDF): 978-1-68331-842-2

Cover design by Andy Ruggirello
Book design by Jennifer Canzone

Printed in the United States.

www.crookedlanebooks.com

Crooked Lane Books
34 West 27th St., 10th Floor
New York, NY 10001

First Edition: November 2018

10 9 8 7 6 5 4 3 2 1

*This book is dedicated to my godmother,
Olive Mary Arthur, a remarkable woman
who lived a quiet life of selfless love.
Gone, but never forgotten.*

Some have asserted that witchcraft is nothing in the world but an imagining of men who ascribed to spells those natural effects the causes of which are hidden . . . But such assertions are rejected by the true faith whereby we believe that angels fell from heaven, and that the demons exist, and that by reason of their subtle nature they are able to do many things which we cannot; and those who induce them to do such things are called wizards.
—St. Thomas Aquinas, The Summa Theologica

CHAPTER 1

England, 1324, during the Reign of Edward II

Nothing quite ages a man like penury, unless perhaps it is disappointment. And in the last few years, Roger Lacy had experienced more than his fair share of both. In fact, had you seen him that night, making his way slowly down the dark village street, you might well have supposed his were the sad, shuffling steps of a vagabond. You might have shaken your head in pity and thought, *There goes a man who has been broken on life's wheel. Just another poor soul who believes that he has little left to live for, and even less to offer the world.* And on any other night, you would have been right. But on that particular night, you would have been wrong, because as pitiful as he might have seemed, Roger Lacy's luck had turned. His luck had turned at last.

The old man tugged at his cloak, drawing it closer against the chill autumn air. It had once been a wealthy man's cloak, made of the finest wool and dyed a rich Lincoln green, but the color had long since faded, and rather like its owner, it was now a drab, shabby-looking thing, with loose threads hanging from the hem and several tears sorely in need of mending.

Roger was ashamed of his attire, of how far he had fallen, but comforted himself that things would be different now. His hand fluttered nervously to the breast of his tunic, and he sighed with relief when he felt the reassuring bulge and crinkle of the precious letters tucked inside. Those few sheets of vellum with their hastily inscribed lines represented a new beginning for him. Tomorrow he could walk into town with his head held high and buy a brand new cloak. If he saw a nice felt cap, he might just buy that as well, and a pair of warm woolen hose and boots made of the supplest Cordova leather.

"As fine as a lord you'll look!" he cackled into his ratty white beard. "Oh yes, indeed. As fine as a lord!"

And didn't he deserve a little happiness after all that he had endured, after years of wandering village to village like a beggar, eating scraps from other men's tables, sleeping more often under a hedge than under a roof? It was almost as though he had been cursed or as if God was punishing him for some terrible sin.

"Now, now, old man," he chided himself. "Things will be better now. The mistress will see to that."

Roger turned his steps from the main street toward the church, feeling an overwhelming need to give thanks, and almost walked straight into the young woman hurrying around the corner in the other direction.

"A thousand apologies, my lady," he rasped, offering her a strangely formal and somewhat wobbly bow.

She was swathed from head to toe in an elegant hooded cloak as black as the night itself. Two eyes glittered with amusement, and from within the shadows of the hood, Roger caught the curve of a cheek and the gleam of an even set of white teeth. *A pretty face,* he thought. And she had smiled at him! He could scarcely remember when a pretty girl had last smiled at him that way, and it filled him with a pleasant tingling sensation that spread from his belly, across his loins, and all the way down to his toes. Then she swept past him and was gone, leaving behind only a faint fragrance of rosewater and lavender.

Roger straightened himself up with a groan. He could only imagine she was off to some tryst. Ordinarily he might have scowled with disapproval and made a bitter remark about loosening morals, but his change in fortune found him in a generous frame of mind, and he could honestly say that he felt nothing but joy for the girl and for her lucky young man, whoever he might be.

Saint Mary's Church now loomed darkly ahead, its square tower rising up to blot out the night sky. He had half-expected to find it closed and was pleasantly surprised when the wicket door opened under his hand and swung slowly inward, its sullen iron hinges squealing in protest at the unexpected visitor.

Inside, the church was vast, dark, and empty. Only a little moonlight managed to sift through the stained glass windows, dusting the nave here and there with a sickly yellow color, and the distant glow from the altar lamps cast not so much pools of light as two reddish puddles. Otherwise, the church was shrouded almost completely in shadow and in even deeper darkness.

And it was quiet. Far too quiet for Roger's liking. As he shuffled down the nave toward the altar, the only sound he could hear was the scuffing and scraping of his own worn-out shoes on the stone flagged floor. It also smelled funny—a vaguely unpleasant odor of mildew, dust, and decay that made his nose wrinkle. Then there were those several rather disturbing shapes lurking in the deep recesses of the transepts on either side of him. Roger supposed they might have been statues or tombs. At least he hoped so. But he did not know for sure. Nor did he particularly feel like venturing into the gloom to find out.

The farther he progressed into the church, the more oppressive and ominous the darkness became, and the more he began to wonder if stopping to pray had been such a good idea after all. He stood a moment, frozen in hesitation, gnawing his lip, tempted to turn around and bolt for the door. But he was more than halfway down the nave now, and it was even darker behind him than ahead, so he swallowed slowly and pressed onward, his limping pace quickening to take him past the heavy oak rood screen separating the sanctuary from the rest of the church, and then up the steps to the altar itself.

Roger knelt down gingerly on stiff, complaining knees and looked despondently at the hands he pressed limply together in front of him. He could no longer unclench them fully since the rheum had set in, and they resembled claws more than anything else, the fingers all twisted and crooked, and the knuckles little more than swollen lumps bedded in wrinkles. Long ago, when he had been the steward of a great estate, many a beggar had come before him, seeking his largesse, honored that a man such as he would even deign to speak with them. Roger supposed that those beggars must have looked much as he did now—men and women in the winter of their years, with one foot already planted firmly in the grave. At the time he had thought them pathetic, naturally, but mostly sad, and had never dreamed that he might one day count himself among them.

Tearing his eyes away from his broken hands, and mentally adding a nice pair of fleece-lined gloves to the purchases he would make in town, Roger had just begun to move his lips in silent prayer when he heard a faint noise behind him. Turning his head stiffly, he cocked an ear and listened with baited breath. There was nothing, only the wind gusting lightly against the windows.

"Is anybody there?" he called out in a croaky voice. Nobody answered. He was alone.

"Silly old fool," he muttered to himself. "I swear you have become as nervous as a clucking chicken."

But there it was again, unmistakable this time: a footfall, soft and furtive, as though someone was trying not to be heard. And there was another, much closer now, almost at the sanctuary itself. An icy finger traced its way down his spine, and he clambered to his feet, greatly regretting his sudden burst of piety.

"Who is there?" he shouted, peering long and hard into the blackness.

Still nobody answered.

"I am sorry if I am intruding," he stammered, licking his lips nervously. "I have leave to be in the village. I just felt the need to pray for a moment."

He waited anxiously, his ears straining against the silence.

"I—I am not a vagabond. I am a guest of Lady Isabella."

Roger offered up what he hoped was a companionable chuckle that soon died on his lips when the hooded figure slowly emerged into the fringe of light spilling from the altar lamps. He felt the hairs on the back of his neck stand up in horror, and he barely noticed the sudden dampness spreading across his loins or the sour scent that assailed his nostrils, because in that dreadful moment Roger Lacy knew that his luck had turned again for one very last time.

CHAPTER 2

H is Grace, Henry Burghersh, the Bishop of Lincoln, plumped himself down onto a well-padded chair and tossed his miter at the nearest table, where it wobbled about uncertainly before toppling over into a puddle of red wine.

"Another long day, Thomas," he said with a sigh, turning to the young man standing in the middle of the room. "I would never have accepted the position had I known it meant sitting through hours of such utter tedium."

The bishop was a stocky, jolly fellow with a florid complexion that bespoke either rude health or high living. He had a high-pitched, almost feminine voice and a cherubic face that had deceived many an opponent into underestimating the shrewd, political mind that had propelled him to the bishopric at an astoundingly young age.

He squirmed about uncomfortably, nestling himself deeper into the cushions. "My back aches fiercely, and my bum has gone completely numb from sitting on that stupid chair they laughingly call my throne. I can't imagine what my predecessor was thinking having the thing made in the first place. I would burn it for firewood, but then I would no doubt be accused of a terrible break with tradition. Sacrilege even." He winced and shifted gingerly from one buttock to the other. "I tell you, it doesn't matter how many cushions you pile on the damned thing, it seems to have been designed as an implement of torture. I swear Bishop Beck must have had an arse made of iron."

By now, Thomas was used to the bishop's complaints and waited patiently for them to run their course.

"And these wealthy burghers will do anything for a few years off their stay in purgatory, you know. The silversmith's wife positively offered herself to me in return for a dispensation of fifty years. Can you imagine?"

Actually, knowing the lady in question, Thomas rather suspected that she would have offered herself for free, but he allowed his benefactor to revel for a moment in his imagined conquest.

"She got quite desperate when I rejected her. Suggested that she might perform all sorts of depraved acts. I was blushing to my toes, Thomas. To my very toes."

Thomas doubted that. Henry Burghersh had been a man of the world long before he had begun his meteoric rise through the ranks of the clergy, and he was rumored to have had quite the appetite where the fairer sex was concerned. Likely he had enjoyed and even encouraged his flirtatious encounter with the lascivious dame.

The bishop narrowed his eyes thoughtfully. "I must confess, some of the things she proposed did sound rather interesting, though, and she still has a shapely figure to her, don't you think? Nice and plump. Just the way I used to like them."

He winked at Thomas and pumped his arms and hips vigorously back and forth to help illustrate his point.

"For a moment I was sorely tempted to take her up on her offer. Sorely tempted. Though I suppose it would have been truly wicked of me," he added as an afterthought. "I shan't tell you what she suggested, Thomas. No, I couldn't possibly do so. It would be too shocking by half. Quite impolitic of me."

He looked up expectantly and was plainly disappointed

when Thomas chose not to inquire any further. So instead, he sighed wistfully and sketched a quick cross over his chest.

"And Baron Linden has been at his scullery maids again."

"Scullery maids, Your Grace? Wasn't it the stable boys last time?"

The bishop stroked his chin thoughtfully. "Hmmm. Yes, I believe you might be right at that. Scullery maids. Stable boys. Either way, it's all a bit off, isn't it? He wanted me to grant him some sort of indulgence and didn't care how much it cost. You should have heard him blubbing away, Thomas: *'Never again, Your Grace. By all that is holy, I swear, never again.'* The same kind of nonsense all drunkards spout after a particularly rough night on the town. Shocking stuff, really. I told him to keep his breeches on and get his sorry arse to his chaplain for confession. Indulgence, indeed! A sound thrashing would be more to the point. And likely he'll get one when Lady Linden finds out."

He eased the shoes off his feet and stretched out his toes, sighing with pleasure.

"The Good Book says that it is harder for a rich man to enter heaven than for a camel to pass through the eye of a needle. I remember reading that once, and I do believe it to be true. Have you ever seen a camel, Thomas?"

"I cannot say that I have."

"No, me neither," continued the bishop with a sad shake of his head. "I understand it to be an utterly terrifying beast. A grotesque, horselike creature, by all accounts, with a huge snout, cloven feet, and two humps on its back shaped rather like a pair of giant breasts. Imagine trying to fit such a thing through the eye of a needle. No, it's a sorry lookout for the rich, I am afraid. I fear for Baron Linden's soul. I surely do."

It was Thomas's turn to sigh. "Why am I here, Your Grace?"

The bishop looked up in mock surprise. "Why, Thomas, because I have missed you. I barely get to see you these days."

After a moment of unimpressed silence from Thomas, he rummaged around on his desk and picked up a sealed letter. "Now that you mention it, however, I should like you to take this letter of introduction to Sir Mortimer de Bray, Lord of Bottesford Manor. He will be expecting you."

"Bottesford?" Thomas asked, taking the proffered papers. "Why am I going to Bottesford?"

"Oh, there's a terrible fuss, Thomas. A dead priest. Murder. The high altar of Saint Mary's has been profaned." He pursed his lips. "A shame that. It's a lovely little village church. I visited once, you know. I remember there was the prettiest oak *reredos* behind the altar that had the most vivid depiction of the Messiah's birth. The look of wonder on the shepherds' faces was almost lifelike. I had half a mind to bring it back with me and would likely have done so if I had been traveling with a baggage cart."

Thomas chose to ignore the apparent laxity with which his benefactor regarded what sounded suspiciously like theft. "How was the high altar profaned?"

The bishop waved his hand dismissively. "Oh, I don't know exactly. I am sure you can get the details once you are there. Anyway, I understand the Dominicans are all up in arms about it, crying heresy and sorcery. You know, the usual things."

"Bottesford is a long way from Lincoln."

"It most certainly is. I suggest that you leave tonight."

"That was not what I meant, Your Grace. What is your interest in the matter?"

The bishop leaned forward and rested his elbows on his knees, fingers steepled under his chin. When he next spoke, all the levity was gone from his voice.

"What I am about to tell you is dangerous, Thomas, very dangerous. I must trust in your discretion." He paused a moment, collecting his thoughts. "I am afraid His Holiness, the pope, is not of an entirely sound mind. He sees heretics and assassins leaping out at him from every shadow. Did you know that he believes his enemies are casting spells against him? Actual spells! He truly believes it and spends most of his time huddled in his chambers, surrounded by the protection of every holy relic he can lay his hands on. How the man became pontiff in the first place, I'll never know. And I fear he gets worse with each passing year.

"Then there is that poisonous snake, his mad inquisitor general, Bernard de Gui, whispering in his ear. Scaring him with tall tales of sorcery and witches. Feeding his paranoia. All so he can expand his own little empire of heretic hunters.

"De Gui is a complete fanatic. They say he has prosecuted a thousand cases of heresy in Toulouse alone, and he is champing at the bit to get his claws into England. He well knows that many of the old customs linger here, and he senses a weakness in our king, as well he might. Edward is not the man his father was. I think he is half mad himself, and still deeply unpopular with the people.

"The last thing we need over here is some sort of inquisition. Nobody will be safe. No," he shook his head, a determined look in his eyes, "there will be no return to the shame of the Templar trials in England if I can help it."

Thomas's eye twitched, and the bishop shot him an apologetic glance.

"I am sorry, Thomas. I sometimes forget. I did not mean to resurrect old injuries, my friend. Anyway, I shan't have that. Not again. And I am not alone in my concerns. There are certain other interested parties who are of a like mind with me. But we shall not speak of them yet."

Thomas replied cautiously. "I have told you that I do not want to become involved in this sort of thing anymore, Your Grace. You know my history."

"It is precisely *because* of your rather unique history that you are most suited to this, Thomas. You of all people know what these fools can be like when they get the bit between their teeth and the stench of heresy in their nostrils."

Thomas dropped down wearily into one of the bishop's fancy chairs.

"These are turbulent times, Thomas. The rebellion has not been forgotten. The Earl of Lancaster's supporters are hiding in the rushes. Mortimer has escaped from the Tower. I doubt we have heard the last of him. And now we are at war with the French."

"I try to stay away from politics, Your Grace."

"Oh, I know you would prefer to hide away in your library, surrounded by your dusty tomes, but the time is coming when we must take part in events lest they simply overwhelm us. He who straddles the fence for too long is likely to get a sore arse, Thomas. A very sore arse indeed."

The bishop lowered his voice and leaned a little closer.

"It is not just fanatics like De Gui who concern me. There are those to whom the Inquisition would be a useful political tool. King Philip used it to purge the Templars, and Edward might easily be persuaded that it serves his own purposes. I do not know if you are aware, Thomas, but I am not exactly in the king's good graces myself."

Thomas was indeed aware. For years England had been teetering on the edge of rebellion. Appalled at King Edward's ineffectual Scottish wars, his extortionate fiscal practices, and the gross excesses of his various favorites, a powerful group of barons, led by the Earl of Lancaster, had finally risen in rebellion. Although he had not exactly *favored* the barons in the ensuing conflict, nor had the bishop been particularly vocal in his support of the king. As a result, with the rebel forces soundly defeated, he found himself completely out of favor at court, and his many enemies were now circling about him like a flock of graveyard crows, only too ready to take advantage of his fall from grace.

"Thankfully, I am not yet friendless. Were the Inquisition to arrive on our shores, however, I imagine I would be one of its first victims. And it would not end there."

"And my reward?" Thomas asked after a considered silence.

"Reward?" the bishop scoffed, his lips twitching. "I would have thought that the peace of the realm and the solace of seeing proper justice done would be more than enough reward for you. And I seem to recall that I already pay you a handsome allowance."

Thomas stared back stonily. It was not the first time they'd had this discussion. The meager allowance to which the bishop referred was actually more in the nature of a retainer, for which Thomas worked damned hard, representing the bishop in any number of those personal and business affairs with which his benefactor would rather not soil his lily-white hands. The arrangement was nevertheless a satisfactory one for Thomas, and certainly preferable to selling his services in yet another pointless border war, but it had never been intended to encompass matters such as these—matters, as he kept telling the bishop, in which he really did not wish to become involved.

"As it happens, however, I have only recently acquired a rather special artifact. Something I think the Church might be willing to entrust to your stewardship. It would make a nice addition to your . . . collection."

"Is it something better than the splinter from the true cross that turned out to be a cutting from a dogwood tree?"

Bishop Henry looked genuinely hurt.

"That was an honest mistake, Thomas."

"An honest mistake? There are no dogwoods in Palestine,

Your Grace. A splinter of the true cross, and it wasn't even cypress wood."

The bishop squirmed about guiltily.

"I swear to you it came with papers, with genuine articles of authenticity."

Thomas rolled his eyes. "So, what is it this time? A hair from the beard of Saint Francis? A toenail shorn from the foot of Saint Andrew the Apostle?"

"Now you are just being mean. You know I would never attempt to foist such things off on you. I am not some petty relic peddler. No, this is a truly precious item left to my diocese by a grateful parishioner who only wished me to say a mass for his soul. I am sure you will appreciate it, and I would rather you become its protector than it lie collecting dust among the other scrolls in the cathedral *librarium*."

Thomas's eyes flared wide. So, it was some sort of writing. That intrigued him. He had always possessed a reverence for the written word and a thirst for the wisdom that an ancient text might impart. The bishop was well aware of his weakness and not at all above using it to his own advantage.

"And must I remind you that I helped you in your time of need, Thomas? That I took you in when all others spurned you?"

"Why not remind me, Your Grace? You do so every time you ask me for a favor," Thomas replied with a wry smile.

The bishop chuckled. "Ah, have I become so predictable? But then so are you. I already know you will say yes. So what say we skip this merry dance and get you on your way?"

He rose without waiting for an answer, patted Thomas companionably on the shoulder, and walked him over to the door.

"And what if I do find heresy? What if there is even sorcery?"

"The chances of that are rather slim, don't you think? These things are usually the work of some criminal with a depraved mind. Thankfully it has been some time since we had an honest-to-God heretic, let alone a necromancer. Should that be the case, however, I expect you to deal with it quickly and quietly. Rumors of heretical practices are quite bad enough. The real thing would be disastrous. We would face the full fury of the Holy See and all its Dominican inquisitors. No, that would not do at all. In the unlikely event that you find heresy, Thomas, I think you know what to do."

The bishop squeezed Thomas's shoulder and gave him a slow, conspiratorial nod. "The same thing you did with Timothy of York."

Timothy of York was a sad old man, full of unspent lust, who believed that communing with demons would give him power over women, and over one widow, in particular, who had tickled his fancy. Incantations had been made, false idols worshipped, and countless chickens sacrificed, Timothy becoming ever more desperate as no demons answered his summons and the widow continued to spurn his advances. The bishop had dispatched Thomas to *make the problem go away*, as he had put it. For some reason, he believed Thomas had done so by *offing* the old man in the most violent fashion and that Timothy's savagely dismembered body now lay buried somewhere under the muddy banks of the River Ouse. He seemed perfectly content with this scenario, and whenever Thomas tried to persuade him otherwise, would simply shake his head, wag his finger in the air, and smile knowingly, as though they were sharing a particularly salacious little secret.

He would be surprised to know that Timothy of York was in fact not dead, but merely living in Dumfries, Scotland, where he no doubt still practiced the dark arts and was still unsuccessful in his attempts at magically wooing Scottish widows, for no amount of dead chickens could change the fact that Timothy was a truly ugly man, with a warty face and breath that could fell an ox at twenty paces.

"Well," exclaimed the bishop happily, stretching and pressing a hand to his aching back, "I shan't keep you, Thomas. You have much to do, and I need a nice warm bath. And then I believe I must visit the prioress at Stixwould. She has some young initiates she wishes to introduce to me. They are quite charming, apparently. Lovely creatures. The prioress has high hopes for them and is keen for me to further their spiritual edification. I must say I am looking forward to it."

The bishop caught Thomas's incredulous look.

"Good Lord, Thomas! You really need to get your mind out of the runnels. What on earth did you think I was suggesting?" He dusted irritably at a speck of dirt on his sleeve. "Honestly, I sometimes wonder about you. For that matter, you could do with finding a nice woman yourself." He stared at Thomas. "And I mean a *nice* young woman, Thomas, not one of your old doxies from the hovels by the River Witham. A good, honest swiving with a nice, clean wench would do you a world of good. You need to stop this mooning about over lost loves and begin to move on with your life. You are becoming quite a bore, what with your fits of melancholy and your prudish behavior. How long has it been since you had a good woman anyway?"

Thomas did not bother to respond. In truth he had not had *a good, honest swiving*, as the bishop had so elegantly put it, for a long time.

The bishop looked Thomas up and down disapprovingly. "And while we're on the subject, it is high time you did something about your appearance. I mean, just look at you, man! What on earth do you do with the money I pay you? I would think you could afford a nice doublet or a cambric shirt. And a bit of color here and there, instead of those dull browns and grays, would help. You really are turning into a terrible rustic. Honestly, I half-expect you to walk in here one day dressed in one of those ridiculous farmer's smocks with your hose rolled down around your ankles and a pair of sod-covered clogs on your feet."

"Why do you care what I look like, Your Grace?"

"I care because you are on my business, Thomas, and being on my business, you represent me. I also hope to see you settled down some day with a nice young woman. You are a handsome man, Thomas, but you are not likely to catch anyone's eye dressed like that."

A sly look came over the bishop's face, and he plucked at his sleeve, trying his hardest to feign nonchalance. "Now that I mention it, I seem to remember that De Bray does have a rather attractive daughter. Cecily, I believe is her name. She seemed a might uptight for my liking; too serious by half, and too skinny as well. Not nearly enough for a man to grab hold of."

He pumped his arms and hips again, to leave Thomas in no doubt of his meaning.

"But I suppose she might do for you. I can see it now. The two of you sitting together on one of the resting benches in her father's garden, a cloud of melancholy hovering above, the sullen silence broken only by an occasional spouting of some old Greek or Roman verse. It will be something suitably deep and morbid— Plutarch's *Moralia*, perhaps, or something of that ilk. And, naturally, each of you will be striving to outdo the other with the profundity of your selection and the gravity of your recitation.

"Yes, I dare say that the two of you should get along very well. And I am sure that if you chip away diligently enough at the ice, you will find underneath a deep pool of good, honest lust just waiting for you to dive in and splash about. Who knows? Perhaps you shall kill two birds with the one stone on this trip, Thomas. Put to bed this heresy business and the girl both."

The bishop chortled out loud, thoroughly impressed with the jape. He liked a good jape, did the bishop, and he liked his own japes best of all.

"You might even return to me in a better humor and rather less of a boorish prude."

"Is that why I am really going to Bottesford, then—to find a bride?"

"Don't be ridiculous, Thomas. You are going to Bottesford on God's work. And I never mentioned marriage. Not that I would for a moment condone relations out of wedlock, you understand. After all, let us not forget, I *am* the Bishop of Lincoln."

And he held out his hand that Thomas might be granted the undoubted privilege of kissing the ring on his finger.

CHAPTER 3

And because it is just that those who by their deeds make mock of the Most High should meet with punishment worthy of their transgressions we pronounce the sentence of excommunication which it is our will they shall ipso facto incur, who shall presume to act contrary to our salutary warnings and commands. And we firmly decree that in addition to the above penalties a process shall be begun before competent judges for the infliction of all and every penalty which heretics are subject to according to law . . .
—Pope John XXII, Decretal Super Illius Specula (1326)

Dame Alice Kyteler turned around in a slow circle, dolefully surveying the meager little cottage that was to be her new home.

A single shutterless window let in barely enough light to see by, leaving full half the room veiled in shadow. But there really wasn't much to see anyway. A crude trestle table stood on one side of the room, tilting ever so slightly where its broken leg had been mended short. There were also a couple of backless benches, a milking stool, and a splintered trunk with shattered locks. That was all. Nothing more.

The hearthstone was cold and unwelcoming.

In one corner of the cottage, the barbs of a bramble bush had forced their way through the crumbling wattle wall, leaving a messy dusting of clay amid the clumps of leaves and soiled straw that lay scattered across the floor. Overhead she could hear the telltale skittering and chattering of birds nesting in the thatch. As if that weren't enough, there was a distinctly musty odor of animal droppings that suggested the presence of mice and made her nose wrinkle in disgust. It was a truly squalid place, the very air inside laden with neglect. Nobody had lived there for some time. And why would anyone want to?

Alice lowered herself warily onto one of the benches before the tilting table, realizing for the first time how far she had fallen. Not long ago she had been one of the wealthiest women in Ireland, with a fine home, a thriving business, and servants at her beck and call. Now she was an exile, chased and harried by the Church at every turn, having only those few possessions she had managed to steal away with her when she fled. And for the first time in her life, Alice was utterly alone.

She took a compact out of her purse, opening it up to reveal a small silver-lined mirror, and watched as the reflection of her fingers traced upward over a finely formed jaw and cheek to touch the faint lines only just beginning to emerge at the corners of her eyes—brilliant, violet eyes, deep with intelligence, but shadowed with weariness after her long journey.

Alice had always loved the tiny mirror, at times taking an almost sinful pleasure in the sparkling glass and in what it revealed. It had been a gift from her first husband. He had been a good man, and in her own way, she believed that she might have loved him—even if only a little.

She hesitated for a moment, lost in nostalgia, and then snapped the compact shut.

Standing up, Alice trailed a finger across the table, surprised to find that the wood was solid English oak, dark and heavy, and the tilt not quite so bad as she had at first supposed. Like her, the table might have seen better days, yet it still stood, sturdy enough, defiantly waiting to serve a new owner, even as nature slowly reclaimed the hut all around it.

The elegant lady smiled to herself. It was not in her nature to give in to despair, and Alice Kyteler was far from helpless. Yes, she had fallen a long way and she had fallen quickly, but she could always begin again. Who knew? This might actually be fun, and it was certainly a sight better than the fate she had left behind. She would be safe here in England, she thought, at least for the time being. Hidden away deep in the woods, in her dingy little hut, with her wonky old table.

CHAPTER 4

It was that time of year when nature finds itself poised in a delicate balance between the seasons, the warm and humid days of summer giving way reluctantly to crisp autumn breezes, the bright colors of the flowers soon to be replaced by the turning of leaves, the fragrant sweetness of summer bloom and of harvest by the earthier scents of damp and rot.

Thomas Lester sat on one of the resting benches scattered judiciously about Bottesford Manor's spacious gardens and looked out admiringly over the abundant meadows, orchards, and fields of the demesne lands.

The harvest had already been gathered, the sheaves carted to the barn for threshing and winnowing, and the flocks turned out into the fields to graze among the white stubble. Michaelmas, falling as it did at the end of September, was a time to take stock, to settle debts, to pay and set rents. It was a time to pause, even if only for a moment, before preparations began for the celebration of Lady Mass and the approach of winter. Soon, the final plowing of the fallow fields would begin, followed by the sowing of winter wheat and rye; the last of the mid and late season fruits would be collected and either boiled for marmalade or laid out to dry, providing a tasty supplement to the villagers' diet during the dead season when nothing grows. The tranquil scene made it hard to imagine that England had only recently been torn apart by war. Or that the embers of discontent still glowed warmly, ready at any moment to kindle a fresh flame that could once again consume the entire country.

Thomas had heard it said that it is possible to feel the weight of a stare. He did not know if that was true, but he sensed a sudden pricking at the nape of his neck.

And turning to the side he saw her.

She stood still and silent, her hands clasped loosely in front of her, regarding him with soft blue eyes set in an oval-shaped face defined by its delicate features and faultless symmetry. His first thought was that his wife had come back to him, and for a moment he held his breath, just for an instant, even though he knew it could not be true. Hawisa was long gone and he would never see her again, but this young woman looked so much like her. She had the same slender build, the same fair complexion, the same russet-brown hair, its coils catching the light with glints of reddish-gold, and the same graceful carriage. Just as Hawisa had once done, she drew the beholder's eye to her as naturally as lavender draws bees.

Yet as he looked closer, Thomas saw that there were also differences. The woman before him had a harder set to her mouth. Her lips, though full and red, were unsmiling and pressed together in what could easily be considered disdain. The eyes that he had at first perceived to be the softest blue betrayed a touch of flint. And she carried herself not so much with grace, perhaps, as with pride. She was elegant—some would say beautiful—and well worth the looking at, but at the same time she struck him as aloof and unwelcoming.

Nevertheless, the memory of his wife made Thomas smile. And he realized at once his mistake. The woman's eyes first widened in shock and then narrowed, fixing him with a look as withering and as cold as winter ice, a look he rather suspected she had perfected at a young age.

Thomas was a good-looking man by any standards, of a little above average height, well built, with wide-set hazel eyes and a broad, handsome face that reflected his Saxon heritage. A tousled thatch of wavy brown hair, left somewhat unkempt and unshorn, fell about his brow and ears in a becoming way that might have charmed a village girl, but to this highborn lady probably appeared uncouth. From the simple, mud-splattered homespun and leather he had chosen to wear for travel, she might take him for a freeman, and at best a yeoman farmer. In either event he was someone who worked the land for a living, not a man of any particular substance in her eyes.

She stared at him because her birth and position gave her the right to do so, but she did not countenance the same in return. Nor did her regard in any way invite familiarity.

Thomas knew that she now expected him to make his reverence and withdraw, so he decided not to do so, instead returning her gaze and stretching his mouth wide in an insolent grin.

And for a long moment they both just stood there, the one taking the measure of the other, a gentle breeze whispering through the grass, stirring the carefully tended beds of flowers and herbs, filling the air with the heady scent of mint and lavender, and carrying with it the hails of the distant apple pickers and the strident, belligerent song of a robin, one of the few birds stubborn enough to brave the changing weather.

"Sir."

So absorbed was he in the silent struggle of wills that Thomas had completely failed to notice the young maidservant who now stood at his side, addressing him in an insistent voice.

"*Sir,*" she repeated, "I am told to bring you to the hall."

Thomas wrenched his eyes away from his inquisitive companion with some difficulty.

"His lordship said to bring you *now*, sir," she added more urgently; and with one last look at the woman who had reminded him so much of his dead wife, Thomas turned to follow.

The maid led him across the garden, walking determinedly at his side, a surprisingly neat little pair of leather ankle boots peeking out from beneath the skirts she held aloft to keep them free of the mud.

"You serve his lordship?" Thomas asked conversationally.

"I am Lady Cecily's maid," she replied with an evident note of pride.

Thomas remembered De Bray's daughter was named Cecily and wondered whether it was she whom he had just seen.

"Ah, an important position. You have done well for yourself. And what is your name?"

"My—my name?" It was another few steps before she answered. "I am Hunydd."

Hunydd was young, perhaps eighteen or nineteen, smaller than most, robust and healthy looking, with a round, open face, a flush of color high on her cheeks, and bee-stung lips that liked to smile a lot, he thought. Hers was an old Welsh name that Thomas had encountered from time to time along the border, pronounced "Hee-nith" when she spoke it in the distinct and charming singsong lilt of her native land.

"A pretty name," he said smiling down at her. "Did you know that Prince Hywel of Gwynedd once wrote a poem about a girl named Hunydd? She was his *lover*," he added, leaning closer and speaking in an exaggerated, conspiratorial whisper.

Hunydd was quiet as they entered the courtyard, and Thomas wondered whether he might have offended her, but after a time she leaned toward him and spoke in a whisper to match his own.

"What did he say about her?"

"What did he say about who?" Thomas teased.

"*Hunydd,*" she said. "What did Prince Hywel say about Hunydd?"

"He said that he would love her until the crack of doom."

"*The crack of doom,*" she repeated slowly, her eyes dreamy.

They crossed the courtyard, passing a variety of buildings that serviced the needs of the manor and its inhabitants. There was a small stone chapel, a smithy, kennels, kitchens, a stable, and a motley collection of less well-constructed cob outhouses where the servants and guards slept. Further out, closer to the wicket fence surrounding the manor, Thomas could see the large threshing barns, haylofts, granaries, and animal enclosures you would expect to find on any prosperous country estate.

"And do you suppose that he did?" Hunydd asked. "Do you suppose that he truly loved her like that?"

"I expect so," replied Thomas evasively, suddenly finding the dog kennels completely fascinating.

Prince Hywel had been a notorious plunderer of young women's chastity and had bedded a string of lovers, likely having promised them all the same thing. In fact, the selfsame poem that spoke of Hunydd also happened to mention at least seven other girls, and the *crack of doom* came soon enough for the young prince who had died bloodily, albeit at the hands of his own family rather than a cuckolded husband. All details, Thomas thought, that Hunydd probably did not need to know.

"His lordship is busy today, Hunydd. Is something amiss?" he asked, congratulating himself on the subtle change of subject.

Once he had presented his papers to the steward, Thomas had fully expected to be admitted to the lord of the manor, but instead he had been made to wait half the afternoon already.

Hunydd's face took on a guarded expression, and she seemed to wrestle with herself a moment over what to say. "I am sure I do not know, sir," she finally responded, "but I think it might have something to do with the black monk. He is waiting in the hall now."

Thomas felt a sudden chill travel down his spine, and his fingers drifted reflexively to the pendant around his neck, touching the iron in what might have been considered a pagan gesture had the pendant itself not been molded into the rough shape of a Celtic cross.

Hunydd gave him a sidelong glance, her eyes lingering on the talisman.

"I don't like him—the monk, I mean," she continued, watching as Thomas tucked the pendant back inside his jerkin. "He is not very nice, and he is always scowling. He yelled at the steward, you know. And I don't like the other ones he brought with him. Well, not the rough-looking one, at least. It makes me uncomfortable how he looks at me. The other monk is nice enough, I suppose, though he does not smile much either. But at least he doesn't scowl, and he doesn't shout at people, and he doesn't look at me like . . . that."

She paused her nattering a moment and looked up at Thomas with a pair of black eyes as round and inquisitive as those of the robin he had heard singing in the garden.

"Why do monks wear black do you suppose?" she asked.

Thomas was beginning to wonder whether Hunydd might be just a tad simple. *Touched by the moon,* as they would have said where he had grown up in Cumberland.

"Not all monks wear black, Hunydd," he explained, "though the Benedictines do. I think wearing a plain color like black is meant as a gesture of humility. In so doing a monk rejects vanity and worldly things, and accepts a life of poverty, as did Christ."

"Oh," she mouthed slowly, her lips making a circle. "I had always imagined Christ wore white. But the monk is not a Benedictine," she said assuredly with a little nod of her head that sent a lock of raven black hair tumbling across her face. "And he is not humble; he is rude. He called the steward all sorts of names. It made me blush fiercely."

Thomas suspected the man in question was not a monk at all, but a Dominican friar—one of those wandering preachers charged by the pope with correcting doctrinal error and rooting out heresy wherever they found it.

Hunydd was still trying to describe the monk, her dislike of the man growing more evident by the second. "His face is all pinched and scrunched up," she said, pulling a funny face of her own. "Like he smells something bad or like a midge fly is biting his bottom."

Thomas laughed out loud at the evocative description, and Hunydd's face broke into an answering smile that brought a sparkling dimple to her right cheek as they climbed the steps to the Great Hall.

The manor house was constructed like a Norman keep, its three stone and timbered floors rising above a stone undercroft. The hall itself was a long, timbered room with vaulted ceilings, dominated at the far end by a raised dais and a large oak table, on which sat several candelabra and a large silver saltcellar. Beyond that was a paneled partition that would lead to a narrow staircase and the family chambers on the second floor. The trestle tables, for those who sat "below the salt," were pushed aside against the walls, which were decorated with a variety of smoke-blackened tapestries, stuffed animal heads, brightly painted shields, and weapons of a various and gruesome nature. Cresset torches and tall candelabra added to what little light flowed in from the open doors and narrow windows. And off to the left side, a large fireplace was built into the wall—a surprisingly modern addition at a time when many halls still boasted a central hearth.

The hall smelled of timber, smoke, and dog shit, masked only ineffectively by the more fragrant scent of herbs that had been deliberately crushed into the rushes scattered underfoot.

Thomas paused at the top of the stairs, nodded to the guard, and allowed his eyes to adjust to the dimly lit interior. A sly-looking character lounged just inside the doorway, doing his best to appear casual and disinterested, the fingers of his right hand caressing the hilt of a wicked blade tucked inside his belt, while his eyes roamed restlessly around the hall, pausing only long enough to leer at Hunydd.

Thomas had seen his type before. Many times. He was the kind of man who waited in the dark for those foolish enough to wander the back alleys at night. A man who would not hesitate to slit a throat for money, and not someone Thomas would have expected to find in the manor of a country lord.

Even Hunydd sensed a predator and shrank away from his stare, tugging at Thomas's arm like an impatient child.

Sir Mortimer de Bray sat in a high-backed chair, swathed in furs and huddled before the fire. He was surrounded by a group of attendants and petitioners, and at first glance did not look to be in particularly good health. In fact, he looked utterly haggard.

Ignoring the thug for the time being, Thomas followed Hunydd across the room and took a place at the edge of the gathering, just in time to see a rather corpulent Benedictine monk emerge from the throng to address Bottesford's lord.

"Who is the monk, Hunydd?" Thomas whispered.

"That's Prior Gilbert. He's funny." Hunydd's smile was replaced by a sudden look of concern. "It's not wicked to say he is funny, is it, him being a monk and all?"

"Oh, I dare say you can be forgiven. I am sure you did not mean to speak ill of him."

"Oh no, not at all," she exclaimed. "Prior Gilbert is nice. But he *is* also funny. Sometimes."

The prior cleared his throat loudly, folded his hands comfortably over an ample belly, and tucked his head into his chins.

"My lord," he began, "allow me to present Friar Justus.

He has come to us all the way from London at the request of His Grace, the Archbishop of Canterbury, to investigate the recent . . . uh"—the prior paused and looked upward as though searching for heavenly guidance—"the recent *disturbing* events. Naturally, we have opened our house to Justus and to his . . . um . . . companions."

With that, Friar Justus himself stepped forward, and a ripple of interest passed through the assembly.

The Dominican immediately struck Thomas as an arrogant man. There was no hint of Saxon pallor to him, but rather the olive skin and dark piercing eyes of a more heated clime. Already above average in height, he contrived to make himself taller yet by standing stiffly erect with his hawk-like nose held proudly aloft. And although he was clothed in the simple white woolen tunic and black mantle of his order, he wore those clothes regally, and along with them an air of condescension quite at odds with the humility and quiet grace usually to be found among mendicant friars. The staff he held limply in his hand might have been a scepter; the close-clipped ring of silver hair, a crown; and the polished rosary beads hanging from his waist, a chain of office. Here was a man, thought Thomas, who believed he stood apart, whose pursed lips and sour expression suggested that he was all too ready to be displeased with everything and everyone he saw before him.

Thomas had to smile to himself, recalling Hunydd's description. She had him exactly.

De Bray regarded the friar from under his bushy gray eyebrows.

"So, you are a Dominican?"

Friar Justus spread his arms wide in a self-effacing gesture and inclined his head by way of acknowledgment.

"A hound of God," added De Bray, using a derisory but commonly used epithet for the Dominicans.

"We do not choose to call ourselves such," replied the Dominican coolly, "but yes, I am of the Order of Saint Dominic, or the *Black Friars,* as you sometimes refer to us here in England."

He spoke with an inflection that marked him as a foreigner. Thomas supposed he might be French or Italian, perhaps, but not Norman. And his voice was curiously strained, the words coming out accompanied by a slight crepitation that suggested either prolonged overuse or a deep malignancy of the throat completely at odds with his otherwise robust physical appearance.

At this point, the young lady who had subjected Thomas to such intense scrutiny in the garden emerged from behind the dais, and everybody watched in silence as she walked unconcernedly across the hall to take a place at Sir Mortimer's side. The Dominican looked at her and then back at De Bray, evidently expecting some form of introduction. When none was forthcoming, he shrugged, wearing an amused half smile on his face, as if the entire incident was just one of those discourtesies one might expect to encounter in rural England.

"You suspect some devilry here?" asked De Bray.

"It is difficult to know for sure without an investigation, but a man killed in the holy church, his body draped most rudely across the altar in the manner of a pagan sacrifice, mocking the crucifixion of our Lord . . ." The Dominican let his words hang in the air for a moment or two. "Yes, there is much here of concern to His Grace, the archbishop, and to our papal father."

Thomas doubted very much that the pope knew or cared about the goings on in rural England, but the Dominican was speaking figuratively. The archbishop was the pope's representative in England; and the Dominican, the representative of the archbishop. As far as Friar Justus was concerned, therefore, he was speaking with the full authority of the papacy, especially on the subject of heresy.

De Bray tugged anxiously at his beard. "Roger Lacy's murder happened on my land. Surely it is a matter for me and for the county sheriff."

"This *sacrilege* happened in God's house, sir," retorted the Dominican. "In a church, I might add, whose priest had only recently died in the most mysterious, the most *disturbing*, of circumstances."

This last pronouncement set off a flurry of whispers among the audience and caught De Bray completely off guard. His face darkened with anger.

"What are you talking about? There was nothing unusual about Father Oswin's death. It was well known the man had a weak heart."

"So you say," said the Dominican with a barely concealed smirk. "So you say. And perhaps Father Oswin was simply old and infirm. Yet his death is a surprising coincidence that bears examination. I am sure you can understand that His Grace might be concerned."

Prior Gilbert, now standing with the rest of the gathering, frowned deeply. He took a half step forward, clearly intending to speak on the subject, but met the Dominican's stony gaze, thought better of whatever he was about to say, and quietly retreated once more to the safety of the assembly, mopping at his sweating brow with the sleeve of his habit.

"As I was saying," continued the Dominican, turning his attention back to De Bray, "perhaps it is true that Father Oswin died of a heart ailment, and perhaps not. Regardless, there is much of concern here. We find ourselves living in a time of wickedness. Pagans practice openly. Cultists and false apostles roam the countryside. Sorcerers conspire against the lives of pope and monarch alike. And who can forget the shocking heresies of the Templars, only so recently uncovered?"

De Bray glowered angrily. "The Templar trials were more than ten years ago. Their heresies are of no moment here, if indeed what is said of them is true."

"Oh, I assure you the allegations were true," retorted the friar. "I was a witness to all that transpired and had the sad task of taking down the confessions of those beasts. I am not surprised at your skepticism, my lord. Who could have believed the Templar Order capable of such terrible crimes against God, against nature even? I myself struggled to accept the truth of it. Only imagine that such heresy hid in the very bosom of Christendom. We must be constantly on our guard. Why, this very year the Bishop of Ossory uncovered a witch practicing her foul arts in Ireland!"

"I have heard of this case, Friar." The young woman laid her hand lightly on De Bray's shoulder and spoke in a crisp, clear voice, commanding everyone's attention. "And I do not believe the matter is nearly so simple as you say. It is my understanding that most of the allegations against Dame Alice Kyteler were gleaned from the confession of some poor maid who was tortured for days by the bishop's men; whipped repeatedly until she told them what they wished to hear. England is not Ireland. Our law does not condone the torture of helpless prisoners, and I would remind you that the Inquisition has no power here and never has. While we greatly respect the Dominican Order and all its good works, you are not inquisitors in England."

It was bravely said, and Thomas found himself reconsidering his first impression of her. In fact, it would be fair to say that his admiration soared, and he regarded her now with great interest. She caught his eyes upon her, and Thomas quickly looked away, feeling red creep up his collar.

For his part, the Dominican stared at her blankly for a moment before directing his attention back to De Bray.

"The young lady speaks for you, my lord?" he asked.

"This is my daughter, Cecily."

"Your *daughter*?" said the Dominican with an affected air of surprise. "My apologies, I had rather supposed her to be your *wife*."

He stared pointedly at the hand on De Bray's shoulder, which Cecily immediately snatched back with a sharp intake of breath as if the fingers had been singed by a flame.

De Bray shifted uncomfortably in his seat. "My wife is not well and is at present recuperating in her chambers."

"I am sorry to hear that. I understand Lady Isabella to be a rare beauty, and I had hoped to meet her. Yet I now see that your daughter too is a delight to behold"—the Dominican offered Cecily a little bow and an ingratiating if somewhat condescending smile—"and so bold to speak her mind in the company of men. How refreshing! Though I fear in this instance she may have ventured into matters of which she can have but little understanding."

He turned very deliberately to Cecily.

"Dame Alice Kyteler is a monster, madam. She is a weirding woman, one of those hags who go by night and consort with demons and other foul creatures." The Dominican seemed to grow in stature as he spoke, his voice rising to fill the hall, engendering all the assurance and power of a Biblical prophet. "She is a succubus who crawled up from hell itself to seduce and then poison her husbands. For years she has denied the true faith, corrupting those about her and forcing them to do her filthy bidding, condemning their souls to eternal damnation. So foul and wicked has she become, that she is no longer able to tread consecrated ground, and the very fruits of the earth despoil and perish in her presence.

"That she has fled from justice only confirms her guilt beyond all doubt. But mark my words. She cannot"—he raised a bony finger and punched it angrily into the air—"she cannot escape God's judgment."

He glared at Cecily for a long moment, and then around the hall, daring anyone to challenge him.

"Deus Videt Omnia!" he declared loudly. "God sees everything!"

Cecily opened her mouth to respond but snapped it shut when she saw the two fingers her father held up in warning. A wise decision, thought Thomas.

"In any event," the Dominican continued in a much calmer tone, "I fear we have wandered terribly from the matter at hand. I mention Alice Kyteler merely by way of example. There are many others.

"And you appear to have completely misunderstood my mission, Lady Cecily. I am come merely to *investigate* those things that have transpired here. This is not an inquisition. There are certain formalities we like to pursue should it come to that: a second inquisitor, for example, formal hearings, arrests, and I daresay some suitably solid dungeon with all appropriate appurtenances to facilitate the interrogation of those accused. No, this is not an inquisition, my dear. Not yet."

He allowed the implicit threat in his words to settle over the hall like a cold shroud and then beckoned to a figure hovering a respectful distance behind him, as a dutiful servant might, at heel and near to hand, but not so close as to draw attention from his master. The young man, also dressed in the Dominican black, might have been a little past twenty, and he possessed a boyishly smooth face, a fair complexion, and tow-colored hair trimmed neatly in a tonsure. He took a pace forward and held out a scroll that Friar Justus promptly snatched from his hand.

A pair of steely blue eyes flashed briefly in anger, only to be quickly veiled and lowered once more in submission.

"I assure you that I am here with all due authority from the archbishop," said the Dominican. "Perhaps you would like to review my mandate. I am sure that you will find everything in order."

De Bray gestured wearily to a priest standing behind him. "Give it to my chaplain, Father Elyas. He shall read it."

The chaplain had been standing so quietly that Thomas had not yet noticed him. He wore a nondescript, somewhat frayed, and worn black robe and had a bland, unremarkable face that might pass unnoticed as neither comely nor unattractive.

The Dominican gave the chaplain a curious glance, his eyes lingering on the shabby robe and the slightly overly long black hair of his tonsure. "Father *Elyas*? I had understood Father *Clement* to be your personal chaplain, my lord."

"Clement passed away this last year. Elyas joined us from Oxford, where he was studying."

"An Oxford man, no less!" exclaimed Justus, handing the parchment to Elyas with a mock bow. "I am indeed humbled to find myself in such august and learned company."

Elyas offered no reaction to the unsubtle flattery and simply proceeded to scan the scroll with a bored expression.

"I am saddened, my lord, to hear that you have lost yet another member of the clergy. That is most unfortunate. There appears to be some sort of epidemic hereabouts for us priests. Perhaps Father Elyas and I should be cautious of something in the air," said Justus.

The Dominican began a wheezing, hissing sound that might have been a laugh but sounded more like a ragged pair of worn-out bellows, and then stood smiling crookedly at any of those in attendance who dared to meet his eye, until Elyas finally rolled up the scroll and nodded to De Bray.

"You see, all is in order," he announced smugly. "I was sure it would be so. And as a precaution I had already taken the liberty of speaking with Sir Hugh Despenser. I am sure your chaplain saw his personal seal affixed to my papers alongside that of the archbishop."

The casual mention of the king's favorite, Hugh Despenser, had the desired chilling effect on all those present. Thomas had never met the man but knew of his reputation. Despenser had been a landless knight before he married a wealthy heiress, a marriage that had elevated him to a position of power. Somehow, he had gained the king's favor, and soon the two had become inseparable, leading to more than one scandalous rumor. As Despenser's power grew, so did his arrogance and greed. There was said to be no depravity to which he would not stoop for advantage or wealth. So offensive had been his conduct that the king had been forced to exile him for a time him to avoid civil war. The rebellion came anyway, Despenser returned, and with the rebels now defeated, he had begun settling old scores in the most gruesome fashion. Nobody in their right mind would wish to draw his attention, let alone his ire.

"Apparently the king is very concerned about recent attempts to use magic against his council, and I dare say it would only take a matter of days to obtain royal approval for my investigation. I was certain I would not need to go so far, however, given that I have the archbishop's mandate, and when Lord Despenser has affixed his own seal thereto, which is as good as a royal order these days, or so I am told . . ."

De Bray leaned forward, gripping the arms of his chair.

"Your point is made, Friar. Begin your investigation, but there will be no violence done to my people, do you hear?"

"Perish the thought," responded the Dominican, with a shocked expression. "And perhaps this is all a misunderstanding. I suppose it is entirely possible that Roger Lacy was merely praying at Saint Mary's when, rather like Father Oswin, his heart failed him, and he collapsed across the altar, remembering to assume the posture of a crucified martyr as he did so. But, nevertheless, one must investigate to be sure."

De Bray's gaze wandered across the assemblage, finally settling on Thomas.

"Yes, a crime has been committed and must be investigated. On that we can agree, and I have already asked Thomas Lester here to investigate on my behalf."

Another ripple went through the audience chamber, and all heads swiveled to Thomas at the same time. Still standing next to him, Hunydd gasped aloud and then quickly clapped a hand to her mouth. This was not at all what he had expected. Nor did he remember ever agreeing to investigate a murder that was being touted as some kind of insane pagan ritual. Thomas was about to disavow his involvement, when he happened to look into De Bray's eyes and see something there, a helplessness, a pleading, that gave him pause and made him hold his tongue.

"I really do not think that is necessary," began the Dominican.

"Damn it all! I am lord here. I am responsible for the king's peace and exercise the power of the noose over my own people. I shall have whomever I want investigate wrongs on my land."

The sudden show of passion visibly drained the last of Sir Mortimer's strength, and he collapsed back into his chair, doubling over, his entire body racked by a deep, phlegmy cough.

Justus waited for the worst of the fit to subside before responding. "As you will, my lord. I should be glad of the young man's assistance, of course. So long as he is not in my way."

Still coughing, De Bray waved a dismissing arm.

"Then I think we are done here," announced the Dominican, making clear to all assembled that it was his decision to end the audience and that he was doing so out of sympathy for the state of their lord.

With that, he turned to leave, took two paces, and then hesitated.

"Forgive me, my lady," he said, addressing Cecily with another fawning smile. "I could not help but notice how you dress your hair. I must ask, is it customary for women of rank in these parts to leave their heads uncovered?"

The strange remark took everyone by surprise, including Cecily. Her cheeks flushed crimson, and for a moment she was lost for words. "I am not yet married," she finally managed to say.

The Dominican's eyebrows shot upward. "You surprise me, dear. Not married yet? A delightful creature such as yourself?" His eyes wandered slowly and deliberately over her figure, "And at your advanced age?"

Thomas squinted at Cecily. He could not imagine she was yet past twenty.

"Still, I would think some kind of a net," the Dominican said, waving a languid hand, "or better yet a wimple. But who am I to say? The fashions of young ladies today—I can hardly keep up."

He hissed out another wheezing laugh.

"But now that I think about it, I seem to recall that your mother was Irish, was she not?" He did not wait for an answer. "Yes, I am sure of it. And perhaps this is how young women attire themselves in Ireland. As you said, the Irish do have some strange customs."

Cecily appeared even more startled by the reference to her heritage. "I–I really cannot say," she responded, looking away. "I know very little of Ireland."

The Dominican smiled complacently. "Ah well, that may be for the best. In my own experience, it is a land full of superstition, bogs, and turf huts." He glanced ruefully to the doors, thrown wide open to let in the weak afternoon light. "And I do believe it may be even more damp there than here in England."

Without another word, and with a brief reverence toward the lord of the manor, Friar Justus walked sedately out of the hall, parting the gathered petitioners around him like the Red Sea, the only sounds piercing the silence he left behind being the steady clunking of his staff against the timbered floor and the slapping of Prior Gilbert's sandals as he bustled after him.

★   ★   ★

De Bray heaved himself up and limped toward the antechamber, gesturing irritably that Thomas should follow. Once inside he collapsed into the large chair behind his oak desk and breathed out a great sigh of relief, as if the short walk had been a monumental task.

Thomas had heard Sir Mortimer de Bray described as a gruff soldier who had obtained his wealth fighting on the borders of Scotland and Wales. The man huddled before him bore little resemblance to the ferocious border reaver of legend. What must once have been a ruddy, fleshy face was now gaunt and sallow, the pallid skin stretched tightly over hollow cheeks. Deep grooves etched into the corners of his mouth lent him a look of permanent grief, and his eyes were a dull gray, sunken deep in bruised sockets, the embers of life flickering behind them closer to ash than flame. He had the appearance of a decrepit old man, a sense of weariness and constraint clutched as tightly about him as his blanket. If ever Thomas had seen a man resigned to death, this was he.

Cecily took a position at her father's side. A brief flicker of concern flashed across her face when she looked down at him, and then she raised her chin and turned her attention to Thomas.

"Who is this, Father?" she asked, her eyes following Thomas as he seated himself.

"I'm sorry, my dear—I thought you had heard. Thomas will be helping us with this matter at Saint Mary's. I am hoping he will stay awhile." De Bray offered Thomas a tired smile. "I shall be giving him some land near Redmile."

This was news to Thomas, but Cecily did not give him an opportunity to question the gift.

"How much land?" she asked tersely.

"I don't know—a few acres. Does it matter?"

Apparently it did matter to Cecily.

"I was thinking of the old Bekley cottage," added De Bray. "There hasn't been a tenant there for the best part of a year."

"A few acres!" Cecily spluttered. "That cottage has nearer one hundred. And I don't even know this man," she added, barely sparing Thomas a glance.

"I am quite decided, dear," her father interrupted with an upraised hand to make clear his decision was final. "I have already directed the steward to draw up the papers. We could use a man like Thomas around here."

Cecily looked Thomas up and down disdainfully. "A man like *him*?" she scoffed, making clear that she was no more impressed with him now than when she had first seen him in the garden. Thomas did his best to sit up straight and tugged self-consciously at his tunic, wishing he had worn something just a little less shabby.

De Bray ignored her comments. "Thomas, you heard that Dominican hound?"

"I did, my lord. I heard what he said."

"And you will investigate the death of this Roger Lacy on my behalf?"

Thomas hesitated. He had not come here expecting to go head-to-head with a Dominican inquisitor and had no desire to be drawn into such a conflict. In fact, it was exactly the kind of thing he desperately wanted to avoid. On the other hand, he had promised the bishop he would at least see the lay of the land, and one hundred acres of Midland soil was quite an inducement.

"Is this not a matter for the sheriff, my lord?"

"Who is to say?" replied De Bray. "There is room for disagreement. The sheriff may want the murderer before the royal courts once he is found, and the archbishop claims it is an ecclesiastical matter. Yet these are still my lands. Henry believes you can help me. He speaks very highly of you, Thomas. Very highly indeed."

De Bray tapped a letter lying on the desk with his fingers, and Cecily's eyes lingered on the paper, no doubt planning to read it as soon as the opportunity arose.

"And after today's audience, I fear things may become complicated. We may well have need of you and your particular experience. I sense Friar Justus is a dangerous man, and I need someone I can trust. A man of my own."

"What about one of your guards or the village constable?"

"No," he replied, poking a finger stiffly at Thomas, "I need *you*."

Thomas had to wonder what the bishop had written that could render him valuable enough to merit a hundred acres of prime land. And of what De Bray was really afraid.

"I fear the bishop may have overstated my qualities . . ."

Cecily's patience with the conversation had finally been exhausted.

"Really! This is becoming absurd!" she declared. "If you are to hold land at our leisure—a most generous tranche of land, I might add—then you must expect to do dutiful service, as do all our tenants. My father, apparently soon to be your lord, has given you a command. It is not yours to question him!"

And just like that, what was left of Thomas's recently acquired admiration for Cecily fell, shattered and broken. She spoke with the air of one born to wealth, and Thomas wondered if what he had taken for boldness might in fact have been nothing more than a noxious brew of arrogance, pride, and vanity.

After a long moment, he spoke in a deliberate voice. "No man is my master, Lady Cecily."

De Bray sighed with exasperation.

"You misunderstood me, Cecily. Thomas is a freeman. I am gifting him the land outright. He will be our neighbor, not our tenant."

"You are *gifting* him the land?" she asked, her eyes wide with disbelief. "Nearly one hundred of our best acres. Surely you jest?"

De Bray smiled benignly. "Thomas, you will have to excuse my daughter. She has my best interests at heart, but I am afraid she has inherited her mother's Irish temper." He patted her hand. "I confess I have indulged her, perhaps because she reminds me so of her mother. She was a wonderful woman, my Mairead. A man could never wish for a better match. I believe that is why I have held off from forcing Cecily into a marriage. No man has ever been good enough for her, and she will not be persuaded, nor less yet commanded. But it is high time she was wed. The Dominican was right about that. Yes, let her pester someone other than me for a change. Though I am sure she will find fault with whomever I choose for her, and she will doubtless peck away at the poor fellow as she does at me, like a clucking hen, at least until her belly swells and she has a few young ones at heel to keep her mind occupied."

Though she bore it in silence, in his peripheral vision Thomas could clearly see Cecily bridle at being spoken of in such an uncouth manner. He might have been more sympathetic had she herself not been quite so rude.

De Bray coughed into his hand. It was the racking, wretched cough of an unhealthy man, and he doubled over, hacking away again, his whole body shaking from the fit, before slowly recovering. He dabbed at his mouth with a linen wipe, stuffing it discreetly into his sleeve. Not quickly enough, however, for Thomas to miss the spots of blood on the white cloth.

"Forgive me, Thomas. This last year has not been kind to me. All my sins are coming home to roost, I am afraid."

Cecily immediately began fussing over her father, offering him water, plucking at his blanket, his condescension toward her completely forgotten.

"Enough, enough!" said De Bray sharply, tugging the blanket away from her. "I understand you have reservations, Thomas. Henry has explained your . . . background to me." He tapped the letter again. "But you of all people know what these heretic hunters can be like." De Bray bit down, embarrassed. "Please, Thomas. We need your help."

De Bray was a proud man, and the plea took a lot out of him. Cecily's lips parted in astonishment. Thomas had the sense that, if she had disliked him already, she detested him now. He had to admit he felt a little less than heroic himself, having brought a proud man in declining health to the verge of pleading. *Thomas Lester, emissary of the Bishop of Lincoln, and heroic humbler of sick old men.*

Thomas knew he should steer clear of the rocks, but not for the first time, the siren song was drawing him in. He nodded once, and the old man heaved out a relieved sigh.

"Excellent! We must find out the truth, Thomas, before this man creates a truth to suit his own purposes. And you might want to roust out the Bottesford constable. He is also the watch captain and may be of some help. He knows the villagers, and they respect him." De Bray frowned uncertainly. "At least, after a fashion."

Thomas could hardly miss Cecily rolling her eyes. Her reaction did not exactly fill him with confidence at the constable's abilities, and he felt a queasy sensation in his stomach. The look Cecily now gave Thomas made clear her doubts extended also to him.

CHAPTER 5

The strange coterie crossed the courtyard, Friar Justus striding out in front, his staff rapping angrily against the cobbles, robes billowing and flapping in the breeze, while those following after spread out on either side of him like the wings of a flock of migrating geese.

Having recovered from the rigors of the audience, Prior Gilbert waddled along to the Dominican's left, somehow managing to keep up a steady stream of jovial banter, punctuated only by the occasional gasping breath. He was at present pointing out all the sights: the church, the two mills on the river below, the meadow and apple orchard—even the famous local cluster of ancient oaks.

Friar Justus paid scant attention to the Benedictine. As a man who had experienced firsthand the many splendors of Paris and Rome, who had beheld the mighty Coliseum, who had worshipped at the great cathedral of Notre Dame and cried at the beauty of the Rose Window, he was not inclined to be impressed by the rustic charms of Bottesford village.

Justus suddenly realized with a start that the prior had ceased his gabbling and was looking up at him expectantly.

"I was just asking whether you had met Bernard de Gui," he explained in response to the Dominican's questioning frown. "I know my abbot in Leicester is a great admirer of his. I cannot say that I have read his works myself, but I understand they are quite brilliant, and I have heard him described as one of the finest ecclesiastical scholars of our time. As soon as I heard of your visit, I set out to commission a copy of *Practica Inquisitionis*, and I expect it to arrive from Grantham any day now. I assure you, it shall find a place of honor in our library."

Prior Gilbert probably imagined that he was ingratiating himself to Justus by flattering one of the more famous members of his Order. He was not. De Gui had been nothing when Justus first met him, no more than an upstart lickspittle, and yet he had gone on to sit at the pope's right hand, his star shining brighter with every passing day, while Justus had been left to rot in England, where it was always drizzling and always cloudy, as though God Himself had thrown a pall over the entire country.

"So, have you met him? Have you met the great man himself?"

"Many times," Justus replied through gritted teeth.

"How marvelous!" The prior clapped his hands gleefully, an ecstatic look on his pudgy face.

Justus felt a headache coming on. He had believed with all his heart that the Templar trials would bring a new age of enlightenment to England. But that had been over a decade ago now, and the English church had lapsed once more into apathy. Lady Cecily had been right about one thing: the Holy Inquisition had no power and little respect in England.

When he had heard of the events at Bottesford, Justus had sensed a real opportunity. Here at last was a chance to pursue his true calling, especially now that he had the attention of the king's favorite, Hugh Despenser.

The man had a fearsome reputation and had been accused of many evil things. Theft, murder, and rape—of both women and men; the list of accusations went on and on. Justus, however, could only speak as he found, and he had observed no such evil tendencies. On the contrary, Despenser had struck him as a God-fearing man who also happened to be extremely sympathetic to the Dominican's cause, having for some time feared that his own enemies were practicing magic against him.

It was Despenser's support that had finally convinced the archbishop to grant the Dominican a warrant to investigate the sacrilege at Saint Mary's. Even then, the order had been tepid, and Justus had been forced to broaden its mandate somewhat, using rich vermillion ink and a quill with a fine, thin nib. He had felt uneasy doing so but comforted himself that he acted with the best of intentions, and he was sure he had only made his papers reflect what had actually been intended.

Prior Gilbert was huffing and puffing to keep up and was now describing the celebratory meal he had arranged to welcome his distinguished guest.

"I have some sherry wine brought all the way from Spain. We brew a decent ale, if I do say so myself, but there is nothing quite like a drop of sherry wine to please the palate after a hard day's devotions." The prior chuckled down into his chins. "I believe it will go nicely with the roasted pheasant. We shall have a nice ragout of fresh vegetables harvested from the fields hereabout. I assure you that you will never have tasted finer, crisper leeks or more delectable mushrooms. And fruit, perfectly ripened and picked from our own orchard. I even have some walnuts from the manor garden. Lady Cecily knows they are a terrible weakness of mine and she is always kind enough to send me a few." He patted his voluminous belly.

How very Benedictine of him, Justus mused dolefully. That order had sunk so low, its adherents wallowing in gluttony and vice. You could tell a Benedictine monk these days as much from the girth of his waist rope as his traditional black habit. In this regard, Prior Gilbert might be a sad sack of a man, but he was an exemplary representative of his Order. Greed, avarice, fornication—it seemed that no sin of the flesh was beyond its members' grasp. Justus had heard sordid tales of frequent, almost bacchanalian dalliances between monks and nuns, and he suspected that half the monks were secretly sodomites, and a good many of the convents, houses of pleasure. He had to wonder, what was the price of a good sister these days, and were they more or less expensive once they had completed their novitiate? These were excellent questions. He would have to ask the fat prior before he left.

He turned his attention to the young friar plodding mutely alongside him. Justus's superiors in London had been very keen for Dominic to accompany him, insistent in fact. Likely they had identified him as a promising candidate for advancement, someone who might benefit from learning at the feet of a great scholar; and so far, Dominic had not disappointed, attending diligently to his master's every command and absorbing each gem of knowledge Justus bestowed on him with a refreshing quietude of a like rarely to be found among his peers.

Their more roguish companion called himself Guy de Hokenham, but Justus had never believed him and imagined that he had gone by several other names in the course of what must have been a less than honorable life. Whatever his name, it could not be denied that Guy was a bad man. Justus had found him wallowing in a London dungeon, awaiting the noose for rape and murder. Or was it murder and ravishment of the corpse? He could never quite remember. In either event, Justus had procured Guy's freedom for a surprisingly small amount of money. A good investment, as it happened. Guy might be a bit of a rogue, but he had proven useful and possessed certain qualities that recommended him. He was obedient, loyal, and had no qualms whatsoever about performing the somewhat seedier tasks that Justus from time to time sent his way.

At just that moment, Guy hawked up loudly and spat a meaty gob of phlegm at a dog that had been unfortunate enough to cross their path, catching it plumb on the snout. The poor creature yelped and skittered away, causing Guy to laugh out loud and look about him to make sure everyone appreciated the jape. Friar Dominic's lip curled up in revulsion, and even Justus felt his stomach churn a little in disgust. Guy didn't seem particularly bothered that nobody else was amused, and continued to tramp along with his long-legged, easy gait, still laughing at the hapless hound.

"This Thomas Lester," said Justus, turning to address Prior Gilbert and catching the poor man mid-sentence so that he almost choked on his words. "What know you of him?"

"Nothing at all, I am afraid. Although, now that I think of it, the steward did mention that a young man arrived on horse this afternoon with a letter of introduction from the Bishop of Lincoln."

"A letter from Henry Burghersh? How very interesting." The Dominican chewed on that morsel a moment or two. "And the woman—the one who found Father Oswin's body. You say she was the vicar's maidservant?"

"Yes. Agnes had served him as such for some years, I believe."

"Then we shall begin with her on the morrow." Justus looked up at the sky, now dulling red as the sun sank fast toward the horizon. It galled him to waste even what little was left of the day, but there was nothing to be done about it. "Something bothers me about Oswin's death, Gilbert. It niggles at me. It . . . disturbs me greatly. Does it not seem to you a little too coincidental that the vicar should die so soon before the blasphemy at your little church? After all, what better way for a wolf to expose the flock to its predations than to first be rid of the shepherd?"

Gilbert chose not to respond to this inherently sound logic, which was perfectly acceptable to Justus. He preferred the man be silent, and he was already quite decided on the matter.

The sacrilege at Saint Mary's was a good start, but more would be needed were he to petition for an inquisition. Proof that a member of the clergy had been poisoned, along with a few sundry other misdeeds, might suffice. And once an inquisition was begun, the heresies would then sprout forth like so many ugly weeds. Such had been the case during the Templar trials once the king had at last acceded to the use of more *stringent* interrogation techniques. Unexpectedly, Justus had discovered that he was rather skilled at that particular craft. Truth be said, he had rarely found anything in life he enjoyed quite as much as the challenge of winkling out a confession from a recalcitrant sinner.

Friar Justus breathed in deeply and smiled at the recollection of happier days and the prospect of more to come. His headache was completely gone, and he was beginning to feel a bit peckish. Perhaps he might enjoy the Benedictine's feast after all.

CHAPTER 6

Lady Isabella de Bray watched the Dominican from the shadowed window of her parlor, her fingers twisting thoughtfully at a loose lock of golden hair. He looked angry and more than a little mean. A part of her, a fairly large part she had to admit, hoped the audience had been particularly unpleasant and that he had berated her husband cruelly. She allowed herself to imagine the scene awhile as the friar strode off into the distance, a smile playing at the corners of her mouth.

Now a young man was crossing the courtyard—a very *handsome* young man. Isabella did not know him and was just wondering to herself who he was and what business he could possibly have with her husband when he suddenly stopped, turned, and looked right up at her. She gasped, spun away from the window, and pressed herself flat against the paneled wall.

Her window provided a wonderful view of the courtyard and of the little road that wound its way up to the manor, and she had seen some very interesting things from there of late. All Cecily's sneaking about, for one: her strange little comings and goings at all hours of the day and night. Yes, Isabella very much liked to *watch*, but she did not like to be *seen*. No, not at all.

She remained as she was for some time, not daring to move, her chest heaving against the fabric of her dress, until she finally plucked up enough courage to poke her head around for another quick peek. He was gone and she breathed out a sigh of relief. Perhaps he had not seen her after all.

Still more than a little shaken by her experience, Isabella retreated to her desk, on which was propped a large oval mirror. The mirror was her most cherished possession, a gift from her grandmother, and the one thing she had insisted on bringing with her from her home when she had been married. Most mirrors were just polished pieces of metal, but this was not. It was real glass set in a beautiful walnut frame, and the reflection it provided, though not perfect, was clearer than most, especially when the sun was up and light streamed in through the parlor window.

Isabella smiled at herself. The young woman in the mirror smiled back.

She had always known that she was pretty. Pride is a sin, or so the priests said, but that she was pretty was simply the truth, and what harm could there be in thinking it? Besides, everybody else agreed. Hardly a day would go by without someone complimenting her on her flawless complexion, her large gray eyes, or her thick tresses of golden hair. And she saw how men's eyes would follow when she entered a room, and how they would linger, only to be snatched away guiltily if she turned to face them. She knew what they all wanted from her.

"Men are like that," she said to nobody in particular.

Her reflection nodded its agreement.

When she had been just a little girl, scarcely eight years old, Isabella had once slipped away from her maid to listen to a wandering preacher in the market square. He had been one of those doom-speakers, and she remembered him as a frightening man with wild eyes, a ragged gray robe, and a face smeared with ash. The doom-speakers always drew a large crowd, and she had wormed her way to the front, where her maid would not see her.

The preacher had told them that the day was coming when

they would all be judged for their sins. She didn't remember everything he said, but there was something about fire falling from the sky, the dead coming back to life, and a woman from Babylon who would apparently get up to all sorts of wicked things with man and beast alike. He had talked about her a lot.

"And the four horsemen!" she declared happily to her twin in the mirror, proud of herself for remembering. "He said there would be four horsemen: War, Famine, Pestilence, and Death. And Death would ride a white horse. I remember that still. The preacher said he would ride a white horse!"

It wasn't the preacher's stories about the end of the world that had interested her the most, however. It was his tales of weirding women—women who practiced the old faerie magic, cast spells, and used mirrors to commune with demons. Isabella had listened breathlessly and afterward ran all the way home without stopping. She had sat staring at her mirror for hours, peering deep into the glass, looking over every bit of its shiny surface, wondering if anything was inside.

She was still sitting in front of the mirror, nose pressed to the glass, when they had finally found her. Her mother was furious and had the steward thrash the maid with a leather strop.

"It must have hurt terribly. She couldn't sit down for days, the poor thing," Isabella said to the glass.

Isabella's reflection jutted out its lower lip and answered with a sad face.

She hadn't seen any demon hiding in her mirror that day. It was all so terribly disappointing. But then, perhaps the preacher had never meant to say that real demons lived in mirrors. Perhaps he had just meant vanity, the demon of pride. Yes, she was quite pleased at having thought of such a thing. It was so very clever of her. Every bit as clever as anything she had ever heard Cecily say.

Isabella didn't like her stepdaughter. Not one little bit. She didn't trust her. Nor was she particularly fond of her husband. She still remembered her disappointment when she had met him on their wedding day. She had been told he was a famous warrior and had imagined he might be strong and handsome. He wasn't. Instead he was old. And fat. And ugly. And he had never shown her any real affection. Well, at least not after those first few weeks, when he had claimed his marital privileges in such a coarse manner, grunting, pawing, and thrusting at her with that flabby body of his. He hadn't visited her chambers as much since then, and hardly ever after her son was born, which was just as well because she found him to be utterly repulsive. He was even more ugly now, if such a thing were possible, and most of the time he smelled of piss and stale sweat, like an old horse blanket.

"He's disgusting!"

Her reflection grimaced sourly and stuck out its tongue.

Of course, now that he was sick, her husband wasn't quite so fat anymore, and these days he bore another smell. The scent of death, she thought.

At that moment, the door behind her creaked open on its leather hinges and then clicked shut, the iron bolt rasping against metal as it was slid into place. Isabella could sense the man's approach, and the mirror darkened as he loomed over her. Then she could see his hands on her shoulders, the long white fingers with their perfectly groomed nails pressing into her flesh.

"Still talking to yourself, my lady?"

He began massaging her shoulders—intimately, as a lover might. But this man was no lover of hers.

"You really are quite mad, aren't you? If you had not been so pretty, I dare say that your family would have locked you away years ago. Or perhaps they might have left you in a ditch at the side of the North Road, and you would be either dead by now or a toothless harlot turning tricks for halfpennies in a brothel somewhere.

"Where I grew up, they used to believe madness was sent by the Devil, and that those possessed of it needed to be beaten, starved, or even drowned so as to drive the demons from their bodies. That would not have been the fate of a fine lady like you, however. No, such a cure would be reserved for the rustics. People like me. You would have been shut away in a tower, and never heard from again, a secret family shame that nobody would speak of. And perhaps one day, when people had forgotten about you entirely, you might have been disposed of in some discreet fashion, like a babe born with a withered arm or a clubfoot."

It was almost dusk, and Isabella's reflection had become shadowy and vague.

"I wonder whether your son will share your peculiarities. I think he might."

"Don't say that!" She twisted about and looked up at him over her shoulder, her pretty face contorted with rage. "Don't say it!"

"They do say it passes down to the children."

"Don't you say it!" she hissed.

He chuckled. It was a dry sort of laugh, bereft of merriment, full of scorn. Isabella felt tears stinging her eyes and bit her lip, angry with herself for letting him goad her. She knew he enjoyed it, and she had sworn she wouldn't give him the pleasure.

"There now, that's much better," he said, pressing her firmly back down to her seat. "And now that I have your attention, let us discuss those things that I require of you. I am afraid it is a rather long list, but I shall expect you to do it all. And do try not to disappoint me, my dear." He squeezed Isabella's shoulders hard, making her wince in discomfort. "You know what will happen should you do so."

He didn't need to threaten her again. He knew full well she

would do as he asked, and she hated him for it. If there was a demon in her mirror, Isabella imagined she would pray to it. She would strike a bargain and ask it to kill him. Him and her husband both. And she would not care if it damned her soul to hell.

But there was no demon. There didn't need to be. There were enough real monsters in the world.

CHAPTER 7

"So, there's heresy afoot?"

The village constable was a giant of a man, well over six feet tall, with roughly the girth of a bull. He spoke to Thomas in a dramatic rumbling whisper, about as loud as a normal man might talk. "Sorcery is it then? Necromancy?"

"I did not say so," Thomas replied.

"Aye, maybe you didn't, but I heard tell of it. They say as how a witch must have killed that poor old sod at the church. *Murdered* him," the constable added with a sinister leer, "and then laid his body out on the high altar for some foul purpose."

The constable's forehead creased up like a plowed field. "Or maybe it was a demon summoned by a witch as did the killing." He shook his head as if the distinction was unimportant. "Anyway, all spread across the altar he was, arms and legs flung out like he'd been crucified. I saw it with my own eyes. And I heard the pope himself has declared it heresy and has sent one of his black priests here to investigate."

"Did you see a witch or a demon, John?" asked Thomas. "Did anyone?"

Constable John scratched at his bulbous nose. "No. But if there weren't some devilry, why would a black priest be here?"

"He's a friar, John—a Dominican friar."

"He's not a priest then?"

"Well, yes, I believe he has been ordained, but he is still a friar."

The constable considered that for a moment and then shrugged it off, deciding it was all a bit too complicated and not something he really needed to understand.

"No, it's heresy, all right," he declared happily. "*Magic. Sorcery.* And I can't say it surprises me none. You hear all sorts of things these days. Why, just the other day I heard there was some mumper walking around the country saying as how he was the real king. That he had been switched as a baby because he had been born with a crooked leg. He said Edward is nothing but a cesspit digger's by-blow. Well, they took the mumper up and questioned him, and what do you know? It turned out he was being told what to do by the Devil himself, and the Devil had been talking to him through his black cat. *A bloody cat, possessed by the Devil!* Can you imagine it? Now tell me there's nothing wrong with that."

Thomas squinted up drily at the big man. He knew the story, of course. John Deydras was a young clerk in Oxford who turned up one day at Beaumont castle, claiming it as his birthright. According to Deydras, he had been playing in the castle courtyard as a child when a royal servant had allowed a sow or a dog to attack him and bite off his ear. Fearing punishment, the servant had switched the princeling with a carter's child. Deydras was never lame, as the constable had suggested; he was just short an ear. It was an insane tale from a sick man, and a testament to how deeply unpopular King Edward had become. Naturally, the pretender was tried and hung for sedition, and just to be on the safe side, so was his cat.

"It's true, I tell you," insisted the big man, sensing that his story was not being received with quite the seriousness it deserved. "I had it from a pack peddler passing through on his way to Melton.

He swore to it. And that's not all either. I also heard tell that there's been strange goings on in Bristol at the crossroads where they hung the rebels. Aye, all sorts of strange things, they say. *Evil* things. Like a giant crow that flew down and alighted on the gallows, cawed three times three, flapped its wings up and down, and then shit and flew away. Everyone knows crows are an evil omen."

This last was a story Thomas had also heard, though in the tale he had been told, the strange happenings had been miracles and the crow had been an angel, and it had certainly not defecated on the gallows. He supposed which story you believed depended on who you had supported in the rebellion.

"Tell me, John, have you done any actual investigation beyond listening to superstition."

The constable looked at him defensively. "Aye. Of course I have. I've looked all over for strangers and runaways."

He said *strangers* with the same sinister connotation he had reserved for *sorcery*.

Villages were tight-knit communities. The villagers lived together, worked together, married each other, and looked to their lord for protection and comfort, rarely leaving home unless it was to go to the local market town after harvest. Most of them were villeins, feudal tenants who belonged to their lord and could not marry or leave without his permission. And by law, they were responsible for any of their people who did commit a crime, so it was always useful to find a stranger to pin the blame on. Even if no crime had been committed, it was not unusual in some places for the watch to round up any strangers wandering the streets at night and throw them in the stocks on general principle. And there they would stay until someone vouched for them, which was none too easy because, well, they were strangers. Unfortunately for John, the only stranger in Bottesford on the night of the murder had met his grisly end in Saint Mary's Church.

"I've been all the way over to Barrowby," he added.

Barrowby must have been all of a staggering five miles away. In his mind's eye, Thomas could see the constable's wife packing him up as if he were off to France.

"His lordship sent word to the sheriff as well, though we are not likely to see him or his men."

That much was certainly true. Country justice was usually left to the lord of the manor, the royal assizes only swinging by a few times a year to dole out the king's justice in the most serious cases. Thomas suspected that the sheriff would want little enough to do with the strange goings on at Bottesford. At least, not until it was time to collect the taxes.

They crossed the village green, surrounded by several clusters of mostly single-room cottages, and walked past a set of empty stocks that were leaning to the side where they had sunk into the mud at some point over the last wet season. Young children were happily playing around them. The girls were taking turns to poke their heads and hands through slats, stick out their tongues, and blow giant raspberries at the boys, before scampering away, shrill voices shrieking with delight.

Constable John coughed and walked by, pretending not to notice.

"Alehouse is right there," he said waving a hand to the far side of the green. Apparently, Roger Lacy had visited the alehouse the night he was murdered, a fact that Thomas found curious, as it sounded like Lacy was scarcely better off than a beggar, without a penny to spend.

What passed for the village alehouse was really just a larger cottage with a bushel sign out front to let people know ale was brewed there. It would be a stretch to call it a tavern. The inside was not much more than a large pot room, with a straw-covered earthen floor and an odd assortment of tables, benches, stools, and barrels. It was a place where locals might gather to share a companionable drink or to hear the latest news from the occasional wandering peddler, or simply to gawk at travelers getting some refreshment while their horses were shod. The door and shutters were propped full open, letting some light and a welcome breath of fresh air into what might otherwise have been an ill-lit and musty little room.

The place was empty, save for three men, all clustered around the same trestle table, drinking ale and eating rye bread and cheese. They were all of an age, perhaps in their mid-thirties. Two of them, fresh from the fields, were dressed in the soiled smocks and clogs of the country so despised by Bishop Henry. One had a huge bushy beard that looked like he was trying to make up for his thinning hair. Another had an unfortunate face, all squashed and scrunched up, as though it had been smashed repeatedly against an anvil. The third, a stocky, bull-like fellow with almost no neck, was dressed in a shabby tunic, his woolen hose rolled down to display thick calves and a pair of hairy shins. He looked to be the leader of the group and was holding court, braying loudly, when they entered.

A bored-looking pot girl flitted back and forth, trying to look busy. She seemed a little too young to be the alewife, so it was probably her mother who did the brewing. Her face broke into a welcoming smile at the prospect of two new customers.

Talk at the table had ceased, and the three patrons eyed the newcomers distrustfully. Thomas could tell from their sullen expressions that they would not be inclined to be of much help.

"Good morrow, friends," he said cheerily, and three pairs of suspicious eyes followed him as he dragged a stool across the floor and sat down at the table with them. Bushy Beard's beaker had paused halfway to his mouth, and he was now regarding Thomas over its rim.

"Another jug for me and my friends here," said Thomas, catching the girl's eye and slapping the tabletop.

She smiled widely and bustled off in a flurry of skirts. Thomas had not offered John a seat, and there was no room for him anyway, so he just stood awkwardly behind, looming over them all.

The pot girl set down a fresh jug and filled a wooden mazer for Thomas, slopping ale liberally over the table. Thomas downed half his ale in one giant swig and smacked his lips appreciatively.

"By God, that's good stuff!"

Actually, it was a bit too sweet for his liking, but decent enough. An honest brew and not one that was likely to risk the alewife being dragged to the manor court for selling watery ale. The girl rewarded him with another smile and refilled the bowl he held out to her. The others at the table sat motionless, watching him, beakers held in unmoving hands.

Thomas gestured to the girl to leave the jug and watched her walk away, before turning his attention back to his companions.

"We can buy our own drink." It was No-Neck who broke the silence.

"I don't doubt it, friend. But why turn down free ale? I am Thomas Lester."

"We know who you are and why you're here. And we don't need no free ale."

The constable leaned down and whispered, comically loud, out of the side of his mouth: "The mouthy bugger who looks like he swallowed a bullock is Tom Attwood. He has a mill on the river off the north fields. The ugly one with the scabs is Adam, and that one hiding behind his beard is Will Peck."

Thomas paused and turned about. "Thank you, John." The tone and stare were intended to convey to the constable in no uncertain terms that he should stay quiet.

"Right you are," said John. "I'll just grab myself a beaker, then, and have a sip or two to wet the old whistle." He looked longingly at the jug. "Just a sip or two. To wet the whistle, like."

Thomas took another mouthful. He had to admit the ale was growing on him. The alewife had managed to do something with the grains that gave it a surprisingly tasty apple flavor. It wasn't too sweet at all. And it was fresh, probably brewed that day. He licked his lips and topped off his mazer, reminding himself not to be so quick to judge.

"John says that the old man who was murdered at the church stopped by here for a drink the night he was killed. Were you here that night, Tom?" Thomas directed his question to the no-neck miller. "Did you see Roger Lacy?"

"I don't remember," was the surly response.

Thomas turned to one of his companions, the ugly one.

"How about you? Adam, isn't it? Do you remember him?"

"He don't remember nothing either," growled No-Neck with a warning glance at his friend.

John had ventured to pick up a mazer and was reaching for the jug when he decided that he had heard quite enough. He slapped the table loudly with a meaty hand.

"By Christ and all that's holy! The gentleman is here on business from his lordship. You'll answer his questions or you'll answer to me."

The pot girl was bringing over another jug and stopped dead in her tracks. Her eyes flicked nervously from one to the other, and she backed away a few steps.

"Now see here, John," began No-Neck.

The constable was having none of it, and Thomas just

managed to pick up his mazer before the big hand came crashing down again.

"Answer. The. Question," he growled, each word punctuated with another mighty thump of the table that made all three men flinch and sent beakers rattling and bouncing about, one of them toppling over and rolling all the way across the table to fall on the floor with a loud *thunk*.

Thomas smiled. The big man had his uses it seemed.

"You'll answer the damned question, Tom, or I swear to God I'll be having you."

The threat was accompanied by a giant sausage of a finger jabbing the miller repeatedly in the chest, nearly knocking him off his stool. The miller was a big man, broad in the chest, but John was something else.

"Now, John," the miller started, squirming as far back on his stool as he could without actually falling off, "there's no need to go threatening a man."

He cleared his throat nervously and turned back to Thomas. "Aye, he was here. Sat right over there." He flicked his hand vaguely to a small table set in a shadowy corner. "He didn't speak none. He just sat all alone, looking about him with those beady little eyes of his, every now and then sipping at his ale like it was Rhenish wine, still spilling most of it down his tunic. And he kept cackling away and talking to himself. It was making us all right uncomfortable, him sitting there watching us, listening in on our talk, acting funny. I told Sally to fetch John. I thought to have him thrashed for a vagabond and thrown in the stocks for the night. Daft old bugger, he was, and no mistake. A right bleeding nutcase."

He blinked and looked at Thomas's hard face, suddenly realizing his comments might not sit too well, given the man had actually suffered a far grislier fate.

"Er. Poor old sod, that is to say," the miller added weakly, tucking his chin down into his chest.

Bushy Beard had no such reservations.

"No, you're right, Tom. A right nutter, he was. Wouldn't have surprised me none if he had dragged out a pittance bowl and gone a-begging table-to-table to scrounge up the coin to pay for his ale. Tom was all for tossing him into the street, and I had half a mind to do so myself. You could have knocked me down with a feather when he dragged out that fat coin purse of his and started throwing his money around like he was some sort of lord."

"He had money then?" asked Thomas, surprised at the unlikely revelation.

"Aye, he had money—a right lot of it." Ugly Adam had picked up the tale. "And he made sure to let us all know. Waving his purse about, acting all high and mighty. And him sitting there dressed like a vagabond and looking like a big dog's leavings."

Thomas tried not to look too closely at Adam's own filth-covered smock or the distinctly cowpat-looking material clinging to his clogs. "Tom said he was talking to himself. Did you hear anything he had to say?"

"It was just a lot of nonsense," Adam replied. "*'Fine as a lord! Lucky old Roger!'* And then a bunch of mumbling and cackling. Like Tom said, he was a daft old bugger, and that's all there is to it."

The pot girl, who had been hovering about, pretending not to listen, decided to join the conversation. She had a round face flushed with color and a tangle of mousy brown hair under her linen cap. Thomas would not call her pretty, but she looked well enough and had a full, comely shape and the kind of cheeky sultriness that he imagined men drinking in the alehouse appreciated a little more than their wives might have liked.

"Oh, you be quiet. Don't you listen to them, sir," she said, addressing Thomas. "He was a harmless old man. He wasn't doing anything wrong—just sitting there having a drink, peaceful and quiet like."

"Was he staying here?" Thomas had noticed a couple of old mattresses piled against the far wall that travelers might rent for the night.

She picked up the fallen beaker and set it down again on the table, tossing an accusing glare at the constable.

"No. I did offer him a mattress, but he said he was staying at the priory guesthouse. I can't say that I believed him. I half-think he might have been sleeping rough, under a hedge some-where. I didn't say anything, though. I didn't want to make him uncomfortable." Thomas nodded encouragingly. "He was sad. I felt sorry for him."

Bushy Beard snorted indelicately. "Of course you did, Sally. No doubt it helped that he gave you a shiny penny and waved a full bag of coin under your nose."

"No, that's not it! And I don't care how he was dressed nei-ther. He had nice manners. Anyone could tell he was a gentle-man. He had just come on hard times I guessed."

Bushy Beard huffed dismissively.

"And it's nice to have a man come in here who isn't always pawing at me. And you with a wife and three young ones at home, Will Peck."

"Now see here!" Peck blurted angrily.

They bickered back and forth until John's big hand slammed the table again to quiet them, sending the selfsame beaker roll-ing back across the table and down onto the floor.

Thomas gripped John's wrist and lifted his hand casually from the tabletop.

"And were you three the only other ones here that night?"

They all nodded. Bushy Beard also threw in an added glare at the pot girl.

"And you all left together?"

The question was met with silence. Heads sunk into their beakers, faces became closed and guarded, and little furtive glances were cast in the miller's direction. Sally suddenly realized she had other things to do, even though they were her only customers, and bustled off to the back room.

Thomas had long ago learned that silence was often the best way to encourage someone to speak, and soon enough Tom, the miller, couldn't stand it any longer. "I left first," he blurted out. "I'd had my skinful and needed to work the next day."

"And when did you leave?"

The miller's eyes darted to his friends, who had now found the sudsy contents of their beakers fascinating.

"Did you leave at about the same time as Lacy, Tom?"

"I don't recall exactly. I was drunk. It may have been around then I left," he murmured, his voice trailing off weakly.

The constable interrupted loudly. "By God, you followed him out, didn't you?"

"I did not!" protested the miller. "I just left after he did, that's all. Sure, it was about the same time, but I didn't *follow* him. Why would I *follow* him? What would be the point of that?"

He looked about angrily. Everyone was staring at him.

"Wait, you don't think . . . ?" He laughed half-heartedly. "Now look here. I don't know what you're all suggesting, but I went and slept it off. And that's all I did. I didn't follow anyone, let alone some half-mad old vagabond."

"A half-mad old vagabond with a sackful of coin," added John before Thomas silenced him with an upraised hand.

"Your wife will say you were home, then?" Thomas asked.

"My wife?" He gave John a pleading look. "John, you know how I sleep it off at the mill. Tell him that's what I do." He turned to Thomas. "When I've had a bit too much to drink, I sleep it off at my mill, sir, so as not to disturb the missus and the little ones. You know how it is."

"Is that where you went, Tom? To your mill?"

"I . . . I expect so. I don't remember much. I was well and truly soused."

He looked helplessly at his friends.

Ugly Adam cleared his throat. "Aye, he was right soused, weaving about, could barely get to his feet. We told him he'd had enough and should be on his way. He knows his missus won't have him in the house when he gets like that, so he goes off to his mill until he comes round and cleans himself up."

Tom smiled his thanks for the show of support.

"And did either of you others leave with him?" asked Thomas.

They both shook their heads.

"So neither of you can actually vouch for where he went?"

They looked at each other, and their eyes flicked back to the miller.

"This is ridiculous!" Tom blurted angrily. "You can't possibly be accusing me?"

Thomas eased himself to his feet and tossed some coins onto the table. "Nobody is accusing you, Tom. We are just trying to put things together. Come on, John. We've got things to do."

As they were leaving, the constable leaned over the table, resting his palms flat on its surface so that it keeled dangerously to the side under his weight. No small man himself, the miller shrank back on his stool.

"We'll be back to talk some more to you." John gave Tom one last hard stare, jabbed him again in the chest with his giant sausage finger, and they walked out, leaving a stunned silence behind them.

They had barely stepped out into the light when the constable decided to share his thoughts on what they had just heard.

"Well, I like him for it."

"Who?"

"Tom Attwood. The miller."

"You like him for what, John?"

"It's as obvious as the nose on your face, ain't it?" Thomas frowned at him questioningly. "He's followed Lacy out, gone into the church and done for him, choked the life out of him, taken all the coin, and legged it off into the night."

The big man gave a decided nod, satisfied he had tied it all together rather nicely.

"I thought it was heresy," Thomas reminded him. "Didn't you tell me it was a demon or a witch?"

"Well, I like to keep an open mind, don't I? And, as I said, I like him for it. Always cheating honest folk, putting his fat thumb on the scale. He killed the poor old sod and took his money pouch. You see if he didn't."

Poor old sod seemed to have become the accepted term of reference in the village for Roger Lacy.

"That doesn't seem likely if he was as drunk as they say," argued Thomas.

It wasn't a point the constable seemed to think important enough to disturb his analysis.

"You don't need to be sober to strangle a man. And lots of folk do stupid things when they've tied one on. He got drunk, saw the poor old sod throwing around his money, saw his hefty coin purse, and thought to his self, *I'll have some o' that, I will.* And maybe he wasn't so drunk after all. Maybe he just acted that way." He gave Thomas a knowing wink. "You caught him lying. He's our man. Yes, I am convinced of it."

"Then where is the coin? He isn't exactly living like a lord, is he?"

John narrowed his eyes and stroked his chin thoughtfully, scratching first at his scrubby beard and then his nose.

"He's stashed it," he said decidedly. "Oh, he's no fool—he'll have stashed it right quick. It's probably in his mill, hidden in among the grain or in a sack of flour. Didn't you see how squirmy he was? Wriggling about like he had ringworms up his arse and down his hose when you were asking him questions. Shuffling about uncomfortable-like."

The miller had looked uncomfortable, thought Thomas, but who would not when accused of being a killer?

"And why was Lacy killed in the church, and why was the body splayed across the altar?"

"He followed him into the church, pretending as how he was going to pray himself, and then he offed him. Once he realized what he had done, he took fright, seeing he just killed the man, and he ran. Didn't give a thought to it—just sort of tossed the body aside."

"And he just happened to toss him across the holy altar, arms and legs splayed out like a human sacrifice?"

John didn't find it necessary to dwell too deeply on that complication.

"No, he's our man. You mark my words." He winked again and tapped his nose, a nose that had been broken more than once and had healed a might crooked. "I have a nose for this sort of thing."

Thomas very much doubted that the constable of Bottesford village had ever encountered this sort of thing.

"Where next then?" John asked cheerily. "To his lordship and tell him we figured it out?"

"No. Let's head to the priory."

"Why there?"

Thomas knew it was likely that both Lacy and Father Oswin had lain in the priory's mortuary chapel before being put in the ground.

"I want to hear what the monks have to say about this fellow Lacy, and perhaps they can help us with the Dominican's suggestion that Father Oswin was poisoned."

The constable's jaw sagged.

"By Christ and all that's holy!" he exclaimed loudly, his hands flicking about his chest, tracing a cross, and his eyebrows shooting up into his ragged mop of hair. *"The bloody vicar was poisoned and all, was he?"*

Several bystanders turned to look at them, their faces full of shock.

"Keep your voice down, man," hissed Thomas, giving the big man a withering look.

"Oh, aye," he mumbled apologetically, tucking his head down. "Sorry about that. You caught me by surprise is all."

Thomas sighed and set his mind to the tasks ahead. John Constable plodded along heavily at his side, as simple, straightforward, and uncomplicated as his name.

CHAPTER 8

The vicarage of Saint Mary's was a timbered and thatched cottage sitting next to the much grander church, leaning humbly against that noble edifice as if someone had piled it there purely as an afterthought.

Friar Justus watched from the vicarage window as Thomas trudged down the main street, noted the monstrous creature lumbering along at his side, and then turned to face the late Father Oswin's maidservant, who was sitting nervously in the middle of the room, awaiting his pleasure.

She was far from being a *maid* in the traditional sense and was likely in her early thirties, edging steadily toward her matron years. He supposed she was not unattractive. A little plump, perhaps, and with one of those broad faces so common among the rustics in these parts. At first glance, one might suppose she was dressed modestly enough in a homespun green kirtle that fell down to her ankle boots. Justus noticed, however, that the dress was just tight enough to hint at the full figure beneath and that it was cinched rather saucily at the waist with a plain twist of leather, no doubt intended to emphasize a pair of generous hips. He did not approve of the immodesty, bordering some-what on lasciviousness in his mind, but she had at least thought to cover her hair with a plain cap, even if several unkempt, ragged brown tresses had managed to burst out hither and thither.

The Dominican settled down into the chair opposite her. It was one of those high-backed chairs with padded armrests and deep, comfortable cushions—the kind one might expect to encounter in the family parlor of a country lord rather than in a tumble-down old vicarage. Justus did not like it. He preferred a hard stool that chafed one's backside if planted on it for too long. One should never be too comfortable as a man of the cloth. Comfort is kin to sloth, and sloth is a sin.

The maid had somehow contrived to sit perched atop her own tiny milking stool with all the dignity of a queen on her throne. She seemed to have that knack some women possess of sitting up straight in the most difficult circumstances: shoulders drawn back, head raised, hands resting lightly in her lap—a posture that certainly made the most of her figure, something Justus observed only briefly before quickly averting his eyes from the temptation.

A glance at Guy, standing at the door eyeing the maid with undisguised lust, reminded Justus that not everyone possessed such laudable self-restraint. The Dominican's lip curled up in disapproval. He had no intention of pandering to either the man's deviances or the woman's vanity.

"That will be all for now, Guy," he said with a dismissive flick of his wrist.

The henchman's eyes snapped up, and his face took on an expression that could only be described as surly. For a moment Justus thought he might actually refuse the command, but instead the ruffian shrugged his shoulders and stomped out of the room, making sure to slam the door shut behind him in a parting display of petulance.

Dominic, Justus was pleased to note, appeared completely unmoved by the woman's presence. He was sitting unobtrusively in the corner of the room, his legs folded under him, busily tacking some parchment down onto the writing tray perched on his knee; inkhorn, pumice stone, and quill all ready to hand. Justus smiled with approval and turned his attention back to the vicar's maid, who was now regarding him expectantly.

"Agnes, isn't it?" Justus asked, leaning forward on his staff.

"Yes, Father."

The Dominican found it interesting that she chose to call him *Father*. He liked that. It bespoke a certain respect, and of course it was quite appropriate as he had been ordained and was no simple friar.

"Agnes," he repeated slowly. "What a pretty name."

Agnes smiled back her thanks for the small compliment.

"And a rather popular name as well. It seems that every other young woman I meet hereabouts is an Agnes. No doubt you were named after your mother?"

The pitch of his last word rose, along with his eyebrows, in the traditional manner of turning a statement into a question.

"I was named after my grandmother, sir," she explained proudly. "Though she was *Agneta*," Agnes added, emphasizing the "*ta*" for the friar's benefit.

"A most subtle but no doubt important difference. How clever of your mother to distinguish you so. She must be a very astute woman. Is she still with us, I wonder?"

"No, sir. She passed away five years ago this winter."

"Oh, I am very sorry to hear it," he said, bowing his head and giving her hand a comforting little squeeze before looking up again with a happy smile. "On the bright side, I suppose that would serve to free up her own name . . . ?" He raised his eyebrows again.

"Margery," said Agnes, answering the unasked question.

"How lovely!" he declared. "Why, between Agnes, Alicia, Margery, and Matilda, I believe we might have captured the names of the greater part of the female population in this country. Remarkable." Justus shook his head in wonder. "Truly remarkable."

Agnes offered him a weak, faltering smile, uncertain whether she was being mocked.

"I must say you are quite charming, my dear, and I could happily sit here and talk genealogy and nomenclature with you all day, but I am afraid we must turn our minds to far less enjoyable matters."

Justus made the merest gesture with his finger to Dominic, who up to this point had been watching silently. The young friar dabbed his quill into the small pot of ink and sat up straight, nib poised above the parchment, ready to transcribe at his master's direction.

"Now, pray tell, how long had you worked for Father Oswin?"

"Since my husband died a few years back."

Interesting, thought Justus. *A widow.* He might make something of that.

"And you tended to his . . . uh . . . needs?"

"Oh yes, I did. In that I washed and cleaned and cooked and helped out about the church, laundering the altar cloths, the vestments and the like," she explained hurriedly, having belatedly caught the question's potential double meaning.

"It must have been a terrible shock for you when Father Oswin died. You found him, did you not?"

"Yes, sir. I can't say that I was completely shocked, though. Everybody knew he suffered with his heart."

"So I have heard," conceded Justus. "And yet I believe him to have been poisoned."

Agnes's mouth sagged open in surprise. "Poisoned? No, sir, it was his heart. I am sure of it."

"Ah, so you are familiar with the signs of poisoning then?"

he asked mildly. "Is that correct, Agnes? Do you profess to have some *intimate* knowledge of poisons?"

"I am sure I do not, sir," she replied indignantly. "I know nothing of such things."

"Then I have to ask myself why you would say with such confidence that he was not poisoned. Unless"—he narrowed his eyes and waggled a finger, as though struck by a sudden thought—"unless you wish us to believe such is the case; unless, perhaps, you are trying to *hide* something from us. Is that why you insist that Father Oswin was not poisoned, Agnes? Are you trying to hide something from us?"

"No, Father! I only knew he suffered with his heart. That's all."

"So, isn't the truth, given your professed ignorance of these matters, that you do not know one way or another whether Father Oswin was poisoned?"

Agnes thought hard, her face creasing up in a look that made Justus wonder if she needed to visit the *necessarium*.

"I suppose I cannot say."

Justus crooked a bony finger to his scribe, barely raising it from his staff, rolling it in a circular motion to indicate that Dominic should begin writing.

"Indeed, you would then surely have to agree that it is *possible* he was poisoned. As far as you know, at least. Quite *possible*."

"I suppose so," she replied after another long think. "But . . . but I really do not think—"

Justus suddenly slammed his staff onto the ground, thumping it noisily against the hard-packed earth floor.

"We have been over this! I say he was poisoned. *Poisoned!*" he repeated. "Do you dare to call me a liar, madam? Is that what you are about?"

"N–no, Father, I—"

"Then do you take me for a fool? Is that it? Am I some

addle-brained imbecile, drooling and dribbling for your personal amusement?"

Justus waved his hands about, stuck out his tongue, and rolled his eyes, doing his best impression of a madman.

He then glared angrily at her for a long moment before sitting back and dabbing daintily at his mouth with the sleeve of his robe. "Forgive me, Agnes. These are troubling times. The Devil crouches at our threshold and threatens us all."

Agnes's eyes flicked nervously to the door, almost as though she expected to see some hideous monster lurking there.

"Now, you were telling me how, when you found Father Oswin, you thought to yourself that he might have been poisoned?"

"I did not, I—"

Thump, thump, thump, went the staff, causing Agnes to wince at each blow.

"Are you mocking me, Agnes?"

She shook her head vigorously, a touch of panic in her eyes.

"I rather suspect that you are. You know, my dear, I am surprised you have not yet remarried. Is it not the custom hereabouts for the local reeve to find another man for a young widow such as yourself? Or perhaps, for some reason, you do not wish another husband?"

Agnes's eyes began to water as she stammered out her response. "His lordship has been kind to me. He knows how much I cared for my husband."

"Yes, but it is not quite right for a woman as young as you to be unmarried. It does not sit comfortably with me. It is a widow's *duty* to remarry, especially a widow of your age who could reasonably be expected to procreate. You ought to know this."

He stroked his chin thoughtfully.

"And you say that your husband passed away like your last master. Did he also die of a heart ailment?"

Agnes nodded slowly.

"Well, I must say, Agnes, it is fortunate indeed that I am here to protect you from suspicion. Another sent to investigate these matters might wonder at these coincidences. That first your husband and then your master dies, and both so suddenly and of weakened hearts. And perhaps they might wonder that a comely young widow had not yet sought another husband. They might suspect you of having poisoned both of them. Or perhaps they might suspect you of having tended rather too closely to Father Oswin's needs. That perhaps you whored yourself for the old priest, satisfying your own lusts at the same time; and that you even did so in the church itself, committing the most heinous sacrilege, squealing with delight as you lay together in the very altar cloths you claim to have laundered."

By now, Agnes was gaping in open-mouthed horror.

"But not I," continued Justus. "No, you and I shall be great friends, and I believe I can protect you from such dangerous accusations. Would you like that?"

She barely managed a nod.

"Then the first thing I shall do is see you properly wed. You are still attractive, dear, and you have such lovely hair."

Justus reached forward and played his fingers through the loose locks spilling out of her cap.

Actually, on closer inspection, the Dominican thought Agnes rather plain after all. Her face was far too broad, her nose a little too long, and her eyes a little too close together so that she seemed to wear a permanent squint. All of her features were at odds. There was no true harmony to her face at all, and a complete want of grace in her manner. *Uncouth* was the word that most sprung to mind. *Drab* was another. Justus had also noticed that his fingers caught repeatedly in knotted clumps of what turned out to be straggly and greasy hair. He felt the sudden need to gag and had to resist the urge to shrink away from her and wipe his hands on his habit.

"Did you know that Agnes is an old Greek name meaning 'chaste'?" he asked, not waiting for a response. "It would be a great shame for you to sully your grandmother's lovely name by strutting wantonly about the village, tempting other women's husbands. That would be most unseemly and would raise all sorts of unfortunate questions. Surely you do not want that, do you?"

A vigorous shake of the head this time, accompanied by the most charming trembling of her lower lip and a fat tear that trickled slowly down her left cheek.

"*Excellent!* Then the next time I speak with you, I hope to be congratulating you on your upcoming nuptials. We shall have you wedded, bedded, and your belly filled with a child in no time."

Justus settled back into his seat, for once rather enjoying the plump cushions and noting with satisfaction that Agnes was no longer sitting quite so erect.

"Where were we? Ah yes, you were telling me how, when you found Father Oswin, you thought to yourself that he might have been poisoned. Do you remember that?"

Agnes swallowed slowly, looked down, and nodded.

"I need you to say it, dear. Now what was it you thought when you found him?"

"I . . . I thought as how he might have been poisoned," she replied in a hoarse whisper.

The Dominican's finger gestured once more to Friar Dominic.

"And can you describe what you saw?"

Her brow creased up, and she began a pitiful stammering.

"Perhaps you would like me to help you remember? To refresh your recollection of the scene, so to speak?"

"Yes, yes, I would. I should like that very much, sir," she said, managing to produce a filthy linen rag from her sleeve that she proceeded to dab at her eyes and nose.

"No doubt you saw his blackened and swollen tongue."

"I—yes . . ."

"Froth on his lips, perhaps mixed with blood, and vomit on his shirt. No doubt you saw that also."

"Yes, I think I did."

"And his skin was a most unnatural color, was it not? And his eyes bloodied?"

"Oh yes, now you mention it, I believe so."

"And did you get close enough that you noticed any peculiar smell about him, a strangely sweet or bitter smell?"

"A . . . a bitter smell?" It was more of a question than a statement, and Agnes looked up uncertainly for approval

"Yes, sadly that would make sense. And did you find his face frozen in a rictus of terror as if he had seen the Devil himself?"

"You describe him exact, sir."

Justus smiled indulgently. He doubted Agnes had ever heard the word *rictus* before. Still, there was no need to quibble over the details. This was all going rather well.

"And at that moment you felt sure he had been poisoned, didn't you?"

"I did. I did!" she exclaimed, at last getting into the spirit of her role.

Dominic had stopped writing and was looking at her intently. Justus gestured to him irritably, and he began scratching away again. This was good stuff, and it needed to be recorded faithfully. There needed to be a record of what had transpired here, so everyone would know the truth of the matter. And detailed proofs would be required to petition the archbishop and pope for a true inquisition.

Agnes's face clouded over as she was struck by an inconvenient thought. "At the time, though, I did not say as much."

"Of course not," Justus declared with a little laugh, as if it was the most natural thing in the world for her to have omitted this small detail. "At the time you surely did not think it your place to make such a claim. You no doubt assumed that some clever physician or cleric would examine the body and reach the same conclusion. How could they not? And far better, you thought, to leave such reasoning and investigation to someone with experience of death and an intimate knowledge of poisons. After all, it would be a terrible accusation for a humble maid to make."

Agnes listened intently, nodding along. "Yes, yes, that's how I felt. Best to say nothing than spread wicked rumors and speak out of turn. Best leave it to those who know what they are about."

Justus patted her hand encouragingly, careful to avoid the one in which she clutched the grubby nose wipe.

"Very good. Now, let us go over your story one more time, to make sure we have it exact. And when we are done, you shall put your mark on a piece of paper for me, and we shall have you on your way to picking out a husband in no time."

Justus sighed contentedly, sat back, and wriggled about, getting himself even more comfortable. Young Dominic was staring wide-eyed at him, no doubt completely in awe at the masterful performance. Justus smiled knowingly, resisting the urge to share a conspiratorial wink. What a wonderful opportunity for the young man to see a real inquisitor at work; to learn from the very best. He was fortunate indeed.

CHAPTER 9

Brother Eustace was a willowy man of advancing years, all wrinkled skin and protruding bone. When Thomas had first met him, he bore the kind of grave and guarded expression that one might expect of a mortician, but on introduction his long face broke into a warm, welcoming smile more befitting his role as infirmerer of the Benedictine priory, a man of infinite compassion who eased his patients' suffering as much with his manner as with his tonics and balms.

He tucked his hands into the sleeves of his habit and listened somberly as Thomas explained the purpose of his visit, nodding every now and then to indicate comprehension, and cocking his head to the side in the way of one slightly hard of hearing.

"I regret to say I can be of little assistance to you," he said when Thomas was done, speaking in the constrained and graveled tones of the aged. "If the truth be told, I recall nothing remarkable about Father Oswin's body. To these old eyes, he bore the appearance of a man whose heart had given out on him."

"Did you notice aught strange about his lips or nostrils, a discharge of blood or vomit perhaps, or an unusual smell or markings on his neck that might suggest he clawed at his throat?"

Eustace raised a single bushy white eyebrow. "You know something of poisons and death, then?"

"You might say so," Thomas replied.

The monk eyed him curiously for a moment and then shrugged his shoulders.

"If it is signs of poisoning you seek, I am afraid I must again disappoint you. In all honesty, I did not examine him for such things. I knew Oswin to have a weak heart. He regularly came to me for decoctions of motherwort and chamomile to steady his nerves, and he was always afraid to exert himself overly much lest he do serious harm. I spent my time preparing his body for its final rest, rather than seeking to determine a cause of death that I believed I already knew."

"I understand, and I was in no way criticizing you," explained Thomas. "Would it be fair to suggest, however, that if he had been poisoned, you would likely have noticed?"

Eustace clasped his hands under his chin and looked upward in thought. "Perhaps, though it is not certain. As you are probably aware, several of the symptoms of poisoning are things one might anyway expect to see when a heart gives way. And, depending on the manner of administration, some poisons can be almost undetectable, especially those intended to induce heart failure."

At this point Prior Gilbert swept into the infirmary, all billowing robes and heavy slapping sandals.

"Thomas, I do apologize for not having been here to greet you," he said, a little breathless from having rushed to welcome his guests. "I am so glad we finally have the chance to meet in person."

He seized Thomas's hand in both of his and pumped it up and down before turning to the constable, who had been standing quietly, a deferential pace or so behind Thomas, still a little mortified at having blurted out to all and sundry the possibility that Oswin had been poisoned.

"And I see you brought my good friend John Constable with you. How is Dorothea, John?"

John knuckled his forehead, offering the prior something that was not quite a bow and not quite a nod, but a little of both. "Oh, she's right well, Your Eminence. Right well."

"Still keeping you on the straight and narrow, I trust," chortled the prior pleasantly, with a knowing wink.

John gave an embarrassed laugh. "Oh yes, she does that. And she has some plum jam fresh made that she will be bringing by for you later today. The last of the Lammas plums, she said."

"Ah!" exclaimed Prior Gilbert happily, patting his rotund belly. "Now that is good news indeed. Did you hear that, Eustace? Manna from heaven! Have you met John's wife, Thomas? She is famous in these parts for her jams, you know. A lovely woman, and the prettiest little thing you ever did see."

Thomas had indeed met Dotty, as John called her, and he had rarely seen a more unlikely couple. She was as small as her husband was large, and what little there was of her looked to be made up almost entirely of gristle, skin, and bone. How she managed to bear the weight of the big man on top of her, let alone carry three strapping sons, Thomas could not say, but for all that there was no doubt that she ruled the household, constantly clucking and pecking at the four of them like a mother hen. As for her being pretty, the prior was stretching the truth a little there. Yet she was appealing enough in her country kind of way, and her husband and children completely doted on her. It was a happy family.

"I often wondered why such a charming creature would marry a big, lumbering oaf like this." The prior rolled his eyes at the constable who, far from taking offense, was positively glowing with pride, a stupid grin plastered across his face. "Why, if I were not a man of the Church, I would have courted her myself and might well have stolen her out from under you, John. Indeed, had I known her, she might well have tempted me away from the cloth altogether, and perhaps I would be the constable and you the prior."

John let out a low rumbling laugh, the grin now threatening to split his face.

"And I assure you I would have been stiff competition, even for a behemoth such as you. And the boys?" inquired Gilbert. "Growing fast, I'll wager."

"Like weeds, Your Eminence. Like weeds."

"Well, let us hope they have inherited their mother's good looks. And her intelligence. And her charm as well, for that matter." He reached up to clap a meaty paw on the constable's broad shoulder, all of which produced another rumbling gale of laughter, before turning his attention back to Thomas, a more serious look on his face.

"I understand Sir Mortimer has asked you to investigate that nasty business at Saint Mary's, Thomas. Naturally, we are at your service, though I fear that what assistance we can provide will be little enough. And I am sure you understand that we must do all we can to support the investigation of the archbishop's delegate."

The prior's chubby hands fluttered apologetically in front of him. The message was clear enough. He could not be seen to be favoring Thomas over the Dominican and would prefer if his house were left out of it altogether.

"Of course, Prior. I am grateful to you for whatever help you can provide."

Gilbert gave him a broad, fat-faced smile at having reached what he considered to be a thoroughly satisfactory understanding.

"Well, I apologize for interrupting. Are you all done here?"

"Not quite," replied Thomas.

The prior's face fell, and he clung to his smile like a dead man clinging to his last breath of life.

"I was just about to ask Brother Eustace how he found the condition of Roger Lacy's body."

The infirmerer took up the conversation eagerly, leaving his senior brother looking on awkwardly, wearing a fixed and now entirely inappropriate grin.

"We have a very different story there. The man had been garroted without a doubt. His larynx was crushed and he had scraped knees, split nails, and claw marks on his neck suggesting he fought hard for his life. Or as hard as might be expected of someone in his fragile condition. The blood had pooled underneath him as he lay on his back across the altar, except where it had crusted around his mouth and the deep scratches on his throat. I would say the murderer was a moderately strong individual who first dragged Lacy across the floor on his knees, flipped him on his stomach and then, with his knee pressed hard into Lacy's spine, throttled him from behind while he lay helpless. He then laid the body across the altar, as I am sure you have already heard, binding his feet together and throwing out his arms so he formed the shape of a cross."

Prior Gilbert had slowly turned ashen as the description progressed, wincing visibly at each new gruesome detail.

His report complete, Eustace spread his hands wide and shrugged, as if to say, *What more is there to know?*

"It is as I had thought," said Thomas grimly. "I suppose we would need to disinter the body to discover any greater details."

The prior's eyes bulged in disbelief. He shook his head vigorously from side to side, jowls shaking with passion, horrified at what he had just heard.

"That . . . simply isn't possible, Thomas," he spluttered. "Roger Lacy is well buried now. We saw to it ourselves. I felt it to be our responsibility as he had died in a church over which we have advowson."

From this statement, Thomas understood that a local lord, likely Sir Mortimer de Bray himself, had granted the priory the right to recommend a priest to the benefice of Saint Mary's and to receive a portion of the parish tithes and donations.

"We laid him to rest in the churchyard with all due reverence. I was a little concerned, what with him being a stranger here, that perhaps he might not have been confessed recently. But he was in church when he died, suggesting he was a pious man. I believed it only just in the circumstances, given what the poor man had suffered, to inter him at Saint Mary's. It seemed the decent thing to do. We have said several masses for him, and the chaplain from the manor came down to perform the service. He delivered a wonderful homily, you know. Quite inspiring. A remembrance of which any man might be proud."

Thomas wondered what the chaplain could have said, given that nobody seemed to know much about poor old Roger Lacy.

"Did he have any friends or family?"

Gilbert shook his head, a frown of consternation across his brow. "No, none that we could find. Though we did try," he added defensively. "It appears he had been living rough for some time. But it was a fine service, nevertheless. A wonderful homily by the chaplain; very moving," he repeated, as if it somehow lessened the brutal manner in which Lacy had been butchered.

"I am afraid it would be impossible to disturb the body now, Thomas, completely impossible. The villagers would be mortified. They are all frightened enough as it is, and something like that would only make matters worse."

Gilbert shook his head again and folded his arms in his habit, his entire posture making clear there could be no yielding on this matter.

Thomas was not unsympathetic to the prior. He appeared to be a decent man who was genuinely concerned for the moral welfare of the parishioners and who found himself caught in the middle of the rapidly unfolding events. On the one hand, Prior Gilbert did not wish to offend his benefactor, Sir Mortimer de Bray. On the other, he needed to respect the archbishop's emissary. He could not be seen to be hindering an investigation into suspected heresy, particularly as the sacrilege had occurred in one of the priory's own churches. And there was a not insignificant risk of some blame or disgrace attaching to the priory itself. The same sort of dilemma had faced many during the Templar trials. Unable to safely pick a side, they had mostly tried to stay out of it, waiting until the storm abated. It was not perhaps the bravest choice, but certainly the safer one.

In any case, Thomas had only mentioned disinterment in passing as something that would be helpful, not for a minute expecting to disturb Lacy's grave.

"I agree, Prior. We cannot disturb the poor man's rest now. Is there anything more you can tell me about Lacy?"

"Very little, I am afraid. He had business at the manor—forgive me, at the *castle*. The locals do like to refer to that noble structure as a castle. It seems to be a matter of some pride to them. *Castle* they say, so *castle* it is. And perhaps it once was. Who can say? The Normans threw up so many wooden structures when first they arrived and built some very austere keeps when the land was troubled. Or so I have heard it said."

He looked down in contemplation.

"You were telling me of Roger Lacy?" Thomas urged, concerned the prior was wandering farther and farther from the subject of his inquiry.

"Oh yes, please forgive me. Local history is a bit of a favorite subject of mine. I never was quite as good a scholar of languages as Eustace here. Nor was I particularly gifted at theology, strangely enough, but history has always fascinated me. I would sit for hours pouring through every history I could find. Livy, Pliny, the works of any Roman or Greek historian."

Now Eustace rolled his eyes. "We were discussing Roger Lacy, Gilbert."

"So we were. So we were. He had business at the castle. I cannot say what nature of business, but I am confident it was with Lady Isabella. It was she herself who asked us to prepare a room for him. I would not have turned him away in any case. *Let all that come be received like Christ,*" intoned the prior, respectfully reciting his own understanding of the Benedictine Rule of hospitality.

"Lacy was in a sad state when he arrived and had no money for hostelry. It was clear to me that he had once been a wealthy man and had since fallen on very hard times. He spoke well and even had a smattering of Latin and some small liturgical knowledge. I must say his changed circumstances made him all the more pitiable to my mind. I think the penury had somehow disturbed the poor fellow's wits. He was also in decrepit health, all ulcerous sores, sagging skin, and crooked bones. Eustace did what he could to make him comfortable. It is no surprise Lady Isabella was moved by his condition."

The prior shook his head sadly. Thomas believed the sympathy was genuine. The prior's heart, it seemed, was almost a match for his belly.

"But sad to say, I know no more. I do try not to intrude into other people's business."

"Can you think of anybody else with whom I should speak?" Thomas asked.

"As I said, he had business with Lady Isabella. Her Ladyship tends to be shy of company, but she will surely see you given the gravity of the matter. How much help she will prove to be . . . well, you shall have to judge that for yourself."

Thomas wondered at the prior's apparent reticence with regard to Lady Isabella but thought it unlikely from his tone that any further clarification would be forthcoming. He would indeed have to judge for himself.

"And as to the matter of Father Oswin, I believe the housekeeper found his body. I suppose you might speak with her. Agnes is her name."

Thomas gave John a look, letting him know that they should add a discussion with Agnes to their list of chores for the day.

"What kind of man was Father Oswin?"

Gilbert inhaled slowly, taking the time to measure his words. "The benefice of Saint Mary's is ours to bestow, you know. Or did I say so already? Yes, I believe I did." Thomas tried very hard not to sigh or roll his eyes. "And we are helping out with services as much as possible until we can find a new vicar. Eustace here has been particularly giving of his time. Sir Mortimer has also lent us the services of his chaplain from time to time. A good man that. And naturally we have hired itinerant chaplains when necessary. I had hoped one of them might prove suitable to take up the benefice. Unfortunately, so far, that has not been the case."

"I had asked about Oswin?" Thomas reminded him gently.

"I was getting there," Gilbert responded, a little irritated at having his flow interrupted. "I was going to say that we are being careful in the selection of the next vicar. Father Oswin was not the easiest man to get along with. He was of a taciturn nature. Very strict, intolerant of sin, prone to taking offense, and often most severe in the punishments he doled out after confession. Many a penitent left confession in tears—mostly women, who do tend to be sensitive about these things. And many a hapless child received a sound thrashing at his hands. He was not one to spare the rod. One might even say he was a tyrant. And he was an unpopular man with his parishioners, which is hardly an ideal state of affairs. Other than his maid, Agnes, I cannot think of a one who liked him."

He shook his head sadly.

"I often wondered if Oswin's zeal might have blinded him to some of his own failings. A certain want of the milk of human kindness, so to speak. From time to time, I encouraged him to show a little more understanding, a little more compassion, but to no avail. All that said, and as unpopular as he might have been, I do not believe that anyone in his flock would have thought to hurt him. Or even to disobey him."

The prior coughed uncomfortably.

"But I think I have said more than enough about Father Oswin. There is no need to speak further ill of the dead."

Thomas nodded his understanding. "Friar Justus is staying here?"

"Yes. There is another hard man. I would say he is . . . devoted to his cause." Gilbert looked upward, choosing his words carefully, reluctant to say anything too terrible about his guest but wanting to convey his dislike.

"He is not someone to be gainsaid, Thomas," he added with a meaningful look. "He is not like other Dominicans I have known from the abbey in Leicester. Good and godly men, I found them to be. One fellow passed through here not so long ago and was very fine company and a rather good chess player. He made short work of me, I can tell you, and he even gave old Eustace here a good game."

Gilbert chortled all the way from his belly.

"Friar Justus seems to believe that there is some devilry involved in both deaths," suggested Thomas.

"So I understand," responded the prior gravely. "*Maleficium*—the practice of harmful magic. Poisoning. Sacrifice. I suppose such things are not unheard of, and the pope long ago declared them to be heretical, but I have encountered nothing of the sort in our sleepy little part of the world. Eustace thinks it is all a lot of nonsense." The infirmerer's face was presently wearing a look of disgust. "It is not our place, however, to question Friar Justus's conclusions. The pope has in the main entrusted the investigation of such matters to our Dominican brethren, and I understand Justus has himself served the Inquisition. As such, he is sure to be far more knowledgeable about heretical practices than we could ever be."

There was something very final about the prior's last words.

"Well, I suppose if there is nothing more, the two of you had best be on your way. It is almost vespers, and Eustace and I shall need to tend to our devotions. Do drop by if you need anything else. We are always happy to help. Though, as I said, I doubt there is much more we can add."

The prior nodded decisively to Brother Eustace and turned to the door, firmly indicating that the interview was now concluded.

★   ★   ★

They had only just reached the village when John elbowed Thomas in the ribs. "Now here's a piece of luck. That's Agnes, the vicar's maid, right over there."

He pointed to a pleasant-looking woman huddled in conversation with a man Thomas already knew to be the village reeve.

As soon as she saw them hurrying in her direction, Agnes moved away, waving them off with her hand.

"I have no more to say. Please leave me be."

"I only have a few questions for you, Agnes," protested Thomas. "It shall only take a moment of your time."

"No, I have said all already," she tossed over her shoulder, quickening her pace. "I have no more to say. You must speak with Friar Justus. He said I should tell anybody asking me questions to speak with him."

And with that she was gone, leaving them all a little befuddled.

The reeve and constable exchanged a look of surprise.

"Well if that don't beat all," remarked the reeve. He was a thickset man, with a no-nonsense kind of face and muscled forearms showing below the rolled-up sleeves of his tunic. Just the sort of person you might expect to find in charge of the village. "A full two years I've been asking her to marry again. Several widowers have had their eye on her. Decent offers too. And every time she just shakes her head, smiling real shy-like. She's lucky his lordship is an understanding man. And now she comes up to me saying as how she has to be married, and right quick. And that she's none too particular who the man is."

The reeve watched Agnes walk away, shaking his head in bewilderment, and then shrugged, doubtless attributing it all to the vagaries of women.

"I suppose there is John Dysart. He was interested in her. What do you think of him, John?"

"He's an old man!" protested the constable. "She's already lost one husband. Why would you put her through that again? What about the hayward? He's closer to her age, and I know for a fact he's been right lonely since his missus passed."

The reeve stroked his chin. "Aye, maybe. She'd be a good match for him. Keep him out of the alehouse too, which would be a good thing for all of us."

They left him mumbling to himself and tallying the prospects.

"What do you make of that, John?" Thomas asked when they were out of earshot.

"Mighty strange. It makes you wonder if she's carrying a bundle. But that would not be like her at all. Dotty is friendly with Agnes. I shall ask her to visit. Everybody likes my Dotty."

He puffed his chest out proudly, and Thomas had to smile.

CHAPTER 10

Thomas sprang down from the saddle of his roan and tossed the reins to the approaching ostler. He immediately spied the chaplain walking toward the little stone chapel and hastened to catch up.

"Ah, our intrepid investigator." Father Elyas smiled in greeting, pausing to allow Thomas to fall in step with him. He had a warm, welcoming smile that lit up an otherwise unremarkable face. "It is a difficult task you have been given, my friend. I cannot say that I envy you. May I ask whether you have made any progress?"

Thomas glanced up at the sky. He had woken that morning to a chill wind that carried with it a misting autumn rain. The sky had cleared for the moment, but the clouds were darkening again, and there would like as not be a storm before the day was out. Thomas could scent the moisture on the air and near taste it.

"Only a little, Father. As you said, it is no easy matter."

The chaplain followed Thomas's gaze heavenward and bundled his hands into his robe against the cold. "Well, I wish you well. This is a terrible business, and I should like to see it put behind us as quickly as possible. Some folk may think this matter a curiosity, but I can tell you that many are simply scared. And not just of the murderer. If truth be told, I think some are more afraid of our Dominican friend."

"Perhaps they have a reason to be afraid. Friar Justus is an intimidating man, and his allegations dangerous."

The chaplain sighed. "The Order of Saint Dominic does tremendous good, you know. In my time I have come across many Dominicans, almost all of whom I have found to be selfless and worthy of our respect. Some I even count as friends. Their doctrine, however, can tend to zealotry among the smaller minded. But that man," he said, shuddering involuntarily, as if from revulsion. "I fear there is something truly wrong with his mind. He sees no good, only blackness and night. He has forgotten that Saint Dominic's Order is first and foremost an order of preachers and not an order of inquisitors. I cannot believe his fraternity would condone his conduct were it widely known, and I marvel that the archbishop would give such a man license to investigate this matter."

They walked in companionable silence for a few more paces. "Your charge is more important than you might suppose, Thomas. If we do not reach a resolution soon, more may follow Justus. If there is any assistance I can offer, you need only ask."

"We are of a like mind, Father. And there is perhaps one matter you can help me with. Do you know Tom Attwood?"

The chaplain's eyebrows rose inquisitively. "From the village? The miller? Yes, of course."

"How well would you say you know him?"

"At Prior Gilbert's request, I have performed services at Saint Mary's and still do on occasion. With Father Oswin's unfortunate passing, we have shared the load as best we can. A flock cannot be left long without a shepherd. Tom is one of the parishioners, so naturally I know him. I knew him a little even before, though not as well."

He paused at the entrance to the stone chapel, tilting his

head to the side and eyeing Thomas quizzically. "Why do you ask?"

"Would you say he is a man capable of harming another?"

The chaplain laughed out loud. "Tom? Hurt someone? No, I would not expect so. Not willingly. But wait," he said, turning to face Thomas. "Surely you do not suspect him of playing some part in Roger Lacy's death."

When Thomas did not respond, Elyas stared at him aghast. "No, Thomas. I am sure you are mistaken." He laughed again, but this time the laugh was faltering and distinctly wanting in mirth. "I cannot say he is the most devoted parishioner; a bit of a rogue to be sure. I dare say he owes some tithes, and I have heard grumblings from time to time about his weights and measures, the usual things people like to say about those in his profession. Perhaps he drinks too much. But an evil man—no, I would not think so. Why on earth would you suspect him?"

Elyas listened with an increasing look of concern as Thomas recounted his discussion with the miller and how he had seemingly followed Roger Lacy out of the alehouse.

"I would not dream of invading the sanctity of confession, Father, but has Tom sought your services as a confessor?"

"Yes," replied the priest slowly, narrowing his eyes. "I have on occasion rendered him the sacrament of penance."

Thomas realized he had to tread carefully. Elyas was not a man to take the sacrament lightly, and the wrong question might end the discussion quickly.

"I only ask, would you say it is possible for him to do such a thing?"

Elyas frowned thoughtfully and glanced to the sky once more, weighing his words carefully.

"It is true that the Devil hides his face. We cannot always know what lies in a man's heart. And then many wicked things can be done in the heat of passion or when a man's mind is befuddled with drink. But this," he shook his head again. "I would not have thought Tom capable of such a thing, and nothing would lead me to suspect him. No." His voice was less certain now, and he seemed to be dredging his memory, trying to persuade himself as much as Thomas. "Surely not. I cannot believe it."

"I am of a like mind with you, Father, but I cannot afford to ignore any leads, however unlikely they may be. Can you keep our discussion to yourself?"

"Of course, Thomas. You need not have asked. And as for Tom, do you wish me to speak with him as his priest?"

It was a generous offer, and Thomas considered it for a moment. "No, I do not think it necessary. I too doubt he has any part in this. With any luck, things will soon become clearer. Thank you for your time."

He left Father Elyas standing motionless at the door of his chapel, his brow furrowed in concern.

★   ★   ★

Almost at once Thomas saw Hunydd making her way slowly across the courtyard. She was carrying a pail of water and making slow work of it.

"Hunydd," he called, "I am glad to see you."

She smiled brightly and gratefully set aside the bucket, smoothing her skirts.

"You were looking for me?"

"Actually, I was hoping to speak with your mistress."

For some reason Thomas felt bad saying so, and Hunydd looked a little disappointed herself, even though there was no reason she should have thought Thomas would traipse all the way to the manor house to attend on her.

Hunydd wiped her brow with the back of her hand. "Yes, of course. I shall take you to her at once, sir."

"There is no need to be so formal, Hunydd. If we are to be seeing each other, I think you should call me Thomas."

"Should I? Do you think that would be proper?"

"I believe so, and I dare say nobody will care much. Besides, I should like it."

"Tomos," she repeated slowly as she led him toward the gardens, pronouncing his name a little differently. "Is it also a Welsh name?"

Thomas laughed, not at the question, but simply because he had managed to get her to use his name. He had half-suspected she would not. Hunydd's cheeks reddened, and she turned her face away from him, clearly hurt.

"I am sorry, Hunydd. Have I offended you?"

"I think you are making fun of my ignorance, sir."

He touched her shoulder gently, bringing her to a halt.

"Sometimes people do," she said, jutting out her lower lip. "They make fun of me. They laugh at me and treat me as though I am simple. I do not like it. It makes me feel low." Surely no lower than Thomas felt now. "My mother said that it should not bother me. That it is the people making fun of me that are the fools, and not I."

Thomas accepted the mild reproof, thinking he likely deserved it for his thoughtlessness.

"And she was right to say so, Hunydd. I truly am sorry if I offended you. I did not mean to do so." They began walking again. "Mine is a Greek name, I think. But you are quite right—it is a Welsh name as well. The letters are a little different, but it sounds very much the same."

She nodded, her general good nature already rising above any perceived insult.

"Of course, I'll grant you that neither one is so pretty as Hunydd," he added with a grin. "And I doubt that anyone will write a poem about a man named Thomas Lester. Least of all a Welsh prince."

At that she smiled, and they turned onto the gravel path leading into the gardens.

"And how does a Welsh girl find her way to a little village here in the east of England?"

"I am from his lordship's estates in the marches," she said, meaning the counties bordering England and Wales.

"How long have you been Lady Cecily's maid?"

"Less than a year. My mother said it was an opportunity to serve a great lady; that I could better myself. I am trying to do so, to better myself, though I shall never be so fine as Lady Cecily."

Thomas did not pry further. To his mind there could be only two reasons for her being so far from her home. Either she had caught the eye of the master of the house, which seemed unlikely, given his state of health, or she was a bastard child brought to her father's manor for her betterment, to salve his guilty conscience. Neither possibility merited discussion, and both were potentially painful for Hunydd.

"My mistress can read, you know," Hunydd continued. "I've seen her doing so. All sorts of books she reads, some of them as thick as my arm. And she has such fine clothes—six kirtles, all different colors, and six surcotes to wear over top. Can you imagine such a thing?" Hunydd glanced at Thomas from the corner of her eye. "Many also think my mistress beautiful."

"Your mistress is impressive, Hunydd," Thomas answered. *And a bit of a stroppy cow,* he thought about adding, but didn't. "And it seems that we are both strangers here, you and I. We shall have to look out for each other."

"You are not from Lincoln, Thomas?"

Thomas made sure not to smile—it seemed that now she had it, Hunydd was determined to make full use of his name.

"No, I am from Cumberland. It is in the North, on the borders of Scotland, though I left there as a child and I have rarely lived in the same place for long."

"You have traveled?"

"Yes, across England and to Scotland, Wales, Ireland. Even France."

"France!" she exclaimed excitedly. "I should very much like to see France, Thomas. They say the pope lives in France, in a city where the streets are made of purest gold. Is it true?"

"France is a very rich country, Hunydd. Far more so than England, and the Holy Father does indeed live there in a town called Avignon. I am sorry to tell you that the streets of Avignon are all cobbles and mud, just like everywhere else."

Hunydd looked disappointed.

"But the great cathedral of Notre Dame in Paris is a wonder to behold. It has a giant window made up of a hundred panes of colored glass, as wide and tall as seven men, and all in the shape of a giant rose."

"Truly? It sounds wonderful. I should like to see that."

It was not likely Hunydd would ever see France, or many other places for that matter. If she traveled at all, it would be at someone else's whim, likely only to the new household of her mistress when she married. She belonged to the estate. To leave of her own accord would make her a runaway, liable to be dragged back and punished.

They rounded a bend in the path to find Cecily walking toward them. She wore a fine, cream-colored kirtle with a pale blue surcote over top, and was holding a wicker basket in the crook of her arm. On seeing Thomas, her face lit up and she approached him without hesitation.

"Master Thomas. I had been hoping to see you again." She clasped his hands in a surprisingly familiar way, having apparently undergone a shocking transformation of character from the last time he had seen her.

A look from her mistress was enough to dismiss Hunydd, and like any good servant she melted away as if she had never been there.

"I must apologize for my words when last we spoke. I fear that I might have offended you."

"Not at all, my lady!"

That was a lie. Actually, she had offended him quite a bit. Thomas recalled very well how she had looked at him, as though he had just traipsed in from the field with the remnants of a cowpat all over his shoes. That said, he rather liked the new Cecily, and he fell in step with her as she strolled between the rows of herbs.

"I find you intriguing, Thomas. My father will only say that you are close to Bishop Henry, and resolutely refuses to answer any more questions about you." She laughed. It was a light, bubbly laugh, full of genuine humor. "You are a complete mystery to me, though I confess I tried every artifice at my disposal to tease some information out of the old man. I even tried to steal away the bishop's letter of introduction, but my father was on to me and had already locked it away. He knows me too well."

Thomas was surprised by the admission. He had not expected such candor, nor such interest, and smiled in response. "Perhaps there is little else worth knowing about me."

Cecily tilted her head and regarded him with an amused eye. "Oh, I very much doubt that."

They walked a few paces in silence before she spoke again.

"So, you are in the Bishop of Lincoln's service?"

"I help him from time to time," replied Thomas. "I would not go so far as to say I serve him. Our bond is of an unusual nature."

Cecily waited a moment and, when no further information appeared to be forthcoming, decided on a different tack.

"You do not sound like you are from Lincoln. You are not from hereabouts?"

"No, though I have lived near Lincoln these last few years. Lincoln is as much home to me as anywhere else."

Cecily looked at him expectantly, only to be disappointed a second time.

"I saw you arrive today. You ride well." He smiled at the compliment. "And you speak well. You are no farmer. Yet you do not wear a war belt, and you choose to dress as a simple yeoman. I wonder what it is you do for the bishop?"

Thomas could not help but feel a tad aggrieved. He was wearing the best cotte he had in his baggage and had put on a clean tunic, fresh woolen hose, and smart riding boots before coming to see her. Admittedly he had never followed fashion, but he had hoped to make a slightly better impression this time around. Despite his attire, however, it seemed that Cecily now believed him to be of good stock. He wondered whether she would retrench from him if he declared it to be untrue? Though in all honesty he could not. Instead, he congratulated himself on maintaining a stoic silence and offered her a noncommittal answer.

"I have always liked horses, Lady Cecily, and I had hoped not to be going to war. Besides, now your father has gifted me land, I dare say I shall have to farm it. As for the bishop, from time to time he asks me to act on his behalf or to investigate certain matters of a sensitive nature that come to his attention. I do what he asks, if it suits me. I have no fixed position in his house."

Cecily laughed heartily, tilting back her head, drawing attention, whether consciously or no, to the creamy skin of her throat and the swell of her bosom.

"You are teasing me now. But I shall know more. I shan't be denied."

They both turned at the sound of the Dominican's heavy sandaled feet crunching on the gravel path.

"You would do well to inquire more deeply, Lady Cecily,"

he declared in his wheezy voice. "It is always best for a lady to know the character of a man whose company she keeps."

The Dominican walked up to them and leaned over on his staff, grasping it in both bony hands, close enough for Thomas to smell a lingering dampness on his robes from the earlier drizzle; that, and an unpleasant hint of sweat.

"I see you are gathering autumn flowers for your posies and your potpourri," he said, spying Cecily's basket. "You young ladies do like to surround yourselves with pleasant fragrances. I myself find that I have little use for flowers, though I naturally delight in all God's gifts."

He peered into the basket and sifted through its contents with his fingers.

"And what do we have here? I see Aster. Michaelmas daisies you might call them—a common wildflower. I am surprised to find it in your garden. And here is red yarrow, another wildflower, unfortunately past their best this time of year. You should have gathered these weeks ago, my dear."

He continued prodding at her collection.

"And what is this?" He plucked one of the flowers out of her basket and held it up to the light. "The anemone. You might call it a windflower. What a peculiar choice for a young lady. They have almost no fragrance, you know. If you wish to collect flowers for your bowls of potpourri, might I suggest choosing from the last of the roses over there? They will have a nice enough scent. And certainly you would want some of the lavender."

He gave Cecily a crooked smile. "Or perhaps you are just collecting those flowers you find to be pretty? Young women do incline toward such impractical pursuits. Ah well, as I told you before, I do not attempt to account for the tastes of young ladies."

The Dominican straightened himself up, having finally satisfied his curiosity, and looked around. "Unfortunately, all gardens in this country become ragged come autumn, and there is a distinct want of variety. So very little to choose from. I suppose you do have a decent enough herb garden here, though," he added grudgingly. "That would be of far more interest to me anyway."

Cecily ignored the insults, intended or not, and responded pleasantly: "Yes, it was my mother's herb garden. She spent many hours here."

"Your mother? How strange. Perhaps she thought to use some of the herbs for cooking?"

"Some she did," acknowledged Cecily. "Others she cultivated for their medicinal value. She was an avid herbalist, and the garden was her passion before it was mine."

The Dominican cocked a surprised eyebrow. "Indeed? I had no idea that you had an interest in medicine. It seems every village these days boasts some old hag who claims to know something of physic. Such women often do more harm than good and would as soon rub shit over you as decoct a proper tincture or balm."

He chuckled to himself, pleased with his own joke and not particularly bothered whether it amused or offended anyone else.

"Medicine is an unusual pursuit for a young lady of good breeding, however. I trust that you at least have received proper training, my dear?"

"Yes. I have received guidance from Brother Eustace at the priory. Perhaps you know him?"

The Dominican nodded approvingly. "A learned enough man and decent at his craft. I had a little poke around in his stores when first I arrived and found them to be quite well stocked. You could do worse, I suppose. The fact he can spare time from his work to teach you is a trifle troubling, however. I hope you do not distract him from his real duties."

"Not at all. I rather think that I help him. I also learned a little from the castle physician when I visited Lady de Ross at Belvoir."

Justus scowled. "I had the misfortune to meet the fellow on my way here. He seemed to me a wholly ignorant man and displayed an alarming want of medical knowledge. He had none of Galen's works to hand, and I could not get him engaged at all in a discussion of the beneficial use of emetics. I might add that I found his Latin to be wanting and his Greek almost nonexistent."

Thomas was amazed at how much the Dominican had determined from that single encounter. He suspected Friar Justus formed opinions quickly, and he struck Thomas as an intractable and unforgiving sort. It must have been an uncomfortable interview for the poor physician.

Justus was still droning on. "I despair of Lady de Ross receiving any proper medical care from that quarter—well, anything more than a simple bloodletting that any barber surgeon might undertake. I myself studied at Salerno. Perhaps you have heard of it? I believe it to be widely accepted as the world's foremost medical school. I am not sure where your quack studied. Frankly, I have my doubts as to whether he studied at all. You may be the more learned of the two, my dear."

He huffed out another wheezy laugh.

"I have certainly tried to better myself through study," Cecily replied, cutting short his laughter. "I have copies of Sister Hildegard's work, including her *Physika*."

"How singular! You are full of surprises."

"I am not overly fond of Galen," Cecily added, "and tend to prefer Sister Hildegard's simpler remedies."

"Indeed? The foremost medical mind of our times, second only to Hippocrates himself, and you find Galen to be unreliable, do you?"

"I do not accede to some of his teachings," she replied hesitantly.

"Such as?"

"Such as his suggestion that a woman cannot conceive unless she derives pleasure from the act of intercourse." Thomas coughed and the friar's eyebrows soared. "That perceived wisdom has served to excuse the rape of many an unfortunate woman. If she does not conceive, then she is considered to have suffered but little harm. If she does, she is merely another temptress who willingly—no *eagerly*—consented to the act."

Cecily seemed not to notice the Dominican's darkening visage. Or perhaps she did and simply did not care. Her own face had hardened, and her eyes glinted with malice.

"Nor for that matter do I believe women's wombs are cold, requiring the constant warming of a man's seed. Or that we wander about desperate for a man to spill inside us lest our wombs atrophy and decay. I find that to be just another convenient excuse to blame men's passions on my kind."

This shocking statement was followed by an awkward silence. Cecily blinked, recollecting herself, realizing that she may have said a little too much.

When he finally spoke, Justus's tone was cool and deliberate. "Some of the things you say, young lady, are disturbing, and not only contrary to Galen's teachings but to the wisdom of several of the Church's leading lights. I shall choose to attribute your words to youth, and at another time, when I have dealt with our more pressing concerns, I shall speak with your father and offer to educate you more thoroughly before I leave. To make sure that you have a better understanding of the things of which you speak and of the consequence of espousing certain ill-considered thoughts."

Thomas suspected that the intended *education* the friar had in mind might well involve the vigorous use of a switch.

Justus gave Cecily one final look and shrugged, dismissing the conversation. "It so happens that I am a bit of an herbalist myself, you know."

He turned about slowly, surveying the garden.

"And I find some of the plants here to be of a surprising nature. That plant over there, for instance, with the distinctive violet, almost blue, hooded flowers. That is *aconite*. I think you locals charmingly call it monk's hood. It is quite poisonous. Even to the touch. A small amount will upset the stomach. In larger quantities it is deadly and will stop the heart. And there," he gestured to a large, dense green shrub with spiky leaves that Thomas knew to be the yew. "That shrub, its leaves, its fruit— all are poisonous. And there, *arum maculatum*, called cuckoopint or any number of other revolting names relating it to a part of the male anatomy. Its berries will soon ripen and can surely cause the throat to swell and even choke a man to death.

"In ignorant hands these plants and several others I see about me can do great harm. All of this is all rather well known to the common herbalist. If you like, when we are both at leisure, I should be more than happy to discuss these things with you. I would hate for you to unwittingly poison some poor soul."

"I am sure Lady Cecily is careful in her preparations," said Thomas, for some reason deciding this was the perfect time for him to leap to Cecily's defense.

Justus blinked in surprise and looked at him as though he had just broken wind loudly. The look Cecily gave Thomas was not much better. It seemed she preferred to fight her own battles and did not at all appreciate his interruption or the implication that she was in some way in need of his protection. *Twice a failure then.*

"Thomas! Why I had almost forgotten that you were still here. I must say that I am pleased that Sir Mortimer appears to be taking these claims of heresy seriously, though I find it more than curious that he would ask you of all people to look into them."

"Why should that be curious?"

"Well, your own father was a heretic, was he not?"

The statement delivered in such a matter-of-fact manner struck Thomas like a blow to the body, and for a long time he stood dumbstruck, incapable of responding. Cecily was immediately intrigued, and her glance swung excitedly between the two of them. She could have made a discreet withdrawal, but it was not in her nature, and nothing could have tempted her away now. For his part the Dominican stood complacently, a look of smug satisfaction on his face, glorying in the effect of his words.

"Yes, something about you troubled me from the first, Thomas. Why would De Bray bring someone all the way from Lincoln to investigate what he claims to be merely a murder? Surely such a thing would be more a matter for the sheriff and his own justice. Why not one of his own people? His bailiff or"—and he chuckled here—"even the constable? And then there was your name. *Thomas Lester.* There was something so very familiar about it. Naturally, once I discovered that you are a protégé of the Bishop of Lincoln, everything fell into place. It was as though a veil had been lifted from my eyes. I recalled that the Templar heretic Geoffroi de Leystre had a son named Thomas who had disappeared and was rumored to have been taken in by Henry Burghersh, your very own master."

The Dominican smiled, this time with genuine humor. "*Lester. De Leystre.* It's not a very convincing ruse, is it? I fully understand, of course. Had my own father been a heretic, I too would have been ashamed and might also have been tempted to hide my name, however poorly."

Thomas had listened quietly, the blood slowly draining from his face, and when he did finally respond, it was through gritted teeth and with barely contained anger: "My father was no heretic."

"Do you say not? I was quite sure I had read his confession among the annals. I seem to recall that he admitted to all sorts of things. No, no, I am sure he was a confessed heretic. I would recount for you those things to which he confessed, but I hesitate to do so in the presence of a lady."

He nodded tersely in Cecily's direction.

"And as for your mother . . . let me think." The Dominican tapped his lips with the tip of his right forefinger. "That was not so certain, as I recall. There were rumors that she was complicit in your father's actions, that she too turned from Christ and chose to indulge in some of his, shall we say, more *lurid* activities. And at a minimum, she was certainly guilty of harboring a known heretic, a serious offense in and of itself. Regrettably, she died before we could interrogate her. Perhaps she was truly innocent and died of shame. Who could blame her?"

Thomas was seething, his entire body tensed like a nocked bowstring. He felt a pressure on his forearm and looked down to see Cecily's hand. Eloquent eyes conveyed a silent warning. He nodded his understanding and forced himself to take a deep, calming breath.

Cecily was right. He was being goaded, and he must not rise to the bait. Besides, things could have been worse. The Dominican did not know as much as he thought he did. He did not know about Thomas's wife. If he did, he would surely have mentioned her by now. There was a secret Thomas hoped he might take to the grave.

"Imagine my surprise to find Thomas de Leystre helping us to root out heretics. Such irony. I do wonder, however, whether it might not be better for you to leave the matter in my hands. Some might think that you have, let us say, divided loyalties. There will always be that unfortunate suspicion attached to the son of a heretic, you know." Justus moved his hands up and down in a mockery of balancing a set of scales. *Qualis pater, talis filius.* 'As the father, so is the son,' and all that."

Thomas's father had fled before the Inquisition, seeking

sanctuary with the family he had left behind when he had joined the Templars. Thomas remembered the night they came for him. His father had looked scared then. Scared for them. And scared for himself. The next time Thomas had seen him, he was emaciated, scarcely alive, with the signs of torture on his body, though that was always denied.

"Of course, were you to help me and thereby demonstrate your devotion to the Church, all lingering doubts and past actions might be expunged. I speak of your own actions, naturally. Your father shall forever live in infamy."

The Dominican turned his attention back to Cecily. "You see, my lady, you were quite wrong to suggest when we first met that the Inquisition has no power in England. Your young friend here can tell you otherwise. The Church and God's judgment know no bounds. I am sure you had no notion of Thomas's rather interesting heritage. Nevertheless, you should be careful with whom you associate, lest you sully your own good reputation."

He gave Thomas a final self-satisfied smirk.

"I had really hoped to speak with Lady Isabella today, but it appears she is still unwell, so I shall leave you two for now—the would-be herbalist, and the heretic's son." He clucked his tongue. "And Thomas, should you uncover anything of use in your meanderings, I trust you will inform me at once. I think it would be for the best."

★   ★   ★

"It seems there is much more to you than you would have had me believe," Cecily whispered to Thomas as they watched the Dominican head back to the courtyard. "Oh, never fear—I shall not make you any more uncomfortable by pressing you on the matter.

"He is a most wretched man," she added more loudly once the Dominican was out of sight. "But you must have wished to speak with me. Is it about your investigation, or"—she paused meaningfully—"was there something else perhaps?"

Thomas was not sure, but he sensed Cecily was toying with him and could swear he saw the corners of her eyes wrinkle in mirth. Why *had* he come here anyway? Thomas had asked himself the same question.

"I suspect there is little that goes on hereabouts that escapes your attention, my lady. You certainly have your father's trust and seem to be familiar with the affairs of his estate."

Cecily inclined her head by way of agreement and in acknowledgment of the tacit compliment.

"I felt sure you might be able to shed some light on what happened to Roger Lacy."

Was that true? Did he really believe so, or was it just an excuse to speak with her again? He had to admit that, as much as he had been inclined to dislike her, he had thought of Cecily often enough since their first chance encounter. Her soft blue eyes, the red of her lips against her pale skin, the way a loose lock of hair had fallen so teasingly about her temple. She may even have been so bold as to venture into his previous night's dream. Thomas coughed and recollected himself.

"I understand he had business here at the manor. Did you meet him? Do you know why he was here?"

"Oh yes," she said, closing her eyes a moment in thought. "What you say is true. Lacy did visit here, but I did not speak with him. He asked specifically for an audience with my father's wife."

My father's wife. Thomas found it curious that Cecily chose not to mention Isabella by name.

"Do you know what they discussed?"

"No, but she did come to my father shortly after, asking about a position for Lacy. She was quite insistent. Petulant even. It surprised me as he looked to be such a shabby thing, but she was adamant that he had been an excellent steward on her father's estate. Were it so, I have to wonder why he had fallen on such hard times."

Thomas was certain now. There was no love lost between the two ladies of the house.

Cecily eyed him curiously. "Why do you ask? Surely you do not think someone here could have been involved in his death?"

"Of course not. I just wanted to find out all I could about him. I suppose I too should speak with Lady Isabella."

Cecily looked dubious. "My father's wife is unwell, and I think an audience is unlikely at present. She often seems so, however, and sometimes keeps to her chambers for days. Should you speak with her, you may also find her to be somewhat . . . distracted." She smiled. "But you did not come here to listen to our family's gossip."

"Perhaps I shall return tomorrow, then, and hope to find her in better health."

"Perhaps," Cecily allowed, clearly doubting there would be any improvement.

They were quiet for a moment. Thomas desperately dredged his mind for another topic that might extend their conversation. Cecily saved him the bother.

"Shall I walk you to the courtyard? It is rare for me to receive visitors, especially interesting ones."

She hefted her basket, took his arm, and they fell naturally in step together. It felt easy, comfortable.

"You must tell me all the news, Thomas. Living out here, we are always the last to know anything. I rarely find myself in Lincoln, or any other great city for that matter. We are quite sheltered here. I suppose we should be grateful, as it kept us safe during the rebellion. Nobody bothered us."

"Your father did not cast his lot for either side?"

Cecily gripped Thomas's arm just a little more firmly and drew just a little bit closer—close enough for him to feel the swish of her skirts against his thigh and smell the scent of her perfume, more pleasing to him than that of the flowers in her basket.

"I would say that my father had sympathy for the rebels' cause, but he did not desert the king. Of course, we did not ride to Edward's side either. It has put us in a difficult position now. Once Despenser has done with those who backed Lancaster, I do wonder whether he will turn his attention to those who did not aid the king. Despenser grows bolder by the day. Tell me, is there any news of Mortimer? I suppose he is the leader of the rebels now that Lancaster is dead."

"Nobody has heard from him since he escaped the Tower. It is believed he is sheltering in France, plotting a return. Or at least that is the story I heard."

And since he heard it from the lips of the Bishop of Lincoln, no less, Thomas suspected the rumor to be true, though he did not say so.

"He still has supporters then."

Thomas did not sense that Cecily intended this as a question, and with the courtyard drawing annoyingly close, he chose to concentrate on ambling as slowly as was humanly possible, certainly slower than was acceptable in polite society. Cecily did not seem to object.

"And how goes the war with France?"

"Poorly, my lady. The English garrisons were inadequately manned and unprepared for conflict," Thomas explained. "The French have already seized Angenais and have cut off Bordeaux. If reinforcements are not sent soon, the city could even fall. I believe the king plans to raise another army and lead it to Gascony."

"He will lead it himself?" she repeated, surprised.

"So he has said."

Cecily nodded thoughtfully. "It is said that the king is purging his court of French interests and has even seized the queen's own lands in retaliation. Is that true?"

Queen Isabella was the daughter of the late King Philip of France. Edward had married her at the behest of his father when she was only twelve years old, and there was rumored to be little affection between them. Cecily was venturing into exactly the kind of political waters Thomas tried to avoid.

"*Purging* is a strong word, my lady. For certain, King Edward has responded to French aggression by seizing such of France's property as he might. It is true he has seized the queen's property. And you are not quite so ill-informed as you would have me believe, Lady Cecily," said Thomas with a smile. "I think that I am not the only one here with secrets."

She returned his smile, conceding nothing.

Cecily halted their progress and looked up at his face, her eyes somehow managing to catch and reflect even the faint light of the overcast autumn day in a strikingly azure shade of blue. "Forgive me," she said. "This is a terribly forward question, but you mentioned that you consider no place your home. Am I to understand then that you have no family, no wife?"

"I was married once."

"But no longer? Is it too forward of me to ask what happened?"

Thomas's mind flashed back for a moment to a lake, a clearing in the woods, torn clothing, blood on the ground.

"She was murdered," he said quietly, his eyes distant.

He looked back up to see Cecily studying him intensely.

"I am so sorry," she said and meant it. "I should not have asked. It was inconsiderate of me. I was being far too inquisitive, and now I have caused you distress."

"You were not to know, and it was a long time ago now."

"Did you find the man?"

"Not yet. But I shall one day."

Thomas wondered if he still believed that to be true. He had spent almost all that was left of his fortune in vain pursuit of the truth and was no closer now than the moment he had found his wife's body.

Cecily touched his arm again—a small gesture to show that she understood his grief and sensed his doubt.

"You have suffered much, I think. What was it that the chaplain said the other day? *'Blessed are they that mourn, for they shall be comforted.'* I grieve with you, Thomas, but you should not despair of bringing her justice. I am confident that in time that you shall do so, however long it takes."

By now they had reached the entrance to the courtyard, and Cecily released Thomas's arm. He felt the loss instantly.

"Well, I shall let you be about your business, Thomas. Thank you for keeping me company, and I hope you will come visit me again when we are both more at leisure."

Thomas smiled and, determined for once not to appear boorish, offered a genteel bow. For all the Dominican's insults, Thomas could not regret the afternoon's experience.

★ ★ ★

As for Cecily, she wanted to know more about this interesting young man who seemed to have such a hold on her father. Much more. She watched him cross the courtyard and mount his horse. He did ride well, like a man accustomed to the saddle, not like a yeoman at all. She flushed as her mind turned to quite inappropriate thoughts.

Cecily reached into her basket and lifted an anemone blossom to her nose. The old wretch was right; it really had no scent, but it *was* a pretty flower, and pretty little flowers often had the most surprising properties. The anemone was quite useful in the right doses as a stimulant. Like most plants with beneficial medicinal properties, however, in the wrong dose it could be

quite deadly and could induce a heart failure, especially in someone more elderly. Friar Justus was not so learned as he supposed.

She felt the first drop of the rain that had been threatening
all day. The storm was coming, and she should seek shelter. On
horse, Thomas would avoid the worst of the rain. The Dominican, however, was sure to be caught in its midst. It was a long
walk to the priory, and he might well be soaked to the skin by
the time he arrived. Cecily smiled. There, at any rate, was something to be pleased about. A sudden streak of lightning forked
across the sky, followed almost instantly by the low rumbling of
thunder. *Even better!*

CHAPTER 11

Friar Justus was growing annoyed. He was annoyed, first, at Guy. The man was still sulking at being tossed out of the maid's interview. It was really quite tiresome. This time Justus allowed him to remain in the room. Not because he was in any way influenced by Guy's behavior, but because this was one of those occasions when his presence might serve to focus the subject's mind. So, the ruffian lounged by the door, arse on a table, one foot perched up on a stool, picking away at the wooden doorframe with that ghastly knife of his. He was not big like the constable, but tall and rangy, and he simply oozed threat. Nobody seeing him could doubt the danger he posed, and it was clear nobody was leaving the room until the Dominican was done with his business.

Justus sighed loudly and sat down on the stool. The man facing him across the table was the second reason for his bad humor. Adam was an ugly, dull-seeming character. He was dressed in a disgusting smock that might once have been white but was now a dirty brown and looked like it might well have been used to wipe a giant sow's backside. He sat there quietly, eyeing Justus with a witless expression, his breath whistling through his flat nose, his elbows spread out wide on the trestle table, and a beaker of the piss, which they laughingly called ale hereabouts, clutched in his grubby hand.

Justus sighed again. They had been at it for hours now, and he was getting nowhere.

"Let us go over this one more time, Adam." He tried to sound genial. "Do you recall the night of the murder?"

"Oh, aye, I do. A terrible thing to be sure, but like I already said, I don't remember nothing special-like."

At first Justus had thought to threaten the man. Guy had stalked the room, looming over them, scowling impressively, but the dullard seemed completely unconcerned and had barely given him a second glance. It was time for a different approach.

"I find that hard to believe, Adam. His Grace, the Archbishop of Canterbury, himself is greatly disturbed. I doubt he will credit that those about saw and heard nothing of note. I should hate to see you excommunicated as a heretic sympathizer. Cut off from God's mercy. Denied the comfort of the holy sacraments. Forbidden confession—or even to enter a church."

The Church was so intertwined in their lives that the very suggestion of excommunication was horrible and unthinkable to the rustics. But the dullard did not seem to understand at all.

"Me either, Father. That would be horrible, to be sure. But I don't know as how that means I done saw anything."

What kind of language was the fool speaking? It was as though the man had just opened his mouth and vomited words out onto the table, expecting Justus to pick through the disgusting stew to find some kind of sense. English was just one of several languages Justus had mastered, and was by some margin his least favorite. He thoroughly disliked its guttural sounds. The local dialect was particularly grating, a soft burr emphasizing every other word. People hereabouts seemed to have no sense of grammar, and their language was replete with silly little sayings that Justus supposed were intended to impart some sort of home-spun wisdom but that in truth were utterly devoid of meaning. As if on cue, the dullard rapped the table with his knuckles.

"But as I always say, a blind cock is as like to find himself in a fox's gob as up a hen's arse."

Dear God! What on earth was he talking about?

Justus clenched his staff in a white-knuckled fist, pinched the bridge of his nose between thumb and forefinger, and took a calming breath. He would have to give up soon. If nothing else, he needed some fresh air. He could barely stand the smell of shit emanating from Adam's filth-covered clogs. Maybe he should just have Guy thrash him, then bring him back in and see if he changed his tune. No, that was too risky. De Bray had been very insistent about not harming his people. For the time being, Justus needed to tread carefully.

"I am sure you saw something," he coaxed. "A strange light, maybe, or an unusual creature. Something untoward. Or per-haps you heard chanting from the direction of the church?"

Adam pursed his lips, a pained expression on his face, as if he were trying to scrape the memory from inside his head. "No. No, I think I would remember something like that."

"I feel sure you must. Any good Christian would have felt something strange afoot that night."

Adam simply shook his head and began picking at the scabby remnant of a pink rash, a virulent case of Saint Anthony's fire that had spread across the side of his nose and halfway up his left cheek.

It was in that moment that Justus began to suspect there was something terribly forced about Adam's ostensible nonchalance, and it occurred to him that the man might not be quite as stu-pid as he appeared.

"You know, Adam, in aiding my investigation you would place yourself beyond suspicion. You would also be helping the

Church. We would naturally be grateful for your efforts, and perhaps some small reward would be in order."

The scab picking stopped, and Adam leaned forward, assaulting the friar with breath laden with ale and pottage. Justus felt his stomach lurch but swallowed slowly and somehow managed to maintain a companionable smile.

"Exactly how grateful do you think the Church would be?" He nodded at his right hand, the thumb and fingers of which were rubbing together meaningfully.

Could he be any cruder?

Justus forced himself to lean forward and whisper in an equally conspiratorial manner, though his stomach lurched again and he felt his gorge rising. The things he had to endure in the service of the Lord!

"Very. Grateful. You would not regret your assistance. There would be some gratitude now and more to come."

He spirited a small leather purse from his robes and slid it discreetly across the table, pushing it slowly toward Adam's left hand. Adam glanced down and scooped the purse into his lap.

"Mayhap I did see something after all." He tapped the side of his nose with a well-chewed fingernail and gave Justus an exaggerated wink.

"I was sure you must have," encouraged Justus. "Perhaps, for instance, Roger Lacy mentioned to you that he feared something amiss, that he was being followed or that he was under a spell."

"Aye perhaps he did at that. He was nattering away to himself in the alehouse. I am sure I might have heard him say something of the kind, and it would be no surprise if nobody else could make sense of it."

"Perhaps you also noticed something strange near the church."

"Perhaps I did. If you were to suggest something, I feel sure it might jog my memory." He rapped the table again. "A nod's as good as a wink to a blind man."

From the corner of his eye, Justus could see Dominic staring mutely from one to the other. This was not Justus's finest hour, he had to admit, but it was an opportunity for Dominic to learn that, at times, when the cause was just, one needed to be a little malleable; to bend the rules, only if ever so slightly; and that sometimes the wheels of ecclesiastical justice simply had to be greased.

Justus gestured irritably for the young friar to get scratching away with his quill. It was at last time to create the witness's sworn testimony.

★   ★   ★

Tom Attwood sat at his usual seat in the alehouse, staring down gloomily at the half-empty beaker of ale clutched in his hand. He felt miserable. The bloody constable had as good as accused him of murdering that silly old fool, Roger Lacy. It was ridiculous. Yet, strangely enough, hardly anybody had come to the mill today. They had to be getting their grain ground somewhere and probably had chosen to go to that bastard Sam Bolder. And when he had walked into the village, bored and with nothing to do at what should have been his busiest time of the year, Tom had noticed all the sly looks and the way people slunk away when he approached, like he was clanging a set of leper's bells.

Even Sally was giving him the stink eye, looking at him like he had sprouted a couple of horns out the top of his head and had a forked tail sticking out of his bleeding backside. Usually she would be laughing and joking with him, letting him play a little slap and tickle maybe, making sure she got her tip. But now she was hardly bothering to serve him at all and saying not a single word when she did. As if he hadn't bounced her up and down on his knee when she was a little girl. Aye, and once or twice when she was full grown and all.

A smile flickered across his face, but only for a second or two, to be quickly replaced by another scowl. She wasn't the only one. He saw the other folk in there, looking at him over their beakers, pretending not to. Mumbling to one another. He knew they were all talking about him. Stabbing him in the back, that's what they were doing. How could any of them truly believe he was a killer? They had known him all their lives.

Bastards. That's what they all were. *Backstabbing bastards.*

He took another deep swallow of ale, sloshing a little on the table as he set the beaker down unsteadily to continue his brooding.

Everyone was turning on him. He'd been having a drink or two at the end of the day with his friends every night for years, and now all of a sudden Will said his wife wasn't feeling well, and Adam said he had to speak with the black friar. Now what could he possibly need to speak to that bastard about? Tom didn't know, but he had a sinking feeling it couldn't be good. Maybe Adam was telling tales about him. The very thought gave Tom the shivers. Adam was his closest friend, and there were some things he knew about Tom that were more than a little embarrassing—even sinful. Tom squirmed around on his bench and looked up to see Sally sneaking a peek at him from the corner of her eye before quickly averting her gaze. And there were other things he could say too. Oh yes, Adam had a whole bunch of secrets, and he could be spilling his guts to a bloody inquisitor right now, thinking to save his own skin!

It was enough to turn a man to drink. And it did. He had been steadily drinking throughout the afternoon and, beaker by beaker, his mood had turned dark and bitter, and he had begun to feel more and more sorry for himself. He should really have gone home, but there always seemed to be a good reason for just one more beaker, one more stoup, and one more mazer.

With a dismissive grunt, Tom picked up his beaker lazily and almost missed his mouth, much of the ale dribbling down his chin and neck. He slammed it down angrily and dragged his sleeve across his face. It was time to leave.

He staggered out of the open door of the alehouse, stumbling into the street. Even now he could feel their eyes boring into his back as he walked through the door, making his shoulder blades prickle. And he could hear the sudden murmur of conversation. *Now wasn't that a trick?* Silent as the grave when he was in there, and now he had left, they were all chattering away like starlings. Talking about him, he was sure.

Tom weaved about a moment or two, allowing his head to clear. He had half a mind to go back inside and give them all a piece of his mind. Call them out for the backstabbing bunch of sheep-swivers that they were.

"Ah, they ain't worth it," he grumbled to himself.

So instead, he staggered off, weaving his way out into the field.

At least Mary had stood by him. She had told him to ignore them, that it was all nonsense and would blow over soon enough. A good woman, she was. He hadn't always appreciated her enough and hadn't done right by her. He would do so now. He'd stop drinking and pay more attention to her. He'd buy her a nice new kirtle; one of those fancy fitted ones from Grantham. She'd like that. And he wouldn't touch that Sally again. Certainly not after the way the cow had treated him the last couple of days. No more slap and tickle for her, and she could forget her tips and all.

Hell, he wouldn't be going to the alehouse anymore anyway. Not after tonight. Mary deserved better than that. Why, he would go home now and show her his appreciation. Give her some real attention. Show her exactly how much she meant to him. She'd like that too.

Why not? The boys would be asleep, and she was still a fine-looking woman. Maybe she had a little more meat on her bones now after the children, but he liked that, and she was as fine to him now as the day they were wed. And she enjoyed a good tumble, did Mary, and never made him feel like she was doing him a favor. Not like bloody Sally—always leading him on. All skirts, no stockings, that one. Why had he ever wasted his time mooning over her when he had such a fine woman waiting for him back at home? It all seemed so silly now. Oh yes, a fine woman. He grinned and felt a familiar stirring in his loins.

Tom tugged at his clothes and lifted his cap so he could comb his fingers through his wiry hair. It looked like he had spilled something on his tunic. He sniffed cautiously at it and jerked his head back. *Sweet Jesus, was that puke?* Funny, he did not remember spewing over himself. He brushed at the stain but it stubbornly refused to come away and just smeared across the cloth and made his hand sticky. It was no good.

Suddenly his stomach clenched. Tom staggered unsteadily for a moment or two, a strange but familiar sensation overcoming him, and then lurched to the side, bent over, and threw up onto the grass and all over his shoes. He stood shakily with his hands on his knees, waiting for the sensation to pass. His stomach flip-flopped, and he was once more overwhelmed and sprayed out another gout of foul-smelling liquid.

"Bloody hell!" he gasped and wiped his mouth with his sleeve. He must have drunk more than he thought, and his head was swimming. He should have had something to eat. The ale and the chill night air had done for him, and no mistake.

Tom's ardor collapsed like a pricked bladder. There was no way Mary would entertain him now. And he was not sure he was up to it anyway. She'd like as not kick him out to the byre quick as you like, with a fierce tongue lashing to take with him. She might even take the switch to him. It wouldn't be the first time. Aye, perhaps he'd best sleep it off after all. He would go to his mill. She was used to him doing that, and he wouldn't be disturbed there. A bit of rest was what he needed. Some sleep would take his mind off everything, and maybe tomorrow things wouldn't seem so bad. Maybe tomorrow he could spend some time with his missus.

Tom stood up, swayed about for a moment like a reed of grass in the wind, and then lurched off in the direction of the river and his mill.

When Tom pushed open the heavy door of the millhouse and walked inside, a shape suddenly erupted from the shadows. Tom sensed something looped over his head and felt a rope cord brush roughly against his neck. As drunk as he was, he half-stepped, half-fell backward into the wall, which was a good thing because in crashing against it, the assailant's grip loosened, and he was able to turn to face him, dragging him around to his front. The attacker was not perhaps so big as Tom, but he was strong. Tom could feel his muscles flexing as he strained against him, still trying to force the rope around Tom's neck.

Tom was having none of it. Even in his sodden state, he somehow knew he was in a fight for his life. He did not pause to think but, with the instincts of a wrestler, wrapped his thick muscled arms wide around his foe. They struggled in silence, reeling about like two drunken dancers in a grotesque embrace, feet scuffing, shuffling, and stomping, each of them grunting and straining, each trying to spread his arms wider so he could get the better grip.

Tom had been the village wrestling champion in his younger days. He was the veteran of many a friendly Mayfair brawl, and his old skills had not left him. The cloaked and hooded figure struggling with him clawed at Tom's eyes. But that was an old trick. Tom kept forcing his arms down, to keep the hands away from his face, working all the time to get the outside grip. And then he had it, and he began to squeeze. His attacker was trying to stamp on his instep, to butt him in the face, and even bite him—every dirty trick ever thought of. But he was no wrestler. His moves were predictable and clumsy; and even dulled by drink, the miller had no difficulty countering them.

Tom's eyes gleamed in triumph as he reached that point where could sense he had the upper hand. He was going to win. He had no doubt. The villain was pummeling at him uselessly, but with his upper arms practically pinned to his sides, and at such close distance, the blows were ineffective, falling wildly and without force. Tom could not even feel any pain, probably the one benefit of the drink. Sensing that victory was close, he squeezed harder, spreading his feet for purchase, readying himself to hook his man behind the knee, to heave him up and send him crashing to the ground with one of his favorite throws. It would be over then. Nobody had ever broken free once Tom had him in that grip

"I've got you now, you tosser," he hissed into the man's face, blowing a gale of ale and puke breath over him. "I'll have you on the floor trussed up in no time now, you backstabbing bastard."

His opponent was thrashing wildly now, becoming ever more desperate, bucking and twisting about hopelessly. Tom grimaced and shuffled his feet just a little wider. A little more purchase and a little better grip, and then he'd have him down. And it was then that his right foot slipped. His leg went out from under him and he was falling, flailing backward, his grip broken. His opponent howled in triumph and, not being drunk like Tom, had the presence of mind to twist about, turning Tom to the side mid-fall so he went down hard on his face and stomach, driving the wind from his lungs.

Stunned as he was, Tom could still have got up and made a fight of it, but the ale had made him stupid and slow, and his assailant was on his back whip-fast, pressing a knee hard into him with his full weight behind it, wrapping the rope around Tom's neck and hauling it tight. Tom awoke to the danger and thrashed about with desperation, fighting for his life, but with his head hauled back and the knee forced into his spine, he could not break free. He tried to buck, but he had no leverage, and the man on top of him, for all that he was smaller, was also strong.

Tom clawed at the rope, trying to get his fingers underneath. He felt hard knuckles grinding into the back of his neck, twisting the rope, again and again, ever tighter. His face was going numb, and he could feel the blood welling in his neck. It was hard to breathe, and he could feel the relentless pressure on his neck and spine. And there was pain now—a lot of it. Tom's struggles became ever weaker, and then there was a loud crack, and his body sagged, limp and lifeless.

★ ★ ★

Hunydd led Thomas by the hand through the manor gardens. He could smell the mint, fennel, and mustard. Thomas wondered for a moment why Hunydd was not wearing any clothes, but let it go when she looked back shyly at him, smiling, the sweet dimple flashing in her cheek, a crown of anemone blossoms atop her raven-black hair. She walked on tiptoes, and though he tried his best not to stare, he would not have been human had he not noticed her slender figure, curved in all the right places.

And then she brushed his cheek lightly with the back of her hand and glided away from him with one last smoldering look over her shoulder. Another hand had taken his. Soft. Feminine. Gentle at first, but then insistent. Cecily pulled him closer and melted against his chest, lifting her face up to him, her lips inviting and her eyes that mesmerizing shade of blue. He could feel her arms about him, pulling him toward her. Strangely enough, she was naked as well. He felt her flesh press against him, her body demanding a response from him, her breath hot against his neck, and he remembered the Bishop of Lincoln's words: *"I am sure if you chip away diligently enough at the ice, there is a deep pool of lust beneath just waiting for you to dive in and splash about."*

It had been a long time since he had felt such desire. He leaned down, closed his eyes, and pressed his lips to hers.

And his world shook. It literally shook. He staggered clumsily. And then another quake rocked the ground, and he staggered again. Cecily had pulled away, a bewildered, hurt look on her face.

Thomas's eyes opened wide, and he found himself staring up at the broad face and large broken nose of the constable.

"Come on, wake up, will you?" he bellowed, his heady breath instantly dispelling the remaining fragments of the dream.

The constable shook him again. He was trying to be gentle, but he was a strong man and Thomas rocked heavily from side to side.

"Come on. Wake up!"

Thomas felt irritable and more than a little guilty. Brushing John's hands aside, he sat up and scrubbed at his eyes. As his head slowly cleared, he remembered where he was—Bekley cottage, the house De Bray had gifted to him. It was a modest home, little more than a yeoman's cottage really, and no grand manor by any means, but it had been expanded at some point to add a second floor and had its own enclosed garden with flower beds and fruit trees that should provide a welcome shade come summer and from all sides offered bucolic views of the Vale. Not perhaps a home that a fine lady such as Cecily would appreciate, but they had done well by him, and he only hoped that he might prove worthy of the gift.

"What in God's name are you up to, John? What time is it?"

he asked, squinting out from under his lids at the gray light filtering in through the cracks in the shutters.

"It's not yet dawn, but we've got to go. We have a problem. Its Tom Attwood—he's only gone and bloody hanged himself at the mill, hasn't he!"

★   ★   ★

When they arrived at the mill, they found the miller's wife weeping against Father Elyas's chest. The poor man had folded her in his arms and was doing his best to provide comfort, but looked no less miserable than her. On seeing Thomas, he whispered in her ear and passed her to the care of her kin.

"How is she, Father?"

The chaplain's shoulders slumped. "Beyond consolation. Perhaps with time, she will recover."

Elyas looked wretched himself and wrung his hands together miserably.

"Oh, Thomas, this is a terrible thing, and I am to blame." He looked like he might burst into tears at any moment. "Had I acted when you spoke to me, had I done something, had I reached out to him, then perhaps he would still be alive today."

"I asked you not to do so. If any bear the guilt, then it is I," reasoned Thomas.

"No. I cannot accept that. It would be a cheap consolation to blame another for my own failure. I was his confessor. Perhaps not his parish priest, but I was one of those who had served that role since the passing of Father Oswin. I was his spiritual guide. His soul was in my care, Thomas. *My care!* And now it is damned."

He stifled a sob, took Thomas's elbow, and drew him farther away from the wailing miller's wife.

"You must understand, in taking his own life, he has condemned himself to the eternal flames. We cannot lay him to rest in the churchyard. To my shame, I do not even know when last he confessed. No, I should have spoken with him, Thomas, and I shall have to bear that guilt for the rest of my life. And he leaves behind a family—two young ones and another on the way."

Thomas clapped him on shoulder. "Bear up man! The people here have need of you, especially now. You must be strong for them. How will it be if they see you so forlorn?"

The chaplain inhaled sharply through his nose at the reminder of his duty.

"You are right, of course. Thank you. Forgive my weakness. God shall give me strength. I shall do what I can." His face took on a fierce look of determination, and he stood visibly taller. "I shall speak with Lady Cecily at once. They shall be cared for. I shall see to it. Whatever he did, they share no blame. They will want for nothing."

He gestured to the body hanging from the mill's rafters, two guards standing nearby. "I pleaded with them to cut him down, but they insisted on waiting for you to arrive. Can you imagine? Forcing the poor woman to see her husband swinging from the rafters. Ghastly. My stomach turned at the sight."

Thomas glanced across to where the body hung from the great crossbeam, the face slack and lifeless, a swollen black tongue protruding from blue lips. The body did not swing; it merely hung still like a lumpy sack, twisted at a strange angle from the neck. A stool lay on the ground beneath the feet, tipped onto its side as though kicked away. Coins and a leather purse were scattered across the floor.

Thomas caught the eye of one of the guards and indicated he should cut the man down.

The chaplain's visage collapsed again as he watched in horror. "This is all so horrible. When will it end?"

He quickly turned and rushed across to shelter the miller's

wife from the view, wrapping her in his arms once more, as much for his own comfort, thought Thomas, as for hers.

The constable walked up, his boots squelching in the mud, and spat to the side, the remnant of a pagan custom to ward off evil. Thomas caught himself fingering the iron of his talisman for the same unspoken reason.

"Well, that's that then," said John.

"What do you mean?"

"This just proves it, don't it? He knew we were on to him. He drank himself a skinful last night, got himself right soused to work up some courage; either that or he got melancholy and then decided to end it. He's hung himself and left the proof of his crime all about his feet—all the coin he stole from that poor old sod he offed in the church."

"I am not so sure, John."

"Not so sure? What's not to be sure about? Here he is swinging from the rafters. I'll wager my best cow that's Roger Lacy's coin purse."

Thomas knelt by the body. It all seemed a little too convenient. A scene prepared carefully for them. It looked like someone had just swept the dirt floor clean. Not something a man who was about to hang himself might do. And yet there were a couple of scuff marks he could still see, and a chunk taken out of one of the wattle walls.

There were some of the usual signs of hanging—the bulging eyes, the swollen face, his bowels emptied, the bruised neck. The neck was clearly broken, however, not something likely to happen with the short fall from the stool, even for a man of the miller's weight. He touched the face carefully, tilting it to the side. The skin was cold and clammy, the face puffy. The severe crease and burn under the rope was thinner than the rope itself, and Thomas could see scratch marks on the skin. That would not be unusual. A strangling man faced with death might well struggle with the rope, clawing at his neck in a last, regretful panic. But these marks here were under the rope, not around its edges as one might have expected. Rolling up the dead man's sleeves, Thomas was not surprised to find bruising. He suspected there would be similar bruising in the small of the back, where a knee might have been pressed, and at the back of the neck where knuckles might have ground into the flesh while tightening the garrote.

Like the other villagers, Tom Attwood was sure to be a deeply religious man. Was it really likely he would hang himself and risk damnation? Thomas doubted it.

No, this was just too convenient a resolution for all concerned. The miller was the second victim. And the fact the killer would so willingly give up his ill-gotten gains to implicate the poor man also served to convince Thomas that coin had in fact never been the primary motive behind Lacy's murder. Something else entirely was afoot.

The constable stood by, watching, saying nothing.

"Well there's little more we can do here, John. Cover the body and have a cart take him to the mortuary chapel. Perhaps Brother Eustace will see something we cannot."

The big man shook his head and sighed.

CHAPTER 12

The young, flaxen-haired boy scampered across the courtyard in pursuit of a shaggy dog that had to be twice his size.
No simple homespun for this lad; his was a finer cloth altogether, although he had managed to tear and soil his hose all
the same. He paused the chase long enough to stand and stare at
Thomas with the unashamed inquisitiveness of a small child.
Whatever had piqued his interest did not hold him long. The
dog, noticing its playmate's distraction, bounced around playfully and gave him a chivvying little yap. Thomas smiled at the
boy. And then he was off again, pumping his chubby little arms
as he ran, making mock barking sounds, his face glowing, bright
and happy, full of life.

Thomas watched the game for a few moments before turning
toward the chapel. He hoped to finally visit Lady Isabella before
the day's end, but first he would stop by Father Elyas and inquire
after the miller's family.

The chapel was a surprisingly small but sturdy stone structure
where the manor's servants would attend services. A small area
toward the front of the nave had been screened off and furnished
with comfortable chairs and well-padded kneeling stools so the
family could also worship there, free from the gawking stares of
their servants. The rest of the chapel was austere by comparison,

with not much more than a few rows of old wooden benches seated on the stone-flagged floor. Most of the congregation would have to stand at the back.

The chaplain's cell would likely be located at the front of the chapel, just off the sacristy. As he proceeded down the aisle, Thomas heard a sudden noise in front of him, the distinct scraping of wood being dragged across a floor, and a woman emerged from the shadowed entrance to the sacristy. She was elegantly dressed and wore a hooded cloak. This could only be the mysterious Lady Isabella de Bray. Thomas had heard she was beautiful, and he could see at once it was no lie.

On seeing Thomas, she froze guiltily in place.

"I apologize, my lady, I did not mean to disturb your devotions. I was just looking for Father Elyas."

"He is not here." The response was curt, almost snappish. Realizing she had been rude, Isabella recovered herself and smiled disarmingly. It was an undeniably pretty smile. "I am sorry. It is only that I too was looking for the chaplain, but I have been waiting for some time now, and he does not appear to be coming. I shall return later."

She turned up her hood and, with an apologetic glance, brushed past him toward the door.

"You are Lady Isabella?"

She paused and looked up at him inquisitively. Isabella could hardly be much older than her stepdaughter, Cecily, and she was even more attractive up close. Thomas made sure to look directly into her eyes, startling gray, even in the dim chapel light, resisting the temptation to let his own eyes wander over the richly embroidered and close-fitted dress visible underneath the cloak.

"My name is Thomas Lester. I was hoping to speak with you."

Isabella's eyes flicked to the side, and she clutched nervously at the cloak's ermine-trimmed edges.

"My husband has told me as much, but I am not feeling well

at the moment, and I was hoping to see the chaplain." Her voice trailed off, and she looked about her as though expecting the man might appear at any moment. "He is usually here. But he is not. I don't know where he could be, and I need to make my confession. I waited and waited, but he did not come."

Her eyes snapped back to Thomas. "Do you know where the chaplain is? Have you seen him?"

Thomas shook his head. "I am sorry, my lady. If you remember I was looking for him myself."

"You were? I thought you wished to speak with me?"

"Yes, that also. I intended to seek an audience with you after speaking with Father Elyas."

"I cannot speak now. I am not feeling well, and I have to return to my room. And we cannot speak here anyway. I suppose, if we must, we may speak a little later. Tomorrow perhaps, but only if I am feeling better and once I have found the chaplain." Isabella chewed her lip and looked back down the aisle to the sacristy. "I waited for some time, but he has not come, and I need to make my confession."

Thomas suspected that Lady Isabella might find herself equally indisposed again on the morrow, and scrambled for a subject by which he might engage her in conversation. "I saw a very likely looking young man playing in the courtyard just now. Your son, Henry, I believe?"

In Thomas's experience, people liked to speak about their children, especially when they were being complimented. Isabella, it seemed, did not, and his attempt to engage her in conversation had quite the opposite effect.

"My son? Was he playing with the hounds again? I have told him not to do so. I must leave at once."

She spun on her heel and walked away without waiting for an answer to her questions, pausing only momentarily at the door to look back at him.

"If you see the chaplain, you must send him to me at once. It is getting late, and it is already long past time for my confession."

Thomas made a belated little bow, and she was gone.

★ ★ ★

Isabella congratulated herself on how cleverly she had managed to avoid conversing with the young man. She was not supposed to speak with him. And she would avoid doing so again tomorrow. Isabella's mother had once told her that women should profess to be unwell when they wished to avoid a man's attentions. A gentleman of good breeding would never press the matter, she had said, for fear he might venture into the frightening realm of women's issues. Men could be so silly!

Isabella was less pleased when she spied her son rolling in the grass at the edge of the courtyard. He was filthy! She would send Hunydd to fetch him in later, but she could not stop now—lingering outside her chambers for too long always made Isabella feel anxious. Unsafe.

She drew her hood close about her face and hastened to the side of the manor house, entering by the postern. She always came and went that way so as to avoid anyone who might wish to engage her in conversation. It was not far now. She hustled across the back of the hall, behind the partition, and suddenly paused, flattening herself against the narrow stairwell leading to the family quarters.

There were voices on the stairs. Isabella could make out Cecily's voice, and she was speaking to someone in hushed, sibilant whispers. Isabella felt a thrill of excitement in her stomach. She knew from the urgency of the conversation that they must be up to something wicked, which made it so very much more interesting; and she had long suspected Cecily of plotting against her.

Isabella held her breath and listened intently, but they were too far away, and she could only hear brief snatches, just a few words, nothing that made any real sense. Still, she would be able to tell *him* about the secret conversation. He was sure to be pleased with her. She gnawed a doubtful lip. On second thoughts, he might also be angry that she did not get close enough to find out what they were saying.

Isabella realized with a start that they had finished speaking. She could hear Cecily walking back up to her room, and other footsteps were rapidly descending the stairs toward her. She barely had time to affect a more casual appearance before Hunydd arrived at the foot of the stairs.

Hunydd blinked in surprise at seeing the lady of the house appear as if out of nowhere. "My lady? Do—do you need anything?"

"Not right now, Hunydd. I am just come from taking the air," Isabella replied, fluffing nonchalantly at her clothes.

She could see that Hunydd had something clutched to her breast. *A letter!* It was surely a secret missive. Isabella tried not to stare too intently. She really wanted to ask about the letter, but she did not want to appear too inquisitive. Hunydd might suspect her of spying and tell Cecily. That, and Isabella really did want to be back inside her parlor. She felt like she had been away for an age already and was getting quite anxious. So, with a nod, she began to climb the stairs, pausing only to call out to Hunydd over her shoulder.

"You should fetch Henry inside now, Hunydd. I left him playing in the courtyard. You know how he is with the dogs."

That was good. It made Isabella's story so much more credible, although she was quite certain Hunydd did not suspect her of listening in on the conversation with Cecily. Hunydd was a fairly silly girl, after all.

CHAPTER 13

"This is stupid," grumbled the constable, shifting irritably from one rump cheek to the other. He stood up, stretched, and rubbed his backside vigorously with both hands. "Nobody's coming, and my arse is going numb sitting around waiting. I could be in my bed now, cuddled up all nice and cozy next to the missus. This better not be some sort of wild goose chase, Will."

His ire was directed at the skinny old man lying flat on his stomach, squinting out over the moon-washed field.

Thomas agreed. They had been waiting well over an hour, and he felt more than a little silly himself, sitting with his back propped up against the rickety wooden wall of the byre, twisting his head around every now and then to glance out over the stubble still left over from the harvest.

"Wait awhile, John," said Will, flapping his hand to signal that the constable should return to his hiding place. "Every night about this time, she comes, skips across the field, all quiet and secret-like, and then disappears into the trees over there." He hesitated, chewing his cheek. "Well, perhaps not every night, but most. She's up to no good, I tell you."

Thomas blew out his cheeks in frustration. The constable had brought Will, cap in hand, to him that morning, with a fantastical tale of a young woman dressed in a dark cloak and hood stealing about the village at night, entering the forest from the field right in front of the old abandoned assart where they now waited.

John slumped heavily to the ground. "If I find you made all of this up, Will, I swear to God you'll regret it. I'll be sure to give you a thrashing of the like you won't soon forget. And what are you doing out here at night anyway, when all decent folk should be abed?"

"I don't sleep well since the missus passed. I find it helps to take the air. It's none too good for the lungs to be shut up inside a smoky cottage all the time, you know." He offered a weak, embarrassed chuckle.

"Taking the air, my arse," growled John. "Peeking in good people's shutters more like. I know what you get up to, you dirty old bastard. I should throw you in the stocks."

"Now see here," whined Will, "it ain't like that."

John was idly chewing on a blade of grass he had plucked up from the ground. "Hold on a minute." The constable suddenly glared at Will. "Were you over at widow Margery's cottage again?"

The uncomfortable silence that followed said it was true.

"Why don't you just speak to her instead of peeking in her shutters, you daft old bugger. She's still a good-looking woman, and you have a decent bit of land. You're a few sticks short of a bundle, I suppose, and you're no spring chicken, but she could do worse."

Will squirmed about and shifted position. "I'm shy. And I have spoken to her anyway. We have what you might call an *arrangement*."

John raised his eyebrows. "What sort of arrangement?"

"I like to look, and she don't mind it none. There's a nice big crack in the shutter over one window. If she wanted, she could get it fixed, but she leaves it like that so I can get a decent eyeful."

"What?" exclaimed the constable, appalled by what he had just heard. "She knows you're peeking at her?"

"'Tis true, I tell you. I like looking and she likes to be looked at. It . . . well, it suits us both." Will gave a decided nod of his head.

John tossed the blade of grass aside in disgust. "So that's it then. She's inside getting undressed and all the while knowing you're outside ogling her in her shift?" He sighed and shook his head. "Then she's as daft as you are, and you deserve each other. Did it never occur to you both that you might go inside and, well, you know . . ." He clenched his fist and pumped it in the air a couple of times to finish the thought.

Will squirmed about again. "We sort of like it the way it is. And sometimes she does leave the door unbarred anyhow, and I'll sneak in real quiet like while she's abed and—"

"No! Dear God, no!" The constable waved both his hands in front of his face. "That's enough. I don't want to hear about it. Well then, you're a right pair of daft old buggers and no mistake. I bet neither of you includes that in your confession of a Sunday, do you? Or maybe you did, and poor Father Oswin died of shock."

He punched Thomas lightly on the arm, a happy grin plastered across his face. "There you go. We've solved the vicar's death. He died of shock and shame that he could have a couple of silly old bastards like them in his flock. I guess tonight wasn't a complete waste after all."

Thomas couldn't help but smile. It wasn't the strangest arrangement he had heard of. There was a woman one time on Brayford Wharf in Lincoln, a skinny old bird as he recalled, who made a handsome living out of a local bronzesmith who liked to be tied up and tickled with a goose feather. And then there was the time the bishop had dispatched him to investigate the famous moaning shade in Nottingham that turned out to be a cooper who—

John interrupted his thoughts, grumbling away again. "I think we should call it a night. Nobody's coming. Like I said, it's a wild goose chase."

"I know what I saw," insisted Will, a tad tetchy at being made fun of.

"I think you drink too much."

Thomas tugged his cloak about him and listened to the pair of them bickering away with each other in exaggerated whispers. He looked up at the sky, dotted by stars and a low hanging moon that gave off a strange translucent sort of light, rendering the whole landscape surreal and fanciful. It seemed somehow appropriate for their strange escapade.

John was still haranguing the old lecher. "And how come you don't know who it is if you've seen her so often?"

"Because she moves about at *night*, doesn't she, when it's *dark*. And she's all covered up with a *cloak and hood*," Will sneered. "It's a better moon tonight, though. Mayhap we'll see something. If you ever stop griping and do some watching," he added quietly as an afterthought, almost to himself.

John shifted uncomfortably. "Some forester you are! Your eyes are good enough when they need to be. Good enough to peek into people's shutters." He plucked irritably at the grass again. "And where does this cloaked mystery woman go then?"

"I don't know."

"What do you mean you don't know? Didn't you ever follow her?"

Will turned to stare at his companion. "Follow her? No, that'd be wrong, to just sort of follow her about. I wouldn't feel right about it. What kind of a man do you think I am?"

Will had a strange sense of morality indeed, and Thomas wondered again what he was doing. There he was, at midnight, looking out over a dead field for some ghost of a girl on the questionable say-so of a half-soused dirty old lecher who liked to wander the village at night to see if he could catch his fancy-bird or any of the other village women in their shifts.

"And I don't go in those woods at night anyway," added Will. "There's things in there."

"What things?" Thomas asked.

"I don't know; *things* is all."

The constable chuckled.

"It's true! Everybody knows it." Will began speaking in an awed whisper. "I've seen them: shadows that slip between the trees like they're following you. Stalking you. Things you see from the corner of your eye, but then when you turn, there's nothing there, nothing but darkness. Blackness. You can feel the hairs on your neck standing on end, and you just know something is looking back at you. You want to turn away, but you daren't because that's what it wants, and you know that when you do turn your back, it will be right behind you. Breathing on your neck. Sharp teeth ready to sink into your throat."

The constable was not smiling anymore and was listening with rapt attention, his eyes black and wide. Somewhere off in the trees, a screech owl screamed, well known to be an evil omen, and both men turned their heads and gaped.

Then John gasped softly as Thomas's elbow jabbed him in the ribs.

A shape had emerged out of the mist—the hooded and cloaked shape of a woman.

"See? I told you so," hissed Will triumphantly.

Thomas felt a chill spread through him and settle some-where about his chest. This was not the first time he had known a young woman sneak out at night to the sanctuary of the woods. It wasn't good then, and it could not be good now.

The three of them were silent as they watched her stalk across the field. Every now and then she stopped to look about, but it was not until the owl screeched again, and she turned to the sound, that the moonlight revealed her face. She was still at some distance, but they all saw her clear enough.

"Hunydd," whispered Thomas under his breath. "What are you doing, girl?"

"Aye, it's her alright," whispered the constable, "and no mistake. By God, she's a witch, isn't she?" he hissed. "I always knew there was something strange about her from the first time I saw her. She's Welsh, right? It's old country that. They have all sorts of magic there and hags coming out of every bloody bush and from around every hillock."

The constable frowned thoughtfully. "Perhaps she's away to dance under the moon. Witches do that, you know. I heard tell of it. Aye," he said, nodding to himself, "and maybe she'll do so tonight. Galloping and cavorting about full naked, jumping and skipping this way and that, not a stitch on her but her dignity."

John was looking up to the sky now, his mind feverishly picturing the scene. The snoop was grinning broadly like a loon, letting his own imagination wander along with him. Thomas just stared at them incredulously.

"I bet that's what she's about," John said. "And maybe she summons some demon lover. I've heard they do that too." Will was vigorously nodding his agreement, a silly, half-toothless grin on his face."

John's eyes widened as he was struck by a sudden thought. "And where there's one witch, there's bound to be others. Aye, maybe there's a whole gaggle of them meeting out there in the woods, frolicking under the stars, dancing around, all stretching and turning, and bits all a-wobbling. And maybe then—"

Thomas cuffed John hard around the head, waking him from his reverie. The constable grumbled and rubbed where he had been hit. "I was just saying, is all," he complained sulkily.

"Come on, John. Let's see what she's up to before she's away from us."

Will cleared his throat and spoke in a croaky whisper: "Maybe I should go too, you know, in case you need any help."

"I thought you were afraid of the woods," said Thomas.

"Well, if there's three of us, I reckon we'd be alright."

Thomas just stared at him. "John, if you catch Will roaming about the village at night again, you throw him in the stocks, you hear? I don't care whose cousin or uncle he is." He nodded Will in the direction of the village. "Off with you. And make a proper proposal to that widow. You can still play your games when the two of you are married."

Will pulled a face as sour as curdled milk, annoyed to be missing the fun. But he set off, sidling low to the ground, mumbling to himself in his whiny voice, casting a longing backward glance at Hunydd's receding form, just now entering the fringes of the trees.

"And you," Thomas said to John, "quiet's the word."

The constable scowled. "I can move quiet when I want. You'll see. I'll make no more sound than the quietest of forest animals."

Hunydd moved stealthily through the forest, picking her way with evident familiarity, barely stirring a bush with her passage, making no sound. Had she not been following the remnants of an old, overgrown track, they would surely have lost her. The big man was surprisingly quiet, setting his feet down with exaggerated care.

They had not been following her long when Thomas suddenly sensed something in the trees away to his right. He stood stock still, his hand up, the constable almost blundering into him.

"What's up?" hissed John.

"Shh."

Thomas stared into the trees. He could not say what had caught his attention, but he held his breath, every sense alert. Somewhere just beyond where he was looking, he heard a rustling of leaves, telling of the passage of some forest animal. He had felt something—he was sure of it. Something not right; but he could wait no longer and, with another glance over his shoulder, began moving forward again.

Behind him he heard John blow out the breath he had been holding.

"You scared me there," came his rumbling whisper.

"Hurry up—and be quiet."

They had lost her, but Thomas was not concerned. If they followed the track, they would find where she was going. It had to lead somewhere.

★   ★   ★

The man stood silent and unmoving, scarcely distinguishable from the darkness around him. A shadow in a sea of shadows, making no more noise than the gentle breeze, nothing that could be heard above the rustling of the drying leaves. And yet one of the two men had turned toward him as they passed and had looked straight at him. He had not been concerned. He knew he was well hidden. In fact, he was surprised the man sensed him at all. That one had moved stealthily, like a woodsman. The big man, not so much.

Where had the girl been going? And why would they be following her? What was she doing that could be of such interest to them? On another night, he might have been tempted to follow her, melting into the shadows, as black and silent as the night itself. She had a secret, and secrets were most useful to him, more valuable than gold. Secrets were like keys that, when manipulated, unlocked doors with hidden treasures. Even a small secret could often lead to a larger one or could give him power over the carrier. And he had found that where there was one secret, there were always others, and they tended to intertwine like a spider's web. And he was the spider, feeling the strands quiver as the unsuspecting flies struggled in the web of their own lies and deceit.

He was sure the girl the men were following was Lady Cecily's maid. Was it her own business she was about or her mistress's? He would find out soon enough, and then he might have one or both of them in his power. He shivered as a tremor of ecstatic anticipation passed through his body.

The man looked about him and listened for a while to the scampering and scuttling of some forest scavenger. He loved the night. And he loved the dark. The night was his domain, and he felt comfortable wrapped in its shroud. He felt somehow safer, stronger.

The young maid's secret would have to wait. He could not follow her tonight. He had other matters to attend to.

He turned, a little too quickly, wincing suddenly in pain and stifling a gasp, his hand sliding instinctively to his bruised ribs. The oaf of a miller had been strong. The man had underestimated him, thinking him blind drunk, and he had almost paid the price. *Foolish.* His fingers touched his ribs gingerly. They were only bruised, not cracked. Still the injury served as a fitting reminder, something that would help him remember to be more cautious in the future. He had deserved no less.

Nor had it been his first mistake. He had allowed his emotions to get the better of him with Roger Lacy as well. Of course, the old man had to die. That went without saying, but once more he had been unable to control his temper. He remembered how he had laughed as he splayed Lacy's body across the altar, regretting only that he did not have time or tools to crucify him properly, in mockery to the savior they all worshipped so adoringly. He despised the Church and priests and monks and friars, and even more so the puling rabble that paid them homage.

As he laid Lacy on the altar, he had imagined he was punishing them all, showing them that their God could not protect them. Abusing them as he had once been abused. But what had seemed a just end for Lacy that night had seemed foolhardy in the cold light of day.

Things were becoming complicated. He had not really believed that the miller had seen him. Likely he had not, but he could not take that risk. Besides, the miller's death served as a wonderful distraction. The miller was not the first man who had hanged for him. And who knows? They may even be foolish enough to believe the miller to be the killer, at least long enough to allow him to complete his business and be on his way.

The man walked slowly through the woods. He knew them well enough, and it was not far to where he had left the village girl, Margareta, bound hand and foot. She tensed when she heard his soft footfalls, the sack he had placed over her head jerking toward the sound, a stream of urgent muffled sounds coming from underneath. The sacked head followed him as he walked around her, and she twisted uselessly at the ropes that held her. He knelt at her side, her pleading frantic now. This girl had a secret as well, and it had drawn him to her.

"Shh, now," he whispered, lifting the sack and looking into the large, pleading eyes. "Be still, my sweet. It will all be over soon. And if you behave yourself, I shall be kind to you."

He stroked her cheek. It was smooth and wet, streaked with tears.

She cringed and gagged as he stuffed the rag deeper into her mouth, and then wriggled about like an eel when he lifted her to his chest, making him wince again at the stabbing pain in his ribs.

Perhaps taking her had been rash also. He was sure it was. Nor had it been necessary, but the opportunity had presented itself, and he had been patient long enough, the pressure building up in him day by day. First it was no more than an itch scratching at the back of his mind, getting worse and worse until it was a pounding in his skull. He knew from experience that when the red mist came over him, he could not control it. Perhaps he was indeed possessed by some demon or devil, as the monks had once told him. This girl would relieve the pressure. But he was not foolish enough to think the palliative effect would last long. He needed to be done here, and soon.

He threw the girl over his shoulder and headed deeper into the forest to find somewhere they might become better acquainted with one another. There was plenty of time. The night was still young.

★   ★   ★

Hunydd had led them to a small cottage in a clearing. It was an old forester's cottage, and John was sure it had long been abandoned.

They walked up to the door. Thomas wondered whether he should knock, or whether he should be there at all. Why would Hunydd come to an abandoned hut in the middle of the forest in the black of night? He suspected the answer could not be good. Perhaps she was engaged in a tryst. That seemed to be the most likely conclusion. He found himself surprisingly disappointed at the thought, though he had no reason to be. How churlish it would be to interrupt a rendezvous with a secret lover. What would she think of him?

He glanced at John, who looked just as uncertain.

This was silly. Why had they followed her all the way here if they were only going to turn back around again? That would make the entire escapade a complete waste of time, which it likely was anyway. Thomas straightened his tunic and raised his hand to knock. And there it stayed, knuckles poised over the wood as he was assailed by another wave of doubts. Did he really want to see what was going on behind that door? He could always ask Hunydd what she was about tomorrow. He could be discreet. That would probably be for the best. And perhaps it was not what it appeared to be, after all.

Thomas had almost convinced himself to leave, when the decision was made for him. The door suddenly swung inward, and they found themselves looking at a woman, and not just any woman. Even with her back to the light Thomas could tell from her demeanor and dress that this was a lady—a very elegant lady indeed, and a very handsome one.

"Well, are you coming in, or are you going to skulk out there all night?"

Her tone was both mocking and playful at the same time.

After a moment of standing in discomfited silence, Thomas followed her inside. He walked on stiff legs as if in a trance, the constable crouching down to fit under the lintel, both of them feeling ungainly in comparison with their host. She walked with such grace that she almost *glided* across the floor, and when she moved, Thomas could swear he caught the scent of wildflowers and meadows on a spring morning.

Thomas was vaguely aware of Hunydd, sitting on a stool, eyeing him curiously, but she might as well not have been there because all of his attention was focused on her companion.

By God, this was a woman such as he had rarely seen before. Of no more than average height, she possessed a handsome face, with wide-set eyes. Some might say her mouth was a little too large, her lips a little too full, her face a little too broad, but each flawed feature somehow contrived to make a perfect whole, all the more attractive for its lack of traditional symmetry. And there was something intoxicating about her eyes. About the way she looked at him. Perhaps this is how the Romans had seen Cleopatra, he thought, never renowned as a beauty, but entrancing all the same, and capable of drawing men to her with a single irresistible glance. Even in the dim light he could see her hair was almost silver in hue, and her eyes a violet color. Eyes, he noticed, which were now crinkled in amusement.

Thomas blinked and roused himself from his stupor, realizing with horror that he was gaping. He felt his face coloring and snapped his mouth shut, cursing himself for a moonstruck idiot.

"Hunydd thought she was followed," the lady said, her voice like dripping honey on a hot summer day. "She heard someone crashing about in the woods behind her like a charging boar. You gave her quite a start."

Thomas glared at the constable.

"No matter," the lady continued. "For one so young, Hunydd does not scare easily. Either that or she has yet to learn to fear that which awaits us in the dark. And now that you are here, you must tell me what brings you to my door. It is a trifle unseemly for young men to be visiting a woman alone in her house in the dead of night."

She appeared to have summed them up at a glance and concluded that Thomas was the one to whom she would speak. She gave scant attention to the constable, something John seemed more than happy about. The big man stood awkwardly, even by his standards, and was huddling away in the corner, trying to make himself as near invisible as possible—no easy task for a man his size. Thomas wondered whether his superstitious fears had seized hold of him or whether he was simply in awe of the lady. It was probably the latter, because Thomas was more than a little in awe of her himself.

She had been studying Thomas through narrowed eyes, and her face suddenly lit up in recognition. "I have you now. My niece has told me of you."

"Your niece?"

"Yes, yes, let us not play games. I think you know who I am, do you not?"

Sudden realization dawned on him. Her Irish brogue was hard to miss. He had heard the accent before. The Dominican had said Cecily's mother was Irish, and he remembered the surprising ferocity with which Cecily had defended her countrywoman to the friar. The rest was intuition.

"Yes, I believe so. You are Dame Alice Kyteler."

She inclined her head by way of acknowledgment, and Thomas could not help but notice the graceful curve of her neck and line of her jaw as she did so. One thing was certain: this was no hag. He had imagined Alice Kyteler to be of more than middling age, even elderly, but this woman looked to be no more than in her early thirties, if that. And she managed to combine the grace of a more mature woman with the freshness and vigor of youth in one single intoxicating brew.

"Cecily has spoken of me?" he asked, suddenly realizing that he was in danger of staring again, but also very much wanting to know what she had said.

"Yes, and why should she not notice you? You are a fine-looking young man, after all."

He was startled by her boldness and the brazen way her eyes wandered over him before returning to seize his own once more. He wished he had dressed better. But that would have been silly for traipsing through the forest, and Alice did not seem particularly displeased with what she saw.

"Yes, a fine-looking man. And interesting. Most interesting."

Hunydd sniffed disapprovingly.

"Cecily is related to you through her mother?" Thomas asked.

"Exactly."

Alice turned to John, who was standing in the corner, as still as a statue, a glazed expression on his face, trying not to breathe too heavily, lest it draw attention to him.

"This one I do not know." She looked at the constable expectantly.

The poor man was mortified that she had spoken to him.

"I–I," he began, tilting his head and clearing his throat. "I am called—" He cleared his throat again and snatched the cap from head, twisting it in his hands and bowing deferentially. "That is to say, my name is John"—he coughed—"er . . . my lady." Despite their difference in height, of the two, Alice was by far the greater presence in the room.

"And quite a man as well," she said, looking him up and down. "A veritable titan."

John's cheeks glowed brightly, and he stared intently at the floor as if he might fall through it at any time.

"Come, gentlemen, let me at least play the host. I would not have you find my manners wanting."

Alice gestured to the table, and they sat on one of the benches opposite her, the constable dropping down with an ungainly thump. Alice poured wine from an elegant carafe and set a cup down in front of each of them. John, visibly cheered at the sight, finally managing to recover some of his old self.

"My thanks, my lady," he said, immediately scooping up the cup in a big, meaty fist. Thomas touched John's hand lightly just as the cup reached his lips. John turned to him questioningly, blinked once, and slowly lowered the cup, setting it back down again.

"I . . . tend not to drink too much these days. The missus doesn't like it." He gave a terribly forced laugh and patted his stomach. "And it don't sit none too well with me. I guess I must be getting old."

It was excruciatingly weak stuff, and Alice watched the pantomime with a sardonic expression.

"I see how it is. You have heard the stories that I poisoned my husbands, and now you fear that I might poison you as well."

She set her own cup down on the edge of the table and adjusted her seat, taking her time about it, letting them both stew in the uncomfortable silence. When she finally spoke, her voice was laced with bitterness.

"You should consider that perhaps I was married at a tender age to service the wants of a doddering old man. Perhaps it was too much for his heart, and then perhaps as a young widow I was passed on to yet another doddering old man, even older than the last, to service his wants, and perhaps he suffered the same fate, or perhaps he died of old age. You might also consider that it was my stepchildren, who conveniently stand to inherit everything, now I am gone, who manufactured the charges against me.

"Perhaps you believe the other stories about me as well. Let me see, of what else am I accused?"

She tapped her lips thoughtfully with the tip of her finger.

"Oh yes. I consort with demons. But that is a given, I suppose, when one is accused of witchcraft. And I chanted spells so that all the town's wealth would come to me. Strange that such wealth as I possessed now appears to be going to my husband's children, don't you think? It was not a very effective spell, was it?

"I shall not deign to repeat any of the more . . . lewd acts I am purported to have performed. Those I always find amusing. I think some of the men who put the charges together have very active imaginations, and I suspect their words say rather more about them than they do about me."

The constable frowned, uncertain as to her meaning. As comprehension dawned, he looked aside, his cheeks blushing a bright red for the second time.

"And let us not forget that I am supposed to have summoned my very own incubus, Robert Artisson. A strange sort of name for a demon, wouldn't you say? And they could never quite decide whether his skin was the dusky shade of a Saracen, or ebony like that of an Aethiopian. I must say, either way, it all sounded rather exciting to me. Very exotic."

Alice looked around her in an exaggerated fashion. "Now where could I have put that demon lover? They are never about when you want them. Such tiresome things."

Thomas stared at her in silence. He had never heard a woman speak like this. Not even the women that frequented Lincoln's saltier taverns of an evening. He wasn't quite sure what to say.

"You are the son of a Templar knight, Thomas. I know your story, and I am truly sorry for what you and your family have suffered. I would have thought that you would be more sympathetic to one so wrongly accused. But I shall not take offense. Nor shall I let good wine go to waste."

With that, she picked up Thomas's cup and downed it in one.

Thomas felt utterly ashamed. "If your kind offer still stands, madam, I would welcome some wine."

"I can do it!"

Hunydd had been sitting quietly and now leapt to her feet, bounded across the room, picked up the carafe, and, standing quite deliberately in front of Alice, poured some wine into Thomas's cup. Thomas thought she leaned over just a little lower than she had to, just enough to remind him that there was more than one woman in the room. He remembered how Hunydd had looked in his dream, walking naked through the garden, and quickly crushed the thought.

The constable had wasted no time downing his own wine and held out his cup for a refill, but Hunydd set the carafe down and returned to her seat, where she adjusted her skirts and sat primly, her hands resting lightly in her lap.

"Right, I'll just pour myself some more, then," mumbled John, pouring himself a healthy measure.

Alice returned her attention to Thomas and inhaled sharply when her eyes fell on the cross hanging around his neck.

"What an interesting pendant, Thomas."

Thomas smiled. "It was a gift from someone dear to me."

He made as if to tuck it back into his tunic, but Alice had already plucked it up in her fingers and was now staring at it intently.

"*Cros Cheilteich*," she whispered, her thumb rubbing the surface slowly. She nodded to Hunydd and repeated herself in Hunydd's native tongue: "*Croes Geltaidd*, Hunydd."

Both women were looking intently at the small piece of iron, and the men at them.

"A Celtic cross," Alice explained, "but a very interesting one." Her thumb traced the circle. "Why this do you suppose?"

Thomas shrugged. "I believe the circle represents the resurrection."

Alice smiled tolerantly. "Some say the nimbus represents the sun, or birth and death, the renewal of life. They think the *Cros Cheilteich* a blend—a harmonizing, if you will—of both pagan and Christian beliefs. Others say it is something else entirely. And the tracings here," her thumb now rubbed the cross itself and the faint scratches on its surface, "what do you know of them?"

Thomas shrugged again. The markings were indistinct, barely noticeable, and he had never been able to decipher them. He had always meant to ask his wife if she understood them, but she had died before he could do so.

"This is a precious piece, Thomas," she added. "Very precious indeed." He was surprised at that. The pendant was simple iron and roughly shaped. Nothing special in appearance. It was precious to him, of course, but simply as a remembrance of Hawisa. "You should carry it with you and wear it close. Always."

Alice held his eyes for a long moment and then dropped the cross to his chest and sat back.

"So, Thomas Lester, now you have uncovered me, now you have found me out, what will you do with me?"

She did not appear particularly afraid.

Thomas tucked the cross into his tunic. "I have no interest in causing you harm, and it is true that I am sympathetic to your plight. But you should know a hound is upon you, and it would be best for you to leave. It would be best for everyone."

Alice looked down at the hands folded in her lap. There was something very vulnerable about her in that moment. Thomas felt his heart swell with pity, but the risk could not be ignored.

"Your presence here places your niece in danger, Alice. If the Dominican should find out . . ." He left the rest unspoken.

"Do you think I am not aware of that?" she snapped, her eyes for the first time flashing angrily. "Or of the danger to Hunydd, for that matter? Yet what choice do I have? I am a wanted woman in fear for her life. No matter where I go, the bishop will never let me be. He is a truly terrible and most dogged man."

Alice bit down on her anger, and when she spoke again, it was in a calmer tone. "A ship is being readied to carry me to France with what little fortune I could bring with me. Rest assured, I shall be gone from here soon enough."

Thomas looked about the hut. "You are not concerned, living out here on your own?"

"Not really. Nobody comes around here. And this place, as dismal as it may be, does not seem so bad when the sword of Damocles is hanging over one's head."

The constable frowned in confusion and began looking about him, wondering where the sword was that she was talking about.

"I understand the bishop's men seized my maid, along with several others who were unfortunate enough to have been my servants or friends. I am sorry that they have suffered because of me. I am sure they all spoke against me. Who would not when tortured or even threatened with torture?" She looked at Thomas. "But you, of course, know this."

He nodded grimly, acknowledging the truth.

"People will say anything to end the pain or in the hopes of saving themselves from it," she explained. "They will lie if needed. I do not blame them and feel nothing but pity for what they suffered on my account. And to think it was all done in the name of God. Do you think God would approve, Thomas? I do not."

She sighed and then rose to her feet. "Well, I suppose you must go. And perhaps you can see Hunydd safely home. She is kind enough to bring me some supplies on her mistress's behalf and to carry messages for us, at no small peril to herself I might add."

"I don't mind, mistress," said Hunydd, "and I am careful."

Alice smiled indulgently. "She is also pleasant company and a clever girl. I will send her out in a moment. I have a message for her to convey to my niece. I trust I can count on your discretion, Thomas?"

Thomas nodded, and he and John walked out the door.

Once they were safely outside, waiting for Hunydd, the constable let out a low whistle. "By God that's a woman and no mistake!"

Thomas had to agree. He had never met anyone like her. Such a woman could drive men mad. Mad with lust. Mad with jealousy. She was a woman whom men would fight over. A real Helen of Troy. He wondered whether the Bishop of Ossory had acted out of personal animus. Perhaps he had found his advances spurned or was jealous of her attention to others. Or perhaps her forthrightness and success had merely offended his patriarchal sensibilities.

John interrupted Thomas's thoughts, nudging him with an elbow.

"She's a nice girl that. Hunydd, I mean. A right tasty little piece, I reckon. Tight little curves, pretty face. And if I am not mistaken, she's setting her cap on you."

"That's ridiculous, John."

"Is it now?" He looked at Thomas archly and grinned. "Truth be told, I thought you had your eyes on the mistress, not the maid."

"Why do you say so?"

"Oh, no reason." John treated Thomas to one of his rumbling chuckles. "Or maybe you'd just be liking Hunydd for a roll in the hay? A quick tumble. A bit of the old slap and tickle." He nudged Thomas with his elbow and gave him a wink. "You could do far worse than cuddling up to that on a cold night, I reckon. Yes, I'll wager she would give you a right going over. And she's not likely to boss you about like the other one."

John was enjoying himself immensely, and Thomas pretended to be annoyed.

They were silent for a while, and then John heaved a giant sigh and blew out another soft whistle. "By God, that's a woman!" he repeated.

"John, you understand we had best not speak of this."

The big man scowled at him, genuinely hurt. "I may be a big man, but I'm not daft. Anyway, she seemed alright . . . for a witch," he added jokingly. "And a right looker too."

He sighed loudly again. "It would have been something, though, wouldn't it, to see them girls dancing about under the moonlight?"

Thomas smiled. "I suppose it would at that, John."

CHAPTER 14

With grief we discover that there are many who are Christians only in name; many who turn away from the light which once was theirs, and allow their minds to be so clouded with the darkness of error as to enter into a league with death and a compact with hell. The very thought of it wrings our soul with anguish. They sacrifice to demons and adore them, they make or cause to be made images, rings, mirrors, phials, or some such thing in which by the arts of magic evil spirits are to be enclosed. From them they seek and receive replies, and ask aid in satisfying their evil desires. For a foul purpose they submit to the foulest slavery.
—Pope John XXII, Decretal Super Illius Specula (1326)

The sulfur match sputtered and flared into life, just long enough to light the candle, creating a wavering half-light in the midst of the darkness.

The witch took up the lump of beeswax and began pressing her fingers into it. Pulling, twisting, stretching, and shaping. She worked quietly and confidently, softening the wax with the warmth of her hands, slowly teasing it into the crude shape of a man.

Intense black eyes caught the light and glittered as she drew the figure closer, shaving the wax now with a thin splinter carved from a dog's bone. It had to be bone, not metal. And from a loyal hound, a bitch, sacrificed under a full moon. The witch knew these things. She had learned them from her mother, who had been taught by her own mother before her, and so on for generations past. Every detail had to be attended to and perfect.

Smiling, she began the finer work, etching the lines of fingers, toes, mouth, and even cock, before dabbing on color with the quill of a cockerel feather. A feather from a cockerel strangled underwater, mind, not a pigeon. That was a common mistake that marked the unknowing. The eyes had to be a soft brown, almost hazel. The tincture had taken some time to prepare, and she had tested and discarded several pastes until satisfied she had the color exact. It did not do to hasten such an important aspect. The more exact the poppet, the stronger the spell.

Nothing else was needed. She had already melted a single strand of dark hair into the wax before molding it. It didn't have to be hair, but hair worked well in most cases. She had seen others who would affix the hair to the poppet's head. That made no sense at all to the witch. The poppet had to *contain* the essence of the person, to *absorb* it. And besides, a single hair on a bald waxen head looked plain silly and could easily come adrift.

The witch looked down admiringly. It was perfect, the proportions exact, and the eyes almost lifelike. She passed the poppet high over the flame. Once, twice, three times. There was magic in the number three; even the Christians with their Holy Trinity knew this to be true. And three times was just enough to cause the poppet's skin, as she now supposed it to be, to sweat. Then she held it aloft, and the wax hardened once more, curing any minute imperfections on the surface, and sealing in her work.

Finally ready for the spell, the witch knelt, bowed her head as if in church, and with the poppet cradled to her breast, uttered the same name over and over in soft melodic tones, rocking back and forth in time to her chant, concentrating now more than ever. Over and over she chanted. Back and forth she rocked. By the time she stood again, the witch could sense the power in the air all around her.

She glanced down at the table and picked up a sharp brass bodkin. The hand holding the pin hovered over the figure for a while, as if hesitant or making a decision, and then she stabbed her thumb sharply, deftly, a small bead of dark red blood welling up slowly from the wound. She smeared her thumb across the poppet, turning the pale wax a dark ochre color where it touched.

Blood. Yes, blood was always necessary. Those who wished to gain must always be willing to sacrifice, the nature of the sacrifice proportionate to the extent of the wish and the skill of the practitioner. For someone less skilled than her, something more drastic might have been required. But she had a rare gift. She had been blessed from youth with a talent for the craft, and her conjurations rarely failed. A single drop of her blood would suffice. It would have been better in this instance, for this particular spell, to use her woman's blood, of course. Unfortunately, she was not in flow and time was short, so this would have to do. And it would still work—she was sure of that.

Her task complete, the witch smiled, the corners of her mouth curling up in triumph and genuine pleasure. Yes, this was good. This was very good. Her mother would have been proud.

She threw back her head, tossing her hair behind her, and laughed once out loud. The candle's flame flared in response, burnishing her painted flesh with a warm, mellow glow. She ran her hands over her nakedness, delighting in the smoothness of the skin, the firmness of her breasts, feeling as languid as a stretching cat. It was so easy to become distracted when the mad man's moon was approaching, but she had work to do in the morning. There were herbs to gather. Motherwort. Hyssop. Monk's hood. Rosemary. Nightshade, if she could still find any. And she needed aqua vitae for her tinctures. So much had been left behind.

The witch sucked her thumb, tasting the iron tang of the blood, then licked her fingers and pinched out the flame, returning the room to blackness.

Chapter 15

"**B**loody fool's errand."

John was grumbling away to himself as he thrashed at the undergrowth with a wispy willow wand.

"There's nothing here I tell you."

Thomas ignored him. He had learned to trust his instincts, and his instincts had led him back to the path through the forest, to where he had sensed a malevolent presence the night before.

He could not say what he expected to find. Perhaps the morning light would reveal something he could not have seen at night. Perhaps there would be nothing at all.

"Bloody fool's errand," repeated John.

The constable had taken Thomas's silence as meaning he should not yet abandon the search, and had started beating at the undergrowth again, mumbling under his breath, forgetting how far his voice carried. Thomas wished he hadn't brought him.

"Wild bloody goose chase and no mistake."

Thomas sighed. Perhaps John was right. They had wandered far from the path now, and the chances of finding anything were growing ever more slim, especially with the constable stomping about, trampling everything in his way. And they had been at it for a full hour or more. Thomas was ready to give up himself.

It was still early morning, not long after dawn, and tendrils of mist drifted low to the ground, clinging stubbornly here and there to the undergrowth, giving the air a moist feel, soon wetting to the face and clothes. A familiar beginning to what might have been just another autumn day. Then the clouds parted, and a single shaft of sunlight lanced through the canopy of leaves, revealing the barest hint of white, a mere wisp of cloth lying half-buried among the gnarled roots of one of the ancient trees; something not at home on the leaf-strewn forest floor; something that should not have been there.

Thomas's breath caught in his throat, and he stood stock-still, dread settling like a stone over his heart, as it had done only once before. He approached warily and then hissed in through his teeth, his worst fears realized.

It could not fairly be called a grave. She had been tossed into a shallow pit crudely hacked out between the roots and then covered with a collection of earth, bracken, and brushwood in a meager attempt at concealment. Whoever did this had not expected to hide her for long, but nor had he expected someone to wander so far from the track. Had he cared to do so, he could have dragged her deeper into the forest, where it was darker and where the great oaks grew even thicker. Yet even here she would likely have lain for some time, alone and undiscovered.

Thomas dropped to his knees and began to ease aside the tangle of twigs and foliage. He wanted to drag them off her, to tear them away, but something told him to be gentle. Low to the ground, he could smell the strong odor of mildew, moss, and fern, all the scents of the forest. And now there was another scent, not strong as yet, but the beginnings of corruption.

They had no spade or mattock, so he scooped and scraped at

the soil with his fingers, working around her steadily and with infinite care, her despoiled body slowly emerging from its pitiful grave to the light of a world that had failed her.

She was young, scarcely more than a girl to his eyes, dressed only in the remnants of a torn and muddied shift. Damp leaves clung to tresses of long red hair that was disheveled and clotted with soil. The blackened and purplish bruising on her neck stood out in rude contrast to the deathly pallor of her strangely unmarked face. The blue, bloodless lips would never speak again, but the glassy eyes that stared up at him were eloquent enough. *This was not supposed to happen to me,* they said. *You were supposed to protect me.*

The branches of the ancient tree stretched out protectively above, its leaves falling gently about her like silent tears, and the clouds covering the sun cast her once more in shadow, the heavens themselves having seen enough.

"*Jesu miserere,*" Thomas whispered.

Who could say how she had found her way to this pitiful pass? What horrors she had endured, only for her small body to be hastily cast aside in its shallow grave, with scarcely enough cover to keep off the forest animals.

Thomas was filled with shame and anger. There had been no prayers said over this poor soul. No priest to confess and anoint her. No family or friends to weep at her graveside. No garland to adorn her. No cross to comfort her and mark her resting place so that others might know where she lay.

Thomas choked back a sob. This was all too familiar to him. What had he done to see such a fate twice in one lifetime?

John had watched Thomas's progress in silence, a stunned expression on his face, and now he brushed roughly past him and picked her up, cradling her head gently against his chest. No words were necessary between them. They could have gone for a handcart, but neither one of them would leave her a moment longer where she laid, lost and alone. Thomas would return later on his own to study the ground for any clues, though he had a sinking feeling there would be none.

It was John who carried her back to her home, stubbornly refusing any help, though his arms must have ached. He trudged through the mud of the fields and through the village, his face black with anger and grief, not stopping or speaking until he reached her family's cottage, a shocked crowd by now following silently in his massive wake.

Thomas did not enter the small home. He was still a stranger to them, and so he stood respectfully outside, not yet having earned the right to be privy to their grief. From inside the cottage, he heard a sudden piercing cry of pure loss and despair. It could only be a mother's cry. Tears wet many eyes around him, and dark mutterings filled the air. She had been one of their own.

★ ★ ★

A short time later, Thomas once more stood beside Brother Eustace in the priory's mortuary chapel, the pair of them looking down at another dead body. Neither of them spoke. Neither wanted to peel back the sheet to see what lay underneath.

"She was a lovely girl, you know," said Eustace sadly. "Margareta, full of life, happy, always with a ready smile on her lips. She used to ask me if she could help at the lazar house. We never allowed her to do so, of course. She would have been a fine woman, Thomas. A fine mother. I am sure she is now in a better place."

He looked up and, for the first time, Thomas saw anger in the gentle man's face.

"We must find whoever did this."

Thomas nodded grimly. "The family knew she was sneaking out at night, Eustace. How could they not? They thought it was to see the blacksmith's son. The two of them were soon to be wed, and her family had supposed the meetings to be innocent enough. Let the young be young. In a way they were pleased. They had made the match for her and wanted her to be happy with their choice."

"He's a likely looking lad," said Eustace, still staring at the winding sheet. "It would have been a good match. I think he loved her too. Surely no suspicion attaches to him, Thomas?"

"No," replied Thomas. "His whereabouts are fully accounted for. And I met the boy—he is no monster."

Eustace reached down and reverently drew back the sheet. "Let us see if she can yet tell us anything before we send her to her final rest."

CHAPTER 16

Friar Justus was already attending upon the lord of the manor when Thomas arrived in the Great Hall. Sir Mortimer de Bray sat slumped disconsolately in his chair by the fireplace. His health did not look to have improved in the last few days. If anything, he was worse, and Thomas had to wonder whether he would even make it through the audience.

The Dominican seemed oblivious to Sir Mortimer's discomfort and was already busy hectoring those present in a loud, braying voice.

"Ah, I see your daughter shall be in attendance once more, my lord." Justus looked pointedly at Lady Cecily standing protectively behind her father. "We shall no doubt benefit from her sage counsel. She is such a clever thing and quite the herbalist, I understand."

He inclined his head and offered her a wheezy chuckle and one of his best crook-toothed smiles.

"Who could have suspected it of such a pretty creature? You must be so proud, my lord."

De Bray was too exhausted, too impatient, or just too weak to respond to the Dominican's none too subtle pandering. Nor did Cecily appear particularly impressed, and she chose to respond with a sweet smile and a little veiled condescension of her own: "I am pleased to be of assistance, Friar. And besides, I am anxious to hear the results of your investigation. I was confident from the outset that an experienced inquisitor such as yourself would have little difficulty finding someone, somewhere, willing to confess to something."

"As it happens, I am sorry to say that I have uncovered evidence that rather confirms my worst fears." The Dominican's hangdog expression and sad shake of the head made his professed disappointment almost believable. *Almost.* "Father Oswin's maid strongly believes her master to have been poisoned."

He reached back to Friar Dominic, snatched a scroll from his outstretched hand, and proceeded to wave it about in the air. "Agnes recounts her observations in detail here in her testimony. There can be no doubt. She is quite specific. And the symptoms she recollects are entirely consistent with poisoning."

"But that's preposterous," spluttered Cecily, her eyes wide with disbelief. "She has mentioned none of this before. Why has she waited until now to make such a ridiculous claim?"

"I cannot say. Perhaps nobody thought to ask. Perhaps people were as happy to believe Oswin died of a heart ailment. As you said, my lady, I am an experienced inquisitor. I bother to ask the questions that need to be asked. The questions others, for whatever reason, sometimes choose to avoid."

Thomas could contain himself no longer. "I do not believe this testimony," he announced loudly. "I suspect it far more likely you bullied the poor woman. I am sure you threatened her, and by the time you were done, she would have said anything you wanted."

"*Thomas!* I am shocked!" Justus did not look shocked. He looked contemptuous. "Are you suggesting dear Agnes would perjure herself? What a thing to say. It seems you accept such blasphemous standards as a matter of course. That is very troubling."

Justus beckoned once more to Dominic, upon which the silent brother handed him a second scroll.

"No matter. I also have here the testimony of Adam, a cottager who holds half a yardland hereabouts—a respected man of no little substance. On the night of Roger Lacy's death, Adam recalled . . . now, what did he say?"

The Dominican made a show of unrolling the parchment and browsing through it, jabbing a finger at the text he wanted to read.

"Ah yes, here it is. And I quote: 'As I left the tavern I saw that the moon was shot through with streaks of blood, and I heard a strange and most sinister chanting from the general direction of Saint Mary's Church, and a flapping as of great leathern wings. A cold wind arose, chilling my body and soul, and carrying on it a foul sulfurous odor that assailed my nostrils and did cause my eyes to water. I saw a litter of black cats gathered about the graveyard, staring toward the church, mewling and hissing as if in chorus with some unseen cantor, and I was filled with mortal terror.'"

He rolled up the parchment and held it aloft. "There is more, my lord, much more. Adam goes on to tell of a terrible creature— nay, a demon—seemingly half man, half beast, with cloven feet, horns, and a crown of flies on its head, that emerged from the church and proceeded to dance obscenely on the graves, summoning forth the restless spirits of those buried therein."

De Bray looked as if he were about to be sick and hardly reacted at all to these surprising revelations.

Thomas snorted indignantly. "And Adam also chose not to speak of this terrible vision until now?"

"So now Adam is a liar and perjurer as well? How easy it is for you to slander someone, Thomas. How readily you sully their reputation and accuse them of such a terrible sin. The man did not speak because he was scared and because he feared that nobody would believe him. I cannot say that I am surprised given the recalcitrance I myself have encountered here. He was even reluctant to speak with me at first, and it required all my skill to reassure him and elicit the tale."

Thomas pointedly ignored the Dominican and addressed himself to the lord of the manor. "There was no poisoning, my lord. There were no demons. What we have here is murder, plain and simple. The time has come for this farce to end. Tell the Dominican this is a secular matter, and send him back to London so we can be rid of these distractions and concentrate on finding our man."

De Bray turned tiredly to Thomas. "Is it true? The miller was found out to be a murderer and hanged himself, leaving the evidence of his crime at his feet?"

"I believe it more likely he was himself a victim of the murderer. Brother Eustace and I both examined the body, and we agree. His wounds reveal that Tom Attwood was garroted, just as Lacy was, and then strung up to cover the crime. The money was left there to cast suspicion on him. The murderer was trying to hide his tracks, my lord."

"I fail to see the significance of this supposed finding," scoffed the Dominican. "If the miller hanged himself and was willing thereby to condemn his soul to hellfire, that is yet another sign that something is rotten in your lands, my lord. And in the alternative, if Lester here is correct and the miller was murdered, then that is even worse. The killer leaves twenty pieces of silver strewn around the hanged man's feet, mocking the death of the Betrayer, Judas Iscariot, a clearly blasphemous message intended to ridicule the Church and declare his derision even for God."

Thomas did not feel like pointing out there were not twenty coins, and for that matter, nor were they all silver. He doubted whether the friar would care.

"And what then of the young girl, Margareta?" he asked instead. "How does her death constitute blasphemy? How is it related to the others?"

Let the fanatical bastard make something out of that!

The Dominican mulled the matter over for a while, leaning on his staff. "Ordinarily I might have agreed with you. One local wench more or less would be of little interest to the Holy Inquisition. But given her youth, and in light of what we have already seen here, I think it not beyond question that she was sacrificed to some unholy end." He shook his head sadly. "A virgin sacrifice. Such offerings are common among invokers of demons and necromancers. Another sure sign that we are indeed plagued by some sort of devilry."

"A virgin sacrifice?" exclaimed Thomas. "My God, man! Is there no end to your dissembling? The girl's death was a crime of lust, pure and simple."

"And how do you know this, Thomas?" responded Justus. "What proofs do you bring us today? What testimony? What witnesses?"

"I have nothing firm as of yet, but my intuition tells me—"

The Dominican hooted loudly.

"Oh, your *intuition*. Say no more. I am quite convinced. I only come here with years of experience in the investigation of heresy and with signed testimonies." He brandished the parchments angrily at Thomas. "But I should yield at once to your *intuition* then. Pardon me for my foolishness. I can see that whereas I have spent the last few days investigating, interviewing witnesses, scrupulously compiling evidence of a most heinous and damning nature, you have been far more productively engaged in honing your *intuition*. And your *intuition* has allowed you to divine that all of my work"—he waggled the parchments back and forth again—"all of this is worthless. And what has your intuition yielded us exactly? Where is your killer then?" He looked about him searchingly, to the left and the right. "Did you perhaps leave him outside?"

Thomas spoke though gritted teeth: "There is a vile assassin here, someone who kills without remorse. I do not yet know who he is or why he does these things, but I will. I do know that Roger Lacy was not killed for the coin he carried, and that the miller was a scapegoat, murdered by the same man. I believe Lady Isabella may be able to shed some light on the subject, as Lacy died shortly after visiting her."

Justus retorted loudly, raising his voice to a half-hissing shout. "Again you offer up no killer, Thomas. Only empty theories, devoid of evidence and full of conjecture, whereas I have made real progress." Waggle, waggle went the parchments above his head. "These murders are all but a symptom of a greater evil that needs to be unearthed and torn out by the roots. I tell you, this place stinks of heresy and corruption."

Sir Mortimer had largely been forgotten in the midst of the argument. He now heaved himself up so that he sat straighter in his chair.

"I have heard you both and will now tell you of my decision."

They both turned to him.

"There have been at least two murders here. Leave aside Lacy for the moment. The girl was murdered in my woods. If Tom Attwood was murdered, as we all now believe to be the case, the deed was done at my mill, not in a church. These are clearly secular matters subject to my own jurisdiction and that of the county sheriff. They suggest to me that Roger Lacy died at the hands of the same man, garroted in the same manner as Attwood, whether he died in church or no. It is my judgment that this is a secular matter now. I see no reason for you to prolong your visit, Friar."

Thomas breathed a sigh of relief, and Cecily's eyes glittered in triumph.

"You have heard my father," she said. "It is time for you to leave, Friar."

The Dominican's head snapped to her, a furious look on his face, soon to be supplanted by a sly one.

"By all means, my lord," he said to De Bray. "Petition the sheriff at once."

De Bray narrowed his eyes suspiciously, surprised at the concession.

"Now that would be the sheriff of Lincoln, would it not?"

"It would," Cecily replied on her father's behalf.

"Yes, I thought as much, given that all hereabouts owe their allegiance to Lady Alice de Lacy. If I recall correctly, the Countess of Lincoln is presently at the pleasure of the king's royal chamberlain, Lord Despenser."

Everyone knew that Despenser had imprisoned Lady Alice at the king's direction and that she was now little more than his puppet. Her tale was tragic enough.

"I shall write to Sir Hugh at once. We have become close, you know. Quite good friends, as it happens." The Dominican wheezed away. "And I shall naturally inform him of my findings here. I am certain he will speak to the sheriff on our behalf. In fact, I am confident he will come here personally to ensure that proper justice is done. Yes, I rather think he will climb atop the fastest horse he can find and be here with his men in a matter of days."

De Bray stared in horror. The prospect of that monstrous man visiting his lands, bringing with him his own brand of terror and justice, was undoubtedly appalling to him.

"Or shall I rather have Dominic here write that you have given the Church's emissary freedom to undertake the task that both the Archbishop of Canterbury and the King of England have entrusted to him?"

De Bray tugged at his beard. Cecily looked at him anxiously and was about to speak when he nodded his acquiescence to the friar, turned his head in shame toward the fire, and began coughing into his hand—a long, whooping cough that seemed to come from deep in his lungs and left him curled over, his hand trembling.

Once the fit had passed, Justus addressed him again.

"Thank you for your consideration, my lord. I was sure I could depend on your continued support. And now I really must insist on speaking with your wife, whether she is ill or no. On that Thomas and I can at least agree, and I am more than willing to conduct the interview in Lady Isabella's personal chambers if that would be more convenient for her."

Thomas was not about to let the Dominican speak with Isabella alone, and had plenty of his own questions for the lady. "And I shall accompany you," he declared in a resolute manner intended to leave no room for discussion.

The Dominican's eyebrows rose, even more so when Cecily also chose to speak up: "I too should like to hear what Isabella has to say."

Justus looked from one to the other and then shrugged, as if he couldn't care less. "By all means, my lady. The more, the merrier. Indeed, does anybody else here wish to attend?" he asked mockingly, pausing to look around, first at Dominic and then at his thug, Guy de Hokenham, who as usual was lurking in the doorway and who now grinned back at his master, thoroughly enjoying the jest. "No? Then let us retire to the lady's chamber. I am sure we three shall just about be able to squeeze inside."

They all turned expectantly to Sir Mortimer, silently asking for consent to speak with his wife. De Bray shook his head resignedly. "Go speak with her then, if you must. Do it now, though I doubt you will get many answers from her. At least none that will make any sense."

De Bray beckoned Thomas over to him as Cecily and the Dominican retreated to the staircase that would take them to the family quarters.

"We find ourselves caught in a cleft stick, Thomas," he said when he was sure the others were out of earshot.

De Bray stifled a cough and wiped his mouth, speckling the linen cloth with a few more drops of red.

"I am dying."

He held up a hand to forestall Thomas's protest.

"No, no. It is true, and I have made peace with it. It has come on sudden this last year. You must understand, Thomas, I cannot have that vile man, Despenser, know of our weakness. He will surely use it to strip my children bare of their inheritance. And what shall they do when I am not here to protect them? I must keep him away at all costs, at least for the time being."

"Perhaps the bishop can help," suggested Thomas.

De Bray pursed his lips and scowled, struck by a startling recollection. "Did you know that scoundrel once tried to make off with the *reredos* from our little church? I believe he actually tried to steal the thing! And he would have done so had the monks not come to me squawking and flapping like a flock of hens at the sight of a fox."

He heaved a great shuddering sigh of resignation, and Thomas could hear the breath wheeze and rattle in his chest. "As it happens, I have already written to Henry on the matter, and he will do what he can—I am sure of that. But he has troubles enough of his own and may not be in any position to help.

"Then there is this Dominican and his crusade. The longer this killer goes unfound, the more lies the friar will foster, and the greater his hold over us will become. You must find our man soon, Thomas, lest the black friar make heretics and killers of us all."

He gripped Thomas's wrist firmly. "Do what you have to. Put the lie to the Dominican's theories. Do you understand?"

Thomas nodded and De Bray released his wrist. "Then go. Protect my children."

CHAPTER 17

Lady Isabella's solar was a small yet well-appointed room. A window embrasure with paneled glass looked out over the courtyard. With the shutter thrown wide, the window let in a decent amount of light. That light shone down directly onto the room's dominant feature, a large mirror bolted securely to a desk by massive black iron brackets.

It was a garish and disturbing looking thing. At its center was an oval of murky glass stained a rusty brown at the edges. Surrounding that was a heavy walnut frame, blackened and singed as though it had once been dragged from a fire. Chipped carvings at each corner appeared to depict some kind of creature. What kind, Thomas could not say. But if demons existed, he imagined they would look something like this, and they all squatted on their haunches around the glass, leering inward at whatever might have the misfortune to be reflected there.

Thomas began to feel a little queasy and had to tear his eyes away. The remainder of the room was furnished more in the manner one might expect of a lady's solar, with a variety of ordinary looking tables, chairs, trunks, a cushioned bench, and an elegantly carved aumbry closet. Linen tapestries, depicting a variety of hunting scenes in brightly colored threads, adorned the walls, and several woolen rugs and herb-scented rush mats covered the floor.

Isabella was sitting in a high-backed comfortable chair by a small brazier, as yet unlit, the days being far too warm to waste good firewood. She wore a rather austere, full-sleeved woolen kirtle of a surprisingly dull green, and her golden hair was closely netted on either side of her head by wire mesh cauls held in place by a stiffened silk fillet band around her crown and by a simple linen barbette that passed fully under her chin. It was a modest look, one which the Dominican no doubt wholeheartedly approved, and quite a change from the elegant velvets and lace she had been wearing when Thomas had last seen her.

At her side, under her protective wing, was the same flaxen-haired boy Thomas had seen in the yard. The boy was straining to be away from his mother, his face all frowns and pouts.

Cecily had already seated herself on the bench opposite Isabella. For the moment, Thomas stood by her side, politely awaiting an invitation to sit, while the Dominican chose to ignore such niceties and playfully ruffled the boy's hair.

"What a fine-looking young man," he declared.

A fine-looking young man he might have been, but he was also at present a surly one and was clearly anxious to be outside making mischief. As if on cue, Hunydd entered the room. The startled glance and smile she flashed at Thomas was quickly suppressed, but not quickly enough to avoid the friar's scrutiny. His face clouded over, and he followed her with his narrowed eyes as she took the boy by the hand and led him out so they could talk in peace.

"Be sure to wash him thoroughly, Hunydd," Isabella called after her. "He has been running about with the dogs again. And remind the kennel master that I instructed him to lock them up. I don't want Henry catching their fleas."

"Yes, mistress," replied Hunydd, offering a quick bob and

pulling the boy out after her, not before he could throw his mother one last sulky glare from under his mussed-up mop of hair.

Justus watched them leave and sighed contentedly. "Ah, you must be very proud of him, my dear."

"Yes. I am, Father."

"And so you should. So you should. I am sure, with your guidance, he will be a great lord one day."

Isabella beamed with pleasure. "Thank you, Father."

The Dominican then suddenly winced in discomfort and coughed dryly into his clenched hand.

"Forgive me, my lady. I fear the change of weather and the challenges before me are beginning to take their toll. I am not as young as I once was, and every now and then God chooses to remind me of the fact."

He passed a shaky hand over his forehead, which caused Isabella to rise from her seat and take his arm.

"You must take my chair, Father. You are unwell."

Justus shook his head and smiled weakly. "I would not dream of it, dear. A little hardship is good for the soul. I shall take this stool here, where I can sit close by you."

Leaning heavily on her arm, he lowered himself down stiffly, sighing with relief as he finally slumped onto the seat. Lady Isabella watched the entire performance with a concerned look on her face.

"Should I have someone make up the fire? Or fetch you some water? Or a more comfortable seat, perhaps?"

"You are too kind, child, but I shall be fine in a moment. These spells tend to pass in time."

Only a short while before, the Dominican had been in rude health, strong enough to harangue and threaten De Bray. Thomas marveled that he appeared to have aged at least a decade in the interim. He also appeared to have lost his staff, contracted ague, and developed arthritis, a limp, and a weak chest to boot. The whole pantomime was sickening.

"I am truly sorry we must intrude on you, Lady Isabella. Personally, I would not have thought it necessary, but . . ."

Justus shrugged and gestured vaguely in Thomas's direction, suggesting to Isabella where the fault lay. Isabella turned a sour expression on Thomas and then sat down primly in her cushioned chair, her eyes turned expectantly to the Dominican. It appeared that Thomas would not be invited to take his ease after all.

"Ah but look at you," the Dominican exclaimed, spreading his arms wide, as though he might well embrace her. "You are truly beautiful. I should not believe it possible that you were yet a mother but for the wonderful glow that always seems to accompany motherhood."

The sour look she had tossed Thomas was immediately replaced by another radiant smile.

The Dominican's eyes wandered about the chamber and rested on a prie-dieu sitting in one of the corners.

"I see you have a prie-dieu in your personal chamber, my lady? It is gratifying to see such a thing."

Isabella nodded. "Prayer is a great comfort to me, father, especially in these troubled times."

Thomas looked at the prie-dieu, noticing the embroidery tossed lazily over the armrest, and the velvet slippers all arranged in a neat row across the kneeling stool. It looked more like a piece of furniture than an aid to prayer. Justus, however, leaned over and squeezed Isabella's hand, evidently moved by the open show of devotion. She returned the pressure, an unspoken exchange of admiration passing between them.

"A good woman ought to spend a great deal of time on her knees," he said. "You are a fine example to your sex."

Irritated at being ignored and growing more than a little

tired of the mummery, Thomas coughed lightly to gain their attention.

"We have come with questions for you, my lady."

Justus rolled his eyes and gave Isabella a helpless little shrug, as if by way of apology for the rude interruption. She pressed her lips together in a thin line of distaste and, as pretty as she undoubtedly was, managed to present Thomas with a face that could have curdled milk in an instant. She was still holding the Dominican's hand and seemed to have no intention of letting go any time soon.

"I understand that you had a visit from Roger Lacy shortly before he died?" Thomas asked.

"That is true," she allowed, regarding Thomas with narrowed, suspicious eyes.

"May I ask, what was his business?"

Isabella looked to the side for a moment, collecting her thoughts, and when she spoke, Thomas sensed it was with words measured and weighed and, what is more, with a story carefully rehearsed.

"I knew him from when I was a child. He was steward of my father's estate. I believe he was let go sometime after I left. I do not recall the reason."

"And why was he here?"

"To pay his respects and to inquire after work."

She turned to Friar Justus and directed the rest of her explanation to him. "How could I not pity him? I had admired him as a child, and it saddened me greatly to see him sunk so low. So I spoke to my husband on his behalf. Is charity to those in need not one of the acts of mercy?"

"Indeed it is, my dear," replied Justus, giving her hand another comforting squeeze. "That was so very kind and thoughtful of you. I must now add charity to the list of good graces with which you are so evidently imbued."

Thomas caught Cecily rolling her eyes, as unimpressed by the display as he was. The Dominican's words had a very different effect on Isabella, however. She blushed and simpered like a moonstruck young girl.

Thomas took a step closer to try to regain her attention. "Forgive me, my lady—what else can you tell us of Lacy's visit?"

"I know not. He only asked that I speak with my husband about a position. I did so, as I have said. I gave the poor man a little money and directed him to the priory guesthouse. There is nothing more I can say."

"Surely there is more you can tell me, my lady. You were the last to speak with him. You might know why someone would wish to harm him. Did he not mention anybody else? Did he plan to see anyone else? Do you know who might have wished him ill? Do you know what he intended after he left you? What else did you discuss?"

Isabella listened to his list of questions with a flat expression, looking thoroughly disinclined to address a single one.

"I don't know anything, I tell you."

She sniffled and withdrew a small silk handkerchief from one of her sleeves, dabbing daintily at her eyes, looking up every now and then from under her golden lashes to judge the effect of her display.

"This is all so horrible." *Sniff.* "I heard what happened. I can barely sleep at all for thinking of it. And I blame myself." She dabbed her eyes again. "I gave him money out of pity and I fear someone has killed him for it. I have been quite unwell, you know."

Looking at the pair of them sitting side by side, hand in hand, him acting the doddery old man; and her, the fragile flower, Thomas had to wonder who was the better player. They could both quite easily turn up at the market square in Grantham and put any professional troupe of mummers to shame.

Thomas waited patiently until she appeared to have grown tired of her own antics before venturing another question.

"For about how long did you sit with Roger Lacy?"

"Surely you have pressed Lady Isabella enough," decried Justus. "Cannot you see she is most upset? I am sure the good lady has nothing to hide."

Thomas wondered how he had managed to become the villain; and the inquisitor, the protector of the weak and innocent.

"Look at her," Justus continued, gracing Isabella with one of his crooked smiles. "How could you harangue such a sweet child in this heartless manner? You have brought her to tears with your harassment, looming over her in such a threatening, ungentlemanly manner."

Isabella dutifully took a little shuddering breath and gave another little sniffle.

"My lady, please," urged Thomas, ignoring the Dominican's feigned concern, "is there anything else you can tell us of Lacy's visit that might shed some light on his death?"

"I have told you that I know nothing," she snapped.

Justus rose halfway from his seat in protest. "Really, sir, this is most churlish behavior. Most unworthy. What sort of monster attempts to bully a lady in her own chambers—a God-fearing, charitable lady of good birth at that, and one who has only recently suffered the great shock of losing a dear old friend. You are very ill bred, sir. Very ill bred indeed."

He sat down again and huffed his displeasure. Isabella was clutching the friar's hand in both her own now and looking at him in wonder, as if he was some sort of paladin who had ridden into her chambers mounted on a noble steed to defend her honor and rescue her from the ravishing heathens.

Justus crooned at her in a gentle, wheedling voice: "I am truly sorry for your loss, dear. What happened to Roger Lacy was horrifying. It is small wonder that you have been indisposed. I am a seasoned servant of the Holy Inquisition and have seen many terrible things in my long life, yet what has passed here has shocked even me. Though certain others seem not to be overly concerned . . ."

Another vague nod flew in Thomas's general direction, followed naturally by an accusatory glare from Isabella.

"If it is any consolation, the Archbishop of Canterbury has sent me to investigate the matter, and I shall do everything in my power to find those responsible. Now that I have met you and seen your distress, let me assure you that I shall neither rest nor sleep until I know you are safe and that I have brought some small measure of peace to you."

He patted her hand.

"Now is there anything you wish to tell me?" Justus inquired. "For example, have you seen anything troubling to you? Anything disturbing? Anything at all that might hint at, let us say, heresy or moral turpitude? Anything you suspect might be a little wicked? Even if only ever so slightly wicked?"

Isabella's eyes flicked briefly to Cecily. It was a momentary thing, but Thomas suspected that the look did not go unnoticed by the Dominican.

"Nothing that comes to mind at the moment, Father."

Justus surprised Thomas by not pursuing such an obvious evasion.

"Well, if you do see or hear anything, you must tell me." She nodded eagerly to let him know she would most certainly do so. "And if you have need of counsel, or of a friend, or even a confessor, please feel free to call on me, day or night. I am completely at your service. I know this must have been a difficult time for you. Perhaps when you are feeling better, you and I might have a more private discussion."

"I should very much like that."

"And shall I also take your confession at that time? Would that please you?"

She looked down shyly and nodded.

"I shall even come here to your personal chambers, and we can use your very own prie-dieu. It would bring me great pleasure to confess you like that. I shall perform such a service for you any time you desire."

With one last pat of her hand, the friar rose stiffly to his feet.

"Well, I think we need trouble you no more today."

Isabella leapt up and threw her arms about Justus, embracing him fiercely, her cheek pressed against his chest. A look of absolute shock and revulsion writhed across his face before he was able to master himself and return the embrace stiffly, patting her awkwardly on the back. As he did so, he caught their reflection in the mirror. He was still looking at it when they separated.

"You like my mirror, Father?" Isabella asked ingenuously.

Justus swallowed slowly. His face had turned gray, and Thomas thought he might actually throw up.

"Yes, indeed," he managed to croak. "It is a most . . . interesting piece, most unusual. How came you by it?"

"It was my grandmother's," she declared proudly. "I have had it since I was a little girl. Grandmama told me it was very special and that every young lady should own a mirror so that she might always look her best."

The Dominican stared at the ghastly piece for a long while.

"That is very sage advice. Your grandmother was a wise woman, my dear. But, if I may be so bold, I believe that with or without a mirror you would be quite delightful."

She rewarded his flattery with a girlish giggle and then insisted on lending his elbow her support as he hobbled slowly, very slowly, to the door.

"I am so glad you are here, Father. These events have been

troubling to me, and I find it reassuring to know that the Church has not abandoned us."

"The Church will never abandon you, child. Nor shall I."

Another squeeze. Another sickening exchange of looks, and then they were out the door, Isabella offering no parting words to either Thomas or Cecily.

★   ★   ★

As soon as the door closed, the Dominican straightened up to his full height and stretched languidly.

"Oh dear, Thomas," he scoffed as they walked away, "you acquitted yourself poorly there, very poorly indeed. You really must learn to play the game."

"The game? I was not aware this was a game, and I would remind you that you garnered no information at all that would be of use to us."

"Did I not? I think perhaps your intuition is in need of further sharpening. I do believe the good lady shall come to me soon enough, and I shall know what she knows. Yes, she will open up to me like a flower in bloom on a sunny day."

They took another few paces toward the stairs, the one fuming, the other smug and self-satisfied, Cecily following along with a slightly bemused look on her face.

"Now that I have had time to ponder the matter, Thomas, I recall that I met your father. I was surprised to have heard him spoken of as a great knight. If that had once been so, I am afraid the man I saw was a mere shadow of his former self. Thin, drawn, haggard. Why, there was more of a corpse about him than a man."

The Dominican shook his head sadly.

"Ah, but God's punishment can be severe. *'How are the mighty fallen, and the weapons of war perished!'* I trust you recall that verse from your scriptures, Thomas."

Thomas knew full well he was being goaded and did not for a moment buy the pretense of empathy. He too remembered his father's appearance in those last few days. To him, his father had always been invincible. He could not marry the image of the man he knew to the skeletal creature that lay in its own filth on the straw of that cell. It was said that he had not been tortured, that the king would not condone it, that it was against the common law. But nobody who saw him could have doubted it.

Justus was not yet done with his taunting. "He was in a most pitiable state. Or at least he might have seemed so had I not known of his heresies, of the terrible sins he had committed."

They had stopped short of the narrow staircase leading down to the Great Hall.

"I had mentioned that I read your father's deposition. The truth is that I actually transcribed much of it myself."

Thomas listened in silence, his gut clenching.

"Oh, how he talked, Thomas. Once we had shown him the iron, of course. A taste was all it took. I must confess, I had expected more from him, but that is so often the case. Those who profess to be the strongest are found out to have soft insides, their pretense of bravery a mere facade, nothing more than braggadocio. His bowels turned to water almost at once. And once he had begun to confess his sins, the words came tumbling out in such a rush, I could barely keep up."

He chuckled, shaking his head in wonder.

"Only imagine it, Thomas. There I was, scratching away with my quill like a madman, wearing the thing out, transcribing sheet after sheet of vellum, being most careful to capture every terrible word, every terrible deed confessed. And the list of heresies that came out of his mouth, Thomas. It was remarkable, truly remarkable. I felt ashamed just hearing of the things he had done. Ashamed and fascinated both. Why there were tales of three-faced gods being worshipped, desecration of the sacraments, denial of Christ, sodomy—both young girls and boys. There were other sins that I cannot even bring myself to repeat here. And naturally he wanted to confess all in great detail. He did not have long to live by then, you see."

Thomas's face was dark with anger, and just as had happened in the garden, he felt a firm restraining hand on his arm; from the corner of his eye, he could see Cecily regarding him with an anxious expression.

"You look as if you are upset, Thomas. Have I said something amiss? Why you almost look like you wish to strike me. Do you, Thomas? Do you wish to strike a servant of God, a representative of the Holy See, an emissary of the Archbishop of Canterbury? I am confident that the repercussions of such an act would be swift."

Justus thrust his face forward, nose to nose, close enough for Thomas to believe he could see the mad fanatical gleam lurking behind his eyes, and for a long moment neither of them said anything. Then the Dominican shrugged and smiled complacently. "No, I had thought not."

"There will be a special place in hell for you, Friar—of that I am sure," said Thomas in a ground-down whisper.

"For me?" exclaimed Justus, bemused. "Oh no, I do God's work, Thomas. I am confident I shall find myself in paradise."

"Have your jest. You too will be judged, all the more so for denigrating the memory of a good man."

"A good man you say? I am afraid your memory of your father is distorted. Perhaps that is to be expected of a dutiful son. And I assure you that I take this all very seriously. I never jest. And sooner or later, I shall have my way here."

"Shall you?"

"Oh yes. And why? Because God is on my side, Thomas, and as the Good Book says: *'If God is for us, who is against us?'*

You would do well to remember that verse as well, Thomas. You will find it in Paul's letters to the Romans."

Having said his piece, Justus stalked off, taking his staff from where he had left it leaning against the wall by the stairwell.

Thomas waited until he was sure the Dominican had left and then grasped Cecily's elbow, drawing her back from the stairs.

"Are you mad, woman? Your aunt tucked away in the woods while an inquisitor sniffs around? Have you any idea what would happen were he to find her?"

Cecily looked down at his hand, shocked at the familiarity. "I do not care to be spoken to in such a manner. And in any case, it is not as if I knew he was coming. And even if I had, what would you have me do? Abandon my kin to a mad Irish bishop? It is no more dangerous for her here, and far less so than it was in Ireland."

Thomas drew her farther aside into a small alcove lit by the dusky light from an arrow slit window.

"But what of the dangers? Do you not think of the danger to which you expose yourself? To which you expose Hunydd?"

"Hunydd is helping us of her own free will."

"Her own free will? She is carrying messages to please her mistress. And she may not fully understand the peril. She is a simple maid and will have no protection should your web of deceit unravel. Hers is exactly the kind of artless soul that the Inquisition preys upon. Nor can you seriously expect to rely on her discretion."

"I think you underestimate her. How very like a man to assume that every woman must be a gossiping fishwife. Hunydd understands more than you know. She is perfectly capable of being discreet and is fiercely loyal to me. I trust her above all others."

"You are abusing her loyalty, Cecily."

She held his eyes stubbornly for a moment and then looked away.

"I think you are mistaken. But I understand your concerns, and I shall consider them. Perhaps I am exposing her selfishly. I would not wish her to come to any harm on my account."

She touched his arm lightly with her fingers. Just the slightest touch, almost no weight to it, and yet a shock surged through his body as though he had been struck by lightning.

"Thomas, can I count on your discretion?"

"Of course," he growled.

"Thank you," she said. "I am very grateful. I know you are doing what you can."

They were already speaking in low tones so as not to be overheard, but she now lowered her voice even further, barely above a whisper.

"I am glad we have a moment alone."

She leaned in close, her hand still resting on his arm. Had anyone passed by, which seemed unlikely unless Isabella were to emerge from her room, they might have been suspected of a tryst. Thomas supposed there were worse things of which to be accused.

"There is a madness in England these days, Thomas. Friar Justus is merely a symptom of a greater sickness. I know you too can feel it. Good people live in fear, especially us womenfolk. Our lot is poor even at the best of times." She smiled wryly. "But those of us who are wealthy must now fear the king stealing our lands and marrying us off to whomever offers him coin to fill his war chest. That terrible man, Despenser, got his wife that way, and his wealth with her. Did you know Eleanor de Clare was forced by her grandfather to marry Despenser to settle a debt of two thousand marks? Sold for money, like a piece of land or a prized beast. And when her brother died, Despenser inherited everything through her. And thus a landless knight became one of the most powerful men in the kingdom through

no merit of his own and through ownership of the lands that
rightly belong to his wife. Do you think that fair?"

Thomas did not. It *was* not. But it was both custom and the
law of the land.

"He has used his favor with the king to steal yet more properties from her family. He preys upon us women especially. I
have heard he cheated Elizabeth de Clare, his own sister-in-law,
out of Gower and Usk. He imprisoned Lady Baret and tortured
her, you know, breaking both her arms and legs until the poor
woman went completely mad. And it is well known the king
imprisoned Alice de Lacy, the richest woman in England, and
forced her to yield a great portion of her lands to Despenser.
Can anyone doubt that she is still within their power? Can you
imagine what she must have endured? What she must still be
enduring?

"Nor is this the first time she has been imprisoned. The Earl
of Surrey also abducted her seven years ago in an effort to steal
her lands. What has she ever done other than become a wealthy
woman who owned land coveted by another? And yet she has
become little more than a plaything tossed from man to man. I
shall not let that be my fate!"

Thomas saw that look of determination in her eyes, a look
that was now becoming familiar to him.

"There is worse yet. I have heard an even more shocking
tale. It is said that not only did Despenser encourage the king to
confiscate the queen's properties, but that he also"—she paused
here—"that he also ravished her and that the king has done
nothing about it, frankly preferring Despenser's company to
her own."

Thomas had heard the rumor. It was also said that in return
Despenser encouraged the king to enjoy the company of his
own wife. Thomas found it hard to credit such scurrilous

stories and suspected them to be manufactured and circulated by the king's enemies. He did not believe the king would accept such an affront to the mother of his heir. It was true, however, that almost no woman in England was safe from Despenser, high- or lowborn, and that there was no crime to which he would not stoop to satisfy his greed and lust. Rape, robbery, theft, piracy, and murder—he had been accused of them all from time to time, and likely with good reason.

Cecily had more to say. "The king turns a blind eye to Despenser's deeds and leaves him completely unchecked. Did you know his arrogance and power have grown to such an extent that he was heard to say he only regretted that he could not command the wind itself?"

Thomas did not need to be persuaded. Despenser was an evil man and would bring despair to the kingdom; of that he had no doubt.

Cecily lowered her voice even further, whispering now.

"I have also heard of miracles being observed at the Earl of Lancaster's tomb and at the gallows in Bristol. I am sure you have heard of them as well. Wonderful things. Lepers healed. Lame men who begin to walk again. Blind men made to see. Angels. Sure signs that God sides with the rebels and wants this king gone."

Thomas rolled his eyes.

"You do not believe in these miracles?"

"Who am I to say? I think, however, that sometimes people see what they want to see, and they hear what they want to hear, all so they can believe what they want to believe."

She glared at him angrily, disappointed that he did not display greater faith in what she considered to be clearly favorable portends.

"Then you should consider that we are at war, and Edward is not a capable military leader. He has proven so time and again in Scotland, where he was beaten by Bruce, and in France also, where you yourself said his forces were unprepared and easily scattered. He will bring us to ruin. The true military men who can defend our interests are entirely on the wrong side of this conflict. Mortimer, for one, proved himself a great leader in Ireland. He defeated the Scots there."

"And yet for all that, the king defeated the rebel army at Boroughbridge," Thomas reminded her.

"Only because he tricked Lancaster."

"Is not trickery itself a skill? What discerns trickery from tactics or strategy?"

Thomas was about to add something very clever from Livy's writings about how Hannibal had tricked the Romans at the battle of Trasimene and then again at the battle of Cannae. It crossed his mind that he might also mention the sly ruse employed by Epaminondas to defeat the Spartans. Then he remembered how the Bishop of Lincoln had mocked him, predicting that he and Cecily would engage in jousting displays of erudition, and he chose not to mention any of it.

Cecily pursed her lips in annoyance at his obstinacy. He couldn't help but notice she looked decidedly attractive that way.

She looked toward Isabella's chamber and then the other way to the stairs, making sure they were still alone.

"There are those of us who would yet aid the rebels and see an end to Edward and his favorites. We suffered a defeat at Boroughbridge, but the rebellion is alive and well, especially now Mortimer is free again. And I think the king misjudges his queen. I do not think Isabella is one to sit idly by and allow herself to be abused so."

Cecily licked her lips, deciding how much to reveal. Thomas watched her pink tongue and the lips it touched. He was watching them still when she spoke again.

"There is a man—John of Nottingham—who is willing to help."

"He will help how?" asked Thomas.

"He knows things. He has . . . certain skills. Unusual skills."

Thomas's mouth sagged open. and he stared at her in dismay.

"Good God, woman, you cannot seriously be suggesting employing the services of a sorcerer."

"I only say we are considering it, Thomas. *We.* I am not alone. There are not so many of us now, perhaps, but we are growing in number every day. And among us are powerful people, Thomas. I cannot say who, unless of course you were to join us."

"Join you? I am here because the Bishop of Lincoln abhors exactly the sort of thing you are apparently now considering."

"And what would you have us do? Sit on our hands as the king and his hound plunder the countryside? My father believes in you, Thomas. I know he has his weaknesses, especially now, but he recognizes quality in others. Your own father was a great man regardless of the lies the Dominican tells about him. Could you be less than him? You are a knight's son, Thomas. I do not think you can abjure what is happening in England any more than I."

"I know, I know," he laughed, deciding to repeat Bishop Henry's witty jape. "'One's arse gets sore straddling the fence for too long.'"

Cecily frowned up at him, a look of absolute confusion on her face. It seemed she did not appreciate the jest.

Bloody Bishop Henry.

"I understand your frustration, Cecily. But to turn—" He paused, realizing suddenly that they had begun speaking louder, and he pulled her deeper into the shadows. "But to turn to a magician," he said in a whisper. "This is true madness."

It was then that she chose to reach up on her tiptoes and kiss him fully on the mouth. It was a good kiss. Her lips were warm and soft. As surprised as he was, he returned their pressure, and for a blissful moment he forgot all his worries. Heretics. Rebels. Fanatical friars. Bishops. Kings. For a moment none of them mattered. All that mattered is that he was there with Cecily and she was kissing him, and he her. And he could feel her in his arms and smell a dizzying scent of nutmeg and cloves. And then it was over.

"Think about what I have said, Thomas," she said, slightly breathless. "My father was right, we need a man like you. *I* need a man like you."

Her hand lingered on his arm for another wonderful moment, and then she walked away, tossing a coy glance at him over her shoulder, leaving him stunned and breathless, his heart racing and his mind whirling about in a maelstrom of emotions.

CHAPTER 18

Thomas's thoughts were still scattered as he rode away from the manor. Far from having reached any useful conclusions, things only seemed to be getting more and more complicated: a brutal murderer on the loose; a mad Dominican friar set on finding and expunging heresy, whether it was there or not; a convicted witch hiding out in the woods; her niece, a rebel sympathizer, about to employ the services of a magician to kill the king's favorite or maybe even the king himself. Could things really be any worse?

Thomas heaved a disappointed sigh. Secrets were strung all over the manor and village like the gossamer strands of some great spider's web, and he was no closer to a resolution of the task at hand than when he had begun. The audience with Lady Isabella had been an unmitigated disaster. She had proven completely unhelpful, avoiding all his questions, and he had been unable to press her thanks to the Dominican. Why would she not speak to him? What was it she knew or thought she knew? Was it even possible she was in some way involved? Thomas could not believe—did not wish to believe—that could be the case, but he was certain she was hiding something important under her veil of vapidity.

Time was running out. He must speak with her again, but

alone, when the friar would be unable to shield her. And if Lady Isabella had nothing to add, he was going to need some help, and he had an idea of where he might get it.

Thomas felt the breeze whipping about his face as he spurred his horse to a gallop.

And what was he supposed to make of Cecily's kiss? Did it mean what he thought it meant, or was that just wishful thinking on his part? Was it possible she was merely playing him, using him in her little campaign the way she planned to use John of Nottingham?

His first impression of Cecily had been poor, but perhaps he had misjudged her, as she had him. She also happened to be beautiful. That helped. Could there really be anything between them? He was the son of a knight but depended on the bishop for a living. Of course, he was now the proud owner of an additional one hundred acres of prime Lincoln soil, a strange and unexpected gift. His eyes popped wide as he suddenly remembered Bishop Henry's sly words about Cecily and the secret missive from him that De Bray held so close. Could De Bray have been plotting with Bishop Henry all along? Had the two of them planned to throw Thomas and Cecily together from the start?

Thomas saw a figure on the road ahead of him and slowed his horse to a canter and then a walk.

Hunydd was busy humming to herself and, without looking back, stood aside to allow him to pass.

"And where are you away to, young lady?" he asked, drawing his horse up next to her.

"Thomas!" she exclaimed happily. "I was just thinking about you. I am to go to the priory for the master's medicine."

Her expression abruptly changed from one of pleasure to one of concern. "I have permission from Lady Cecily to go to the priory. I am not running away or doing anything bad."

"I never thought you were," he reassured her. "But it is a

long walk you have ahead of you," he said, looking up at the sky, "and it looks like it may rain again later today. You will want to be back at the manor before that happens. Perhaps I could offer you a ride, at least to the village."

He jumped down and held out his hands. She looked up at the horse, her eyes dancing with excitement. The noble beast tossed its head and blew a misty breath out into the chill autumn air, impatient to be away.

"Wouldn't that be wicked?"

"Perhaps a little, but only a very little, and in any case," he said, looking around in an exaggerated manner, and whispering out of the side of his mouth, "who will know but us?"

Hunydd looked from Thomas to the horse, eager and uncertain at the same time.

"His name is Achilles," coaxed Thomas, slapping the horse's steaming flank. "And he is no mere palfrey but a coarser—a real warhorse. We have ridden into battle together, we two, armor and all. He would barely notice the extra weight. Usually he's none too fond of strangers, or of me for that matter, but I can already sense he likes you."

The roan blew out another great breath and tipped his nose to her. Hunydd reached out hesitantly to touch him, chewing her lip anxiously. "But what if someone should see?"

"Well, you did turn your ankle back there, Hunydd. I dare say it is very sore and makes walking painful."

"No I didn't," she exclaimed. "I can walk perfectly well. I can—"

"I *know*," said Thomas, inclining his head and raising his eyebrows suggestively.

Hunydd's eyes widened and her mouth formed a funny little circle as understanding dawned on her. Not needing another invitation, she nodded excitedly and held out her arms so he could lift her up to the horse's neck.

Thomas climbed up behind her, clucked his tongue, and they were away. Holding her with one arm around her waist, he spurred the horse to a canter and then a gallop. Her hair blew in the wind, and she laughed out loud, holding on tightly to her cap with one hand and to his arm with the other. Thomas laughed along with her and pulled her closer still, holding her safely cradled against his chest, close enough that her soft hair brushed against his cheek and that he caught the clean smell of soapwort on her skin.

As they rode, Thomas could feel the darkness melting away, and he realized that this had been a lucky encounter for him. He had begun to fall into despair. Hunydd's freshness and simple joy in the feel of a horse under her was exactly what he needed to see now. It gave him hope.

He slowed the horse again as they drew closer to the village. The gelding rocked steadily back and forth under them. He was still holding Hunydd close, though there was no longer any real need to do so.

"I heard you humming at the side of the road, Hunydd. Do you sing?"

She looked over her shoulder, eyeing him quizzically.

"Songs my mother taught me. Do you want me to sing now?"

He smiled. "Maybe another time."

She nodded but looked a little disappointed, he thought.

"Do you like Lady Alice?" she asked. "I mean do you *like* her? Do you think her pretty?" She licked her lips. "Do . . . do you think her beautiful?"

In his mind's eye, Thomas could still see those violet eyes. The way she looked at him, the way her lips turned up when she smiled, the way she glided so gracefully when she walked, the swell of her bosom against her dress, and the curve of her cheek. The impression she made was undeniable. He was not sure that *beautiful* was the right word, but he did not doubt many would say so, and her allure was such that she had been able to lead four of Ireland's wealthiest men in quick succession to the altar.

"I had not really thought about it."

Hunydd faced forward again, not entirely satisfied with his response.

"The friar said she is a witch," she offered petulantly.

"The friar is a fool."

"Are they real? Witches, I mean. Are there really such things as witches and demons?"

"Some people think so. There is a tale they tell in Lincoln about the Lincoln imp. Would you like to hear it?"

She nodded eagerly.

"It is said that the Devil sent a pair of imps to the north of England and that they caused great chaos throughout the land. Terrible things they were, with big, pointy ears like foxes; large mouths full of sharp teeth; and ugly, bulbous noses rather like the constable's." Hunydd giggled, liking the comparison. "There was no mischief they would not get up to. They turned over market stalls, made the fruit rot on the trees, turned the milk sour, made women barren."

Hunydd was looking up at him, wide-eyed.

"One day, they made the mistake of flying into the cathedral and began breaking the windows and chasing the fat old monks. An angry angel rose up from the bible left on the altar and gave the one imp such a sound thrashing on its bottom that it fled the cathedral in terror. The second imp was bolder and flew up to the top of the highest pillar and mocked the angel, throwing stones and insults until the angel cast a spell, turning it to stone. And there it sits to this very day, petrified against the pillar for all to see, a constant reminder of God's punishment of the wicked."

Hunydd pouted over her shoulder. "That's silly. An imp would never tread holy ground, and they don't fly. Everybody knows that." She looked down, embarrassed. "At least, that is what old women always said back home when I was growing up," she added weakly.

"Perhaps," allowed Thomas. "It is just a story the locals tell. Anyway, you should get down here if we are to save your blushes."

She nodded shyly, and after dismounting himself, Thomas lifted her down. She was slender, slight in his arms, weighing almost nothing, and yet felt somehow substantial to him. Hunydd pressed against him for a moment when her feet touched the ground, grasping his shoulders as she sought her balance. His hold on her hips lingered perhaps a little too long, and she looked up at him curiously, dark eyes questioning. She was in no hurry for him to let her go, and he was sure that she wanted him to kiss her. It would be a lie to say he was not tempted, if only just for a moment.

And then he thought of Cecily, and another kiss, a kiss that had suddenly become very dear to him and that had brought to life in him feelings he had thought long dead. So instead, he smiled and released her. Hunydd blinked once, smoothed her skirts, and with a last smile, walked stiffly to the village, her shoulders drawn back and her head held high, aware Thomas was watching her. Had he seen her face, he would have seen that the lips he had so nearly kissed were turned up in a smile.

CHAPTER 19

Prior Gilbert sat hunched over his desk, scowling down at the not inconsiderable mess of parchments strewn across its broad surface. The prior had never been one for study. He did not have the patience for it and would gladly have fobbed the work off on someone else had he not thought it necessary to know the comings and goings of his own house. Unfortunately, that meant he actually had to read the accounts, and the various correspondence addressed to him personally, and God only knows how many densely written legal documents. It might be his least favorite task, but it had to be done, and so he kept at it like a heavy-laden ship battering its way through a choppy sea.

He was not at all disappointed when Eustace rapped on the door to announce his presence.

"Gilbert, might I trouble you for a moment of your time?"

The prior smiled his welcome.

"Of course, Eustace. My door is always open to an old friend. Besides, I was just about to take a break. The numbers are beginning to swim before my eyes. I swear I have reviewed the cellarer's accounts three times now, and I simply cannot make them tally. Have you perhaps come to continue our game?"

The prior gestured to a small table before the fireplace, on which sat a wooden chessboard, the stone pieces scattered across its checkered surface in the midst of a fierce struggle. Chess was a secret vice of theirs and had been for a long time now. Strictly speaking, Benedictine monks were supposed to disavow possessions, a complication Gilbert avoided by regarding the chess set as a piece of furniture that belonged to the priory, rather like a stool or table.

"I believe I have you this time," he added with a chuckle and a cheeky wink.

In truth, Gilbert knew he was but a poor player. He invariably lost and half-suspected such few victories as he managed were gifted to him by his friend. But he enjoyed the fray, nevertheless, and most of all he enjoyed the company.

"Perhaps we can play a little later," replied Eustace with an indulgent smile. "For now, I need to talk to you about our Dominican guest."

The prior's good humor dissipated immediately. Friar Justus had been nothing but a nuisance ever since his arrival. He was a miserable man who seemed to find fault with everything: the food was too rich, the music too jolly, the readings too insipid. It seemed that nothing would please him, and Gilbert was secretly longing for his departure.

"Did you know he beats himself?" asked Eustace. "You can hear his cries at night."

Gilbert's eyebrows shot up, and he drummed his fingers thoughtfully on the desk. "A flagellator is he? Well, I cannot say I approve. I doubt God intends for us to punish ourselves in such a manner. But I cannot tell him how to practice his devotion in the privacy of his own cell."

Eustace nodded his understanding. "I had supposed so, as well. However, his wailing disturbs the novices and even more so the young oblates. He has also taken it on himself to *school* our younger brethren. He scolds them severely at times and has even cuffed or thrashed those he finds to be failing in their duties."

The prior glowered angrily. "It is not for him to discipline our charges. He is a guest here."

Gilbert believed the priory should be a happy place where younger novices and oblates could feel at home. He had often been beaten as a child and could not bear to see another chastised unnecessarily.

"There is worse yet, I am afraid," continued Eustace. "His companion, this Guy de Hokenham, as he calls himself, has been accosting the women in the village. I am afraid he has . . . *touched* several of them in a most inappropriate and unwelcome manner."

The prior gaped in horror. He had always been somewhat innocent of the world, having been an oblate, given to the order as a child, and the idea that someone would abuse the local womenfolk shocked him, even more so as that person was a guest under his own roof.

"Why that is outrageous! This is my house and I shall not have it."

Eustace nodded his approval and stood aside from the door meaningfully. Gilbert took the hint, heaved himself out of his chair, and stormed past Eustace at a rolling gait.

The prior was an extremely affable and caring man. But his strength was also his weakness. At heart, Gilbert wanted nothing more than to be liked and was uncomfortable with conflict. Indeed, by the time they had reached the Dominican's cell, the edge was already gone from his anger, and he dithered on the threshold before he finally managed to pluck up the courage to poke his head inside, where he found Justus on his knees in prayer.

"I apologize for interrupting, Justus, but might we have a word?"

Justus's face wore its usual sour look. "As you can see, I am tending to my devotions. I am surprised you are not doing so yourself."

"This is a rather important matter," said Gilbert firmly. "It cannot wait."

He proceeded to relate the charges. He did so in a calm and confident manner and was very clear as to what was and was not acceptable behavior on the part of a guest under his roof. The Dominican listened patiently throughout, an unreadable expression on his face, and once the prior was done, clasped his hands together, steepling the forefingers to his lips.

"I appreciate your candor, Prior. Have you said your piece?"

Gilbert was a little taken aback. He had not expected reasonable behavior from someone he had become convinced was an unreasonable man. Gratified at the way things were going, he relaxed and was finally able to unclench his buttocks.

"Yes. I think that about covers it." He turned to Eustace, who stood by his side, eyeing the Dominican with an inscrutable expression. "Was there anything I missed, Brother?"

"No. I think you were very clear, Gilbert. It only remains for our guest to affirm that from hereon he will comport himself more consistently with our expectations and that he shall immediately curb the outrageous behavior of his servant."

Both monks turned to Justus expectantly.

"*Your expectations?*" Justus scoffed. "I am to comport myself consistent with *your expectations?*"

Gilbert took a step back.

"I find *your expectations* decidedly wanting and entirely unworthy of a House of God. You interrupt my prayer to tell me that I should limit my devotions. That I should spend less time in worship."

"I did not suggest you limit your devotions, Justus," blustered the prior, "only that—"

"Only that I show less zeal, perhaps, in my love of the Lord?"

"Well, I did not say that, so much as—"

"Have you forgotten that your purpose here in this priory is prayer and contemplation?"

"No, I have not forgotten—"

"I have to wonder then why I see lapses all around me." Justus shook his head. "Devotional offices are not kept strictly to the hour. Brothers stumble into matins tardy, several blatantly sleeping through the Office, snoring loudly, having glutted themselves with ale the night before. And during repast there is a persistent hum of talk and, worse yet, laughter. *Laughter. At the table!* And it is not only during repast. I regularly hear your brothers gossiping like fishwives as they work, even as they illuminate."

Gilbert shuffled uncomfortably from one foot to the other. "It is true that perhaps I have not held everyone strictly to the Rule, but I find—"

"And the food! I had been meaning to mention that to you." The prior stepped back even further, unable to complete his explanation, which was just as well, as it was a rather weak one. "The menu regularly includes meat of the quadruped, and even wines. It is most troubling. Is it not surprising if I must beg the Lord's indulgence after sitting through a veritable bacchanalian festival, an orgy of gluttony? And I see full half your brothers skulking away to the *misericord*, where I presume you have given them full license to gorge themselves on animal flesh, a practice that is becoming all too common in the Benedictine Houses."

Gilbert's buttocks were firmly clenched together once more, and he could feel a cold dribble of sweat working its way down between the cheeks. Justus was far from done, however.

"Then there is the chanting of the Office. Have you not noticed that it is entirely off-key? Ordinarily I would not care for music, but this is the *Divine Office*. The performance ought to reflect the glory of God and the deep reverence we have for Him. And yet your precentor squeals throughout like a stuck pig. I should think the sound most offensive to God's ears."

Justus crossed his arms angrily and grimaced.

"And you dare speak to me of women when half the women in your village strut about like common whores, swaying their hips, and thrusting out their bosoms at any man they can find. Is it any wonder that Guy might be tempted? Only yesterday I saw one such temptress here, in these very cloisters, chatting away with the brothers, giving them her coy looks and simpering smiles. I could scarce believe my eyes."

"I believe you may be referring to a lay laundress—"

"*A laundress?* Have you entirely forgotten the Benedictine motto? *Ora et labora!* Work and prayer! Yet you permit lay servants to do much of your work. And one of them a temptress."

Gilbert would hardly describe the snaggle-toothed old crone that laundered their habits a temptress. She was not likely to arouse the ardor of any of the monks, and he was about to say so when the Dominican stood up, looming over him threateningly.

"While we are on the subject of the vices of flesh, I am convinced the cellarer is trading your stores for favors from village women. And I have become very concerned with the close relationship, the *intimate* relationship, between certain of your brothers and one or two of the novices."

Gilbert looked stunned. "Are you suggesting . . . ?"

"I am suggesting that you curb the behavior of your brethren. You seek to lecture me on my duties when your own charges are engaged in forbidden carnal relations."

Seeing his friend hopelessly floundering, Eustace chose this moment to enter the fray, and placed a reassuring hand on Gilbert's shoulder. "The women your man has accosted were no harlots, Justus, but good girls from decent families."

Justus barked out a scoffing laugh. "I think that perhaps you Benedictines spend too much time cloistered away from the world and are naive to the tricks of women. Do you not recall the warning given to us by the prophet Isaiah: '*the daughters of*

Zion are haughty, and walk with outstretched necks and wanton eyes'.
No, I am all too familiar with women and their ways. They all
lust for trinkets and what a man has between his legs."

Far from being cowed, Eustace took a step forward, putting
himself between the prior and Justus.

"Then perhaps you should consider that the villagers are in
pain, having just lost one of their loved ones, an innocent young
girl, to a terrible assault of a lascivious nature. It would be hurtful
for them to see their daughters accosted at this time. Nor are they
likely to accept it without recourse to violence of their own."

Justus harrumphed, grudgingly acknowledging the point.
He stroked his chin thoughtfully. "I suppose that is a fair point.
If it will make you rest any easier, I shall speak with Guy and
warn him of the dangers of the flesh. I shall tell him to arm
himself against the arts and allures of the local slatterns so that
he should not so easily fall prey to their temptations. But really,
Eustace, you act as if it were his fault."

Justus slowly and deliberately knelt down again, assuming a
prayerful posture. "Is there anything else we need to discuss, or
may I finally return to my prayers?"

Gilbert collected himself from the stupor into which he had
fallen. "No, not at all. Well, I am glad we had this little chat."

"Then I shall return to my devotions, and I suggest that you
do the same. It will shortly be Compline, and we should all
ready our minds and spirits." Gilbert turned for the door. "Oh
and, Prior, you should consider including in the liturgy at repast
some passages regarding the sins of women and the temptations
of the flesh. Something from Proverbs or Ecclesiastes should
suffice."

"Yes, an excellent suggestion," allowed Gilbert as he backed
out the door. "I shall do so. We are sorry to have disturbed you.
It won't happen again."

The two monks walked slowly back to the prior's office.

Gilbert gave an embarrassed chuckle. "Well, that went rather well, don't you think?"

Eustace sighed.

★ ★ ★

Justus scratched irritably at his shoulder. The hair shirt was itching terribly, and he would simply have to take it off soon for some relief. It was also making him sweat, and he feared that he was beginning to smell a bit ripe.

The vicar had been murdered; Justus sensed it to be true. A man had been sacrificed on the very altar of the church. Another had been strung up in mockery of the Betrayer's death. An innocent young girl had been defiled and slain. These things were all connected in some as yet unseen fashion.

And then there was the strange look Lady Isabella had given De Bray's daughter—a look that suggested Cecily was hiding some wickedness. Nor had Justus been fooled by Isabella's pretensions to piety. Her efforts to ingratiate herself had been vulgar. So much so that she had instead only raised his suspicions. He thought it likely that she too had something to hide, and tomorrow he would return to the manor house and have it out of her.

Yes, the Devil's fingers were sunk deep into the soil of Bottesford village, and the more stones Justus overturned, the more creeping degeneracy he would uncover. Soon—very soon, he was sure—he would have enough to petition the archbishop for a broader investigation.

The bell for Compline sounded, and Justus rose stiffly, his knees complaining at having rested for so long on the hard stone. As he strolled to the service, he reminded himself to spare an orison for young Maud. Or was it Margareta? Or Matilda? No matter—God would know of whom he spoke.

CHAPTER 20

She was charged to have nightlie conference with a spirit called Robert Artisson, to whome she sacrificed in the high waie nine red cocks and nine peacocks eies . . . In rifling the closet of the ladie, they found a wafer of sacramental bread, having the divels name stamped thereon in steed of Jesus Christ, and a pipe of ointment, wherewith she greased a staffe, upon which she ambled and gallopped thorough thicke and thin, when and in what manner she listed.

—The Lady Alice Kettle,
Holinshed's Chronicle of Ireland (sub anno 1323)

The next morning Thomas found himself once more standing before the door to Alice Kyteler's little cottage.

"Back again so soon, Thomas," said Alice, throwing the door wide in welcome before he could knock. "People shall start to talk."

Thomas flushed and felt the same boyish awkwardness he had experienced on his last visit. Alice sensed his discomfort and laughed out loud.

"Oh, I jest! I do not think that the forest animals will disclose our rendezvous. I am quite secluded here, you know. I suppose that is why my niece chose the place. And it does get lonely, so I am glad of your visit."

She led him inside, taking his arm in a gesture strangely reminiscent of her niece's, and soon had him comfortably seated with a cup of wine in his hand. So comfortable, in fact, that he scarcely even noticed the decapitated chicken she had left hanging in the corner, all plucked and strung up by its feet, the blood still draining from its neck into the small leather pail set beneath.

Thomas remembered his previous incivility and made a show of drinking deeply from his cup. Alice smiled, recognizing and accepting the apology, and lowered herself gracefully— for *gracefully* was the word—to the seat opposite him.

"Has anyone told you what has happened these last few days?" he asked as the last of the unfortunate fowl's blood plopped down into the bucket.

"The murders?" Alice pursed her lips in disapproval. "Hunydd has spoken of them. I believe you were the one who found the girl, were you not?"

She listened intently, observing him with shrewd eyes and saying nothing as he recounted what he knew of the recent deaths.

"Why are you telling me all this, Thomas?" she asked when he was done.

"I thought perhaps you might have some insights," he replied, taking another much smaller and more appreciative sip of his wine. It was an excellent and unusual vintage—a dark earthy red, barely watered, with hints of blackberry, plum, and clove, and something else that Thomas could not easily place. It was certainly not one of the local wines that so often bit like a snake. Nor yet was it a simple Rhenish. This was altogether different— an unusual wine that belonged in a goblet at a lord's table; something to be sipped at and savored, and not what one would expect to find served by an exile living in a dingy forester's hut.

Alice, it seemed, was not sharing the same mellow moment. She quite deliberately set down her cup and pushed it a little away from her.

"Still I find it strange that you should consult me. I am after all a stranger here and, for obvious reasons, rarely leave this cottage. I have to wonder whether perhaps you are hoping that I might perform some kind of divination for you. That I might stir the ashes of the fire or take apart some poor creature, spread its guts with my fingers, peer into its innards, and miraculously see your killer. Is that what you are here for, sir?"

Her voice had become hard, and her eyes flashed dangerously, reminding him again of Cecily when he had first disturbed her peace in the manor gardens.

"Well, sir," she continued in the same mordant tone, "is that what you are about? You take me for a witch and have come here to ask me to scry, is that it? Am I to strip naked for you and dance around a fire under the light of moon and thereby divine your murderer? Am I to summon a demon and consult with it from within my looking glass?"

Strangely enough, her stormy visage and angry tone in some way released him. Thomas almost felt the spell of her presence dissipating around him, and when he chose to respond, he did so calmly and with a smile, letting Alice know that she did not cow him.

"I suppose you could do those things if you wished." Alice arched an eyebrow. "I had expected something a little less dramatic, however. I came to you because you seem to be an intelligent woman whose horizons have stretched beyond the small world of those who live in these parts. I had taken you as someone, like me, who has experienced the darker side of humanity. In truth, I thought I could benefit from your wisdom. I am truly sorry to have given you offense and shall take my leave now, if that is what you wish."

She blinked slowly and, when he made as if to rise, placed her hand over his. Her touch was warm, and when she looked into his eyes, he realized that her own eyes were not violet at all, as he had thought, but a remarkable shade of blue and gray. Perhaps it was just a trick of the light.

"No, Thomas, it is I who must apologize. I have been rude to you, and you have shown me nothing but discretion and consideration. I suppose I have become overly sensitive. Is it any wonder after all the terrible things of which I have been accused?"

He settled back into his seat. "Not at all. You have every right to be bitter, Alice. I think few could have borne what you have suffered with such dignity. There is really no need to apologize."

"None of my suffering was of your doing, Thomas, and it was wrong of me to speak so. An apology was owed and is now given. Though in some ways I find it even more curious that you should seek my counsel—my *wisdom*, as you so nicely put it. I had always supposed it to be rather dangerous for a woman to display too much intelligence. Men do not tend to like intelligent, independent women. My niece is such. She is also proud and far too bold."

Alice looked to the side, her lips pressed together thoughtfully. "I fear it will hinder her. Have you not wondered that she is not yet married?"

He had, and his wonderings had led to some very strange thoughts indeed.

"Perhaps it is for the best. Few men would truly appreciate her talents. My first husband was one such."

Alice cast her eyes down in a moment of reflection, the ghost of a smile playing at the corners of her lips. Then she shook her head and poured him some more wine. "Most men would only seek to break her."

"Forgive me, madam, but why remarry if you felt so? Your fortune was assured. You need not have done so."

"Oh, you know better than that, Thomas. Women in our society are defined almost entirely by the men who possess them. A girl belongs to her father. A wife belongs to her husband. Her body, her property, everything, is his to do with as he wishes. And young widows are expected to remarry, even when they are women of independent means. When the peasant woman becomes a widow, if she does not remarry quickly enough for her lord's liking, the local reeve finds her a new man, and she is forced to wed. After all, she is the property of her lord. Well, it is much the same for wealthy women. The king or our overlord marries us off as reward to men who offer him service, or to pay a debt. It matters not a jot whether that man beats us, ravishes us, or spends us into penury."

What Dame Alice said was all too often true. Thomas could not deny it.

"And God forbid that a woman give in to any of her natural instincts and desires. Why then she becomes the veritable whore of Babylon, one of the true daughters of Eve, who caused the downfall of man. Anyway," she said, smiling to lift the gloom that had gripped them both, "you did not come to me for a homily on the plight of women. I could speak on that subject for hours, I assure you. And, as it happens, I have thought upon the subject of these murders. The Lord knows I have had little else to do."

Alice looked disconsolately around the miserable shack, her eyes passing over the dead chicken as though it were not there.

"I do not need to tell you that this is the work of a truly evil man. Nor is that any great insight. But I do believe all these murders are somehow connected and the work of a single individual."

She touched her fingers to her lips in thought.

"Putting aside the nonsense about heresy and blasphemy, I find it significant that the first two murders were connected to the church."

"The first two? No. The miller was killed and strung up at his mill."

Thomas's eyes drifted unconsciously back to the corner where the chicken's limp form still hung down over the red-stained bucket.

"The miller? I am talking of the priest. The vicar of Saint Mary's."

Thomas sat back, stunned. "The vicar died of a heart failure."

"Are you so sure? He may well have, but I do not think we should assume so and dismiss his death out of hand. On this point, that horrid Dominican may be right. It is a coincidence that cannot be so easily dismissed. In either case, the manner of Roger Lacy's death shows something akin to a hatred for the Church. Why otherwise choose to murder him in a church on a dark night when he could have easily dispatched him else-where? And why else be so extravagant and crude?"

Alice took a sip of her wine and set the cup down.

"The fact Lacy was murdered and so gruesomely displayed at Saint Mary's is one reason I believe this must be the work of a stranger."

Thomas frowned and shook his head to indicate he did not follow.

"The villagers hereabouts do tend to be hopelessly religious. The Church and its sacraments are a great mystery to them. They hold both in awe. I think it unlikely any of the local people would defile their own house of worship in such a fashion, however demented they had become. What is that charming saying? Oh yes—'A bird does not shit in its own nest.'"

Her words caught Thomas drinking, and he spluttered, having to quickly set aside his cup lest he spill the wine all over himself. An awkward silence ensued.

"Oh, I am sorry. Not ladylike enough for you? I understood

that you had fought in the border wars. I had assumed that you were accustomed to such language and worse, no?"

"Well, yes," Thomas mumbled, feeling uncomfortably hot and trying to recall when he might have mentioned his experience as a man at arms. Perhaps Cecily had managed to sneak Bishop Henry's letter away from her father after all.

"You said the fact the murder happened in a church was *one* of the reasons you believe this to be the work of a stranger?" Thomas urged.

"Killers like this enjoy what they do and are incapable of doing otherwise. Any remorse they might feel after the deed is short-lived, and they soon find themselves gripped by the need to kill again. For them it is as intoxicating as carnal pleasure.

"Were your killer a local, there would surely have been other murders here. Nor can such a beast hide his true character for long in such a close-knit community. Unless, of course, he is just beginning," she mused. "But these murders were not the crude slashings of a virgin killer. No, this man has killed before. Many times, I suspect."

"You are a stranger, Alice, and you are at odds with the Church. By your reasoning, you could be the murderer."

"I am a woman, Thomas. Do you imagine I could truly kill a man?"

"An old man weakened by penury, yes I do. Nor are you weak, Alice. And who has cause to hate the Church more? Besides, I am not so naive as to think that women are incapable of killing, just as I am not naive enough to suspect they are incapable of reasoning."

She lifted her cup to him, acknowledging the point. "You continue to impress me, Thomas. I understand what my niece sees in you."

Yet again Thomas felt himself blushing. He was at the same time both greatly pleased and thoroughly embarrassed at the confirmation of Cecily's interest. Alice knew it, and he sensed that she was enjoying his discomfort.

"But you have already said you do not suspect me of any involvement," Alice reminded him.

"Nor do I. Like you, I believe these murders are connected. You might have been able to kill a weak old man, or poison a priest, if that is indeed what happened, but you could not have overcome the miller, however soused he might have been. And only a man can have harmed young Margareta so."

Alice knotted her brows, the eyes underneath turning flat and hard. "Yes. I had assumed the beast used her."

Thomas looked down, the sight of Margareta's despoiled young body still livid in his mind, and for a time neither one of them spoke. Alice was the first to break the silence.

"I always find it curious that we womenfolk are so often spared such details out of some misguided notion that we are sensitive. As though it might overwhelm us. As if we do not endure childbirth. As if we do not bear the losses of children to disease and of husbands to war. As if none of us has suffered before at the hands of a man. With all we must bear in life, I would have thought it more likely men would quail before the ugliness, not we women."

She picked up her cup again, deliberately not looking at him. "You did not consider that I might have summoned a demon? Or that I do indeed have an incubus who performs these tasks for me?"

Thomas answered only with sidelong smile and a bemused shake of his head.

Alice stood up and began to pace the room.

"What do you know of Roger Lacy—the old man who was killed at Saint Mary's?"

Thomas shook his head. "We actually know very little, only that he was once steward at Lady Isabella's family estate, that he had fallen on hard times and had come begging alms and position from her."

"Interesting, after so long? And you say he had coin—it sounded as though he was dressed as a vagabond. Why would he have coin do you suppose?"

"Lady Isabella told us that she took pity on him and that she feared her gift was the cause of his death."

Alice stopped her pacing and turned fully to him. "Do you believe that Lacy was killed for the contents of his coin purse?"

"Not at all. A simple robber does not feel the need to make statements. He does his work and is gone. He departs quickly so as to avoid discovery. Money may have been a consideration in this instance, but not the main one. If it had been, he would never have parted with it in attempting to point the finger of blame at the miller."

"Perhaps Lacy had something else of value then," she suggested. "Knowledge is more valuable than coin, is it not? He once held an important position as steward to Lady Isabella's household. She gave him quite a sum of money and promised him favors. Perhaps she wanted to buy his silence. Perhaps she feared that would not be enough and took other, more . . . drastic measures. He died shortly after visiting her, did he not? Perhaps, if not capable of the murder itself, she might have been capable of directing it."

It was a terrible accusation, and Thomas sat awhile in brooding silence, contemplating the awful implications. He did not want to believe such a thing of the strange and distant woman he had met, even though the possibility had already fleetingly crossed his mind.

Alice was eyeing him shrewdly. "And perhaps it takes one woman to put into words what you already suspect about another," she suggested gently.

"Perhaps, Alice," he conceded. "Yet your theory would not

explain the gruesome display of Lacy's corpse or what was done to Margareta."

"No, but it is possible that Isabella may have unleashed a beast that she could then no longer control."

Alice was right. Thomas had not wanted to admit his suspicions about Isabella for fear of where they might lead him. Her feigned illness had been as convenient an excuse for him as it had been for her. He knew it, just as he knew that Isabella was hiding something. Alice believed it to be something important, the key to the entire mystery. He had to open himself up to the possibility that Isabella was personally involved and perhaps even in some way responsible for the murders. He had to press the matter and set aside the fact that she was the lord's wife, whatever the consequences.

Alice sat down again and rested her elbows on the table. The candlelight glinted from eyes that now looked deep into Thomas's own.

"Saint Thomas Aquinas once taught that man is inherently good and that evil and sin are but aberrations. Those teachings have been repeated by insipid clerics for half a century now as if they are the words of Christ himself. But he was wrong, Thomas. My life has taught me that man is inherently evil, *and* that he is inherently good. He is both at the same time. At the heart of every man there is a monster waiting to be unleashed. It is only the man's goodness that cages his monster. For some men, the monster is weak, and the bars of the cage are strong. For others, the reverse is true. And there are yet other men who present the world with only the convincing facade of a cage. Whose impression of goodness is entirely false. A deception. It is these men that are the most dangerous because their bestial nature is unhindered, always awaiting an opportunity to prey upon the unsuspecting souls around them. I believe you seek such a man.

"And I believe his face is well hidden. The girl's family said she had been sneaking out to some assignation. Yet she was not visiting with her betrothed. It seems likely that our man seduced her rather than abducted her, don't you think? So, he would likely be someone she trusted, someone charismatic and persuasive.

"Sad to say, Thomas, but people are not always so innocent as they would have us believe."

Thomas tilted his head and gave her an amused, lopsided smile. "Do you speak of yourself, Alice?"

"Oh, I never claimed to be innocent, Thomas. Far from it. I am sure I have done things in my life that would turn any confessor's hair white. It is true that I have from time to time sought out experiences of which others would disapprove. That I have tested the bounds of accepted decency, if you will. I have certainly practiced those woman's arts handed down to us by our mothers and by theirs before them. But I see no wrong in that. I have also given generously to the Church and to those in need, both of my labor and of my wealth. And for all my undoubted sins, I am not what they would have you believe. I am no necromancer. I do not summon the dead. I have cast no spells to steal another's wealth. I do not drink blood, nor yet eat young babes. Perish the thought! And though one or two of them may have deserved it, I most certainly did not poison any of my husbands. While I am more than capable of defending myself if needs must, I have always sought to use such skills as I have learned in the service of others. To heal. To comfort. No, I do not claim to be innocent, Thomas, but I do try to be good."

Thomas sat in silence for a while absorbing all that Alice had said, and then rose to his feet.

"You have given me much to think about, Alice. And you managed to do so without a single animal sacrifice," he added, offering her a cheeky wink.

"And without yet removing a single item of clothing," she responded with an even cheekier wink of her own.

"Thomas, there is one more thing of which I would caution you before you leave. You cannot insist on perfect reasoning from the fractured mind of a madman. And aren't all murderers madmen, in their own way? His way of thinking is not yours. He is driven by lusts he cannot control, hence the girl, and by hatred of the Church, hence the message. His beast is now unleashed; the kill is intoxicating to him, and if he is not caught, more deaths will surely follow until he chooses to leave. You must also consider that, should you fail to catch him, soon he may flee, and he will then inflict this misery on others elsewhere. The cycle will renew, others will suffer, and those who have suffered here will be denied justice."

Alice stood and smoothed down her skirts. "You are sure you will not stay awhile longer? As I said, it gets lonely here. And I am most secluded. Nobody is likely to visit me again for many hours." She looked up at him from under her lashes. It was a coy, sultry look if ever he'd seen one, though he half-suspected she was merely toying with him again.

"You are a charming host, Alice, but I must be away. As I said, you have given me much to think about."

Alice nodded and smiled graciously, not evidencing any particular disappointment, and Thomas opened the door to leave, only to pause once more on the threshold.

"What kind of a man am I, Alice?" he asked.

She hesitated barely a moment. "I believe you are a good man, Thomas."

"How do you know?"

"I know because if it were not so, you would never have asked."

CHAPTER 21

"Father Elyas. Might I have a word?"

Elyas had just climbed the steps to the Great Hall and paused to allow Thomas to catch up.

"I have been looking for Lady Isabella, but her maid seems unable to find her. I know she comes to you for confession. Have you perhaps seen her?"

"I have not. However, I believe she was planning on riding to the village to deliver alms. She has been indisposed a fair bit these last weeks, and she is anxious to return to her charitable work now that she is somewhat recovered. Likely that is where she has gone."

A concerned look crossed Elyas's face. "Do you wish me to look for her, Thomas?"

"Thank you, Elyas, but there is no need. I shall head to the village."

"Thomas, please tell me. Is something amiss?" The chaplain's voice had risen to a plaintive whine, and he was wringing his hands anxiously. Elyas inhaled deeply and looked down to collect himself. He looked tired and pale, and the black hair that showed beneath his skullcap was disheveled, as though he had neglected to clip his tonsure and had been scrubbing at it worriedly.

"I am sorry, Thomas. You must think me ridiculous. The terrible things that have happened, Tom Attwood's death—I am all on edge. My nerves are frayed." He folded his hands into his sleeves and offered Thomas a rueful smile. "I must be a great disappointment to you as a priest. I disappoint myself."

"Not at all. Your compassion does you credit. But you really must not blame yourself for what happened to Tom. And we are all on edge."

"Thank you, Thomas. I shall be heading to the village myself soon. People have been avoiding the church after what happened there and the prior has given me permission to hold some additional masses. I thought it might help." He looked up, considering his words. "I thought that honest worship might help cleanse the place, I suppose."

"That is generous of you, Father. I shall be sure to attend."

Elyas watched thoughtfully as Thomas walked back to the stables, and then limped across the hall and ascended the stairs to the guest chamber above the buttery. He stepped inside and winced at a sharp stab of pain in his rib as he turned to close the door behind him.

Lady Isabella stood in the middle of the small paneled room, clutching at the sides of her kirtle.

"I do apologize for my tardiness, my lady. It was not entirely of my own doing. The young man from Lincoln was asking for you again. I trust you have not been encouraging his advances."

Isabella licked her lips nervously. "No. I do not speak to him. I wouldn't do that. You said not to."

"Indeed I did, and I am glad you have done as you were told. But you do not look very happy, dear. You have such a pretty mouth. I do hate to see it pouting so."

"I . . . I do not feel particularly well today."

The chaplain frowned at her.

"Truly, I am unwell," she added hurriedly. "My throat is sore and I have a headache. I think perhaps that I have a fever."

He bolted the door and turned to face her again. "I found my things disturbed today. I trust that was not you, Isabella?"

"No, of course not. I know nothing of that."

"Indeed? Because I should be most angry if I found out that you had been prying among my private things."

"It was not me, I swear." There was an edge of panic to her voice.

"Do you now? And on what do you swear? Are you willing to swear on the life of your son?"

She looked at him blankly and said nothing.

"No? I thought not. You really deserve to be punished, and yet I find myself in a generous mood today. Now tell me, have you been ingratiating yourself to the Dominican as I told you?"

"Oh yes, yes," she replied enthusiastically. "I have. We are good friends now, I believe."

"Excellent, and what information have you obtained from him?"

Isabella averted her eyes and licked her lips again, making it clear without saying that the answer was nothing.

"I see." His voice was tinged with disappointment. "Then what were you able to find out about the nocturnal activities of a certain young maid?"

"I tried," she said, still avoiding his gaze. "I tried very hard, really, but I did not learn anything new."

"That is very disappointing. I had thought at least you could manage that."

He reached out and stroked Isabella's cheek with the back of his fingers, enjoying the way she shivered at his touch.

"I trust you were subtle in your inquiries."

"I . . . I think so," she said weakly, looking down at the floor.

Elyas sighed. Another mistake. He was making far too many of them now. He should have realized he could not trust the discretion of this vacant woman. Isabella was a dim, silly thing, easily coerced and bullied, but far too dull for Elyas to have any confidence she would not let slip something important. Nor had he really needed her assistance. It had been a simple matter for him to wander into the woods again at night and follow the track to the little cottage in the clearing. He had hidden in the trees, watching and waiting, and he had discovered something shocking, far more shocking he believed than even Isabella's dirty little secret; something shocking and yet at the same time so very wonderful.

He held her waist and drew her to him. She was tense, and he could feel her fighting the urge to squirm away from him in revulsion.

"Yet again you disappoint me, Isabella. I am beginning to wonder whether you have truly taken the nature of our bargain to heart."

"What do you mean? I have done what you asked."

"Really? You have failed to obtain any useful information for me. I suspect that, despite what you say, you have been prying into my things, and not for the first time. And to be quite frank, you are beginning to bore me."

Her mouth opened and closed.

"And now you selfishly feign illness. If things do not change, if you can do no better by me, I fear I shall tire of you completely, and I shall have to rethink our agreement. Is that what you want?"

"No!" she exclaimed, her eyes round. "You promised."

"I did. But now I think that you are not living up to your side of our little agreement. I am not so sure that my promise is binding."

"I—I am doing as you asked." She hastened to the desk and

scrabbled about on its surface, lifting a large hunk of jewelry up to him in triumph, her hand shaking slightly. "See? I brought you this."

Elyas harrumphed and took it from her. It was one of the ugliest necklaces he had ever seen. Heavy and jewel encrusted, as though the craftsman had tried to hide his want of skill with ever more jewels and gold.

"Will he not miss it?"

The *he* to whom Elyas referred was her husband, De Bray.

Isabella's face twisted into momentary bitterness. "He does not notice what I wear, and I have many necklaces. He will be none the wiser."

"Hmm, I see."

The chaplain played the necklace though his fingers. It was heavy and gaudy. Disgusting really.

"It is truly ugly." Isabella nodded, thoroughly agreeing with him. "But I suppose it would fetch a fine price for the gold alone. Very well."

He looked up at her expectantly. "And have you brought me any coin. You will recall that I specifically asked you for coin, not hunks of poorly crafted metal."

He tossed the necklace disdainfully onto the cot. Isabella watched its progress and swallowed slowly, twice.

"It is becoming more difficult. That bitch of his, Cecily, counts each coin as if it were her own inheritance and not that of my son." She grimaced, her eyes drifting to the window, and then blinked, suddenly remembering where she was. "But I shall try again. I shall try harder. I promise."

"Then I shall give you another chance."

Elyas stroked her cheek again. Isabella responded with another delightful little shiver. When Isabella had first come to him with her little secret, she had thought he would help her. That he might speak to Lacy on her behalf. She could never have imagined how he would proceed to manipulate and abuse her. That she had placed herself completely in his power.

The death of the village girl had been unfortunate. He had been toying with her ever since he had begun performing services and taking confessions at the village church. Little glances. Little talks during confession. Flattering her. Gaining her confidence. It had been rather easy, and he had enjoyed the hunt. Margareta had all too readily agreed to a meeting and had been willing enough at first when she thought it a romantic and harmless rendezvous, less so when she understood that more was expected of her. And she had struggled. Oh, how she had struggled. He had been forced to choke her into silence.

"I do apologize," he said, suddenly realizing that in his distraction he had begun idly tracing his finger along the curve of Isabella's lips. "I was lost in thought for a moment there. You must think me quite rude."

"I–I really should be leaving," she stammered.

"Really? I had no idea that you were so busy. Because it appears to me that you spend all day in your room, staring at your reflection and talking to yourself. What on earth can you be doing that would require you to leave so soon? Or perhaps you simply wish to be away from me. Is that it? Do I disgust you now?"

He spat out the last words, and she shook her head fiercely.

"No, no. Not at all." She laughed, nervously, desperately trying to come up with an excuse. "I just . . . I said that I would—"

He let her flop and flounder around like a landed fish for a moment and then pulled her roughly to him.

"If I wished you to stay, you would do so."

She squirmed about as he fumbled under her skirts.

"Is that not right?"

She was blinking back tears and nodded, stifling a sob.

"I expect you to do better from now on, Isabella."

When she did not respond, he gripped a fistful of her hair and tugged her head back sharply, forcing her to look up at him. "Am I rightly understood?"

Isabella nodded again.

"Then you may be on your way."

He spun her about, gave her rump a slap and shoved her toward the door. She needed no more encouragement and was quickly gone.

The man who chose to call himself Elyas smiled bleakly. The real Father Elyas lay in a ditch somewhere on the side of the North Road. He had been a nice man, excited about his new position, and he had proved a good companion for more than a few miles. The man who called himself Elyas had felt a little bad about having to kill him, but only a very little. He had needed a place to hide for a while, and it turned out that he rather enjoyed this particular role. So much so that he had stayed on long after it would have been safe for him to leave. Well, lucky for him he did. The old steward had appeared like a gift from God, or perhaps from the Devil. Or just by chance.

Now he would leave Bottesford with a hefty sum extracted from Isabella. And it was time to revisit the little cottage in the woods. There was healthy profit to be made there as well. And then it would be Cecily's turn. He would make sure she paid her due. Oh yes, he would enjoy breaking her. She was likely to prove a much finer conquest than the insipid Isabella. He shuddered in anticipation.

Well, what can these women expect if they insist on keeping such delicious secrets?

CHAPTER 22

The man who chose to call himself Elyas eased the door open, letting it swing inward slowly on its leather hinges. The cottage's only occupant had her back to him and was stirring the contents of the bronze cooking pot hanging over the hearth.

"Oh, Hunydd," she said over her shoulder, "I had not expected you again tonight. Did you forget something?"

She rapped the ladle against the side of the pot and turned around, her eyes widening in surprise.

"I am afraid it is not Hunydd."

She looked scared to him, and her eyes darted nervously from side to side, looking for some escape that did not exist.

"There is no need to be afraid, madam. I am only here to talk. We have much to discuss, you and I."

He let the staff he carried thump against the earthen floor, pleased at how the sound made her flinch. Just a little something to remind her of the physical danger she was in, something to keep her compliant. She would learn to fear him soon enough.

"Who are you?" He was sure he heard a delightful little tremor in her voice.

"My name is Elyas. I am chaplain to Lord de Bray."

She narrowed her eyes accusingly. "You are no priest."

"No, indeed, though I once studied as such. I suppose that I have been many things, but for the moment it suits me to be a priest. A humble chaplain, as you see."

He spread his hands wide in a self-effacing gesture.

"You killed that man at the church."

Elyas saw no reason to deny it. "I see that you are very well informed for someone living like a hermit."

"Why did you do it?"

"The old man had something I wanted; or at least I believed he did. As for the rather garish display, that stems from a little disagreement I once had with the Church. As I said, I once trained for the priesthood. In truth I regret my actions. Not the message," he said bitterly. "The message was deserved, but the act itself was rash, and it has made my life more difficult than it needed to be."

"And the girl in the woods? You killed her as well."

His eye twitched in annoyance. It irritated him that the girl had been found so quickly. He had been careless, and Alice's accusation was a reminder of the fact. It was another sign that he needed to be gone from here, sooner rather than later, before things became uncomfortable.

"A man has his needs. I am sure you understand. Margareta was a sweet but silly girl. Betrothed to the blacksmith's son, I believe. Naturally she had a head full of romantic notions, as they often do at that age, and she had thought that she ought to experience a little of life before she was wed."

"Why did you have to kill the poor child?"

"I had not planned to do so. I thought only to give her an education that she might one day share with her blacksmith. You will laugh at me, but I had even brought a concoction of wild herbs for her to take afterward so as to spare her any complications. I am sure I need not tell you that a tincture of a particular plant, in the right measure, can be quite an effective abortificant. I have found a use for it before. You see, I was quite thoughtful, really, and did not intend her any harm. But then she decided that she would rather retain her chastity. As you can imagine, I was more than a little disappointed. I felt cheated, and she paid the price. And once the deed was done, I could hardly have her speaking of what happened. It would not at all be consistent with the image I have worked so hard to create."

"You did not need to kill her. She would not likely have spoken unless you got her with child. You know the way of the world for we women. The shame and the blame would have been hers to bear. Men ravish women with impunity every day."

"Hmm, perhaps you are right. Unfortunately, she resisted me, and in my passion I was not entirely gentle with her. Had she submitted willingly enough, she would still be alive today. I suppose there is a lesson of sorts in there for both of us, no?"

"How many people have you killed?"

"You make me sound like a monster. I do not kill for pleasure, madam. Truth be told, I would rather not kill at all. Sometimes, however, it is unavoidable. If you must know, the first time was a monk, a Cistercian brother who had made certain unwelcome advances. He did so on several occasions, in fact. Once he even brought one of his brethren with him, and between them they made sure that it was a long and unpleasant night for me."

Elyas grimaced sourly in distaste.

"I was not yet fifteen years old. Anyway, I killed them both. How could I not? There have been others since. I cannot say how many."

That was not true. The number was twenty-four, and he remembered each one vividly. After the monks, he had lured men into back alleys, promising them pleasure and then cutting their throats for the coin they carried. Such a crude living did not appeal to him for long. He felt himself to be above such things and had learned to put his monastic education to good use, assuming positions in good households or serving as an itinerant chaplain. The veneer of respectability allowed him to inveigle himself into people's lives, learning their intimate secrets and using those secrets against them. It had all become a bit of a game for him, really. He had learned the value of both threats and violence, and when best to use each.

And then there were the women. Some he would force to his will. Others he would take as it pleased him. He found that he had less interest in those who offered themselves to him freely. He much preferred to take what he wanted. Or, better yet, to trick some hapless thing out of her chastity, as he thought he had done with Margareta.

Alice interrupted his thoughts. "Murder comes so easily to you, then, that you no longer recollect the deeds?"

Elyas snorted loudly. "You are a fine one to accuse me so. What is it now—three dead husbands? Or is it four? Tsk, tsk, tsk. And I thought I was rash. You really must learn to control yourself. But let us cease these accusations. I find it tiresome. You have nothing to fear from me. I shall not harm you, and I can keep a secret as well as any man—for a price, of course. I am sure you managed to spirit away some valuables. I know you to be a wealthy woman."

Alice stared at him levelly and spoke through gritted teeth. "I need what I brought with me if I am to begin again. It is all I have."

"Oh, I have needs as well, and you are in no position to argue, dear. But I am not heartless. I shall only take half. Let us say the coin. I am sure you have it hidden somewhere around here. You shall still have your jewels, and your . . . charms. I am sure you will soon find some rich old man who would be more than willing to spread your legs. After all, I understand it is what you do best. And you have been well paid for the deed, have you not?"

"And if I give you the coin?"

"I think it fair to say that we have a mutual interest in discretion. And unlike the girl, it is not as if I need fear that you will expose me. I shall not harm you."

Lies. All lies. He had no intention of taking that risk. She would be lying beneath the leaves tonight, in a shallow grave. He would walk away with the coin and jewelry both. He might stuff one of her more gaudy baubles into her mouth as a parting gift. Yes, that appealed to him. He would prize her teeth apart and cram it halfway down her gullet. A sort of symbolic gesture, a profound message that those who found her would struggle to interpret. It was the kind of thing that set him apart from ordinary killers.

"But honestly, Alice—may I call you Alice?" He did not wait for a reply. "Honestly, Alice, it is not as if you have a choice. I could take what I want. All of it, if I were so inclined. I think I am being more than generous with you. And speaking of your charms," he said, setting down his staff on the table, "I believe I deserve a little something in return for my generosity, to seal our understanding. These village girls are well enough, I suppose, but I prefer my women with a little more experience. I find that the fruit always tastes best when fully ripened, so to speak. And I can tell that you are ripe for the plucking, Alice."

There was something exquisite to his mind about having her whore herself and then pay him for taking his pleasure. He'd had no such intentions when he had set out that night. But then he had imagined her to be a woman well past her prime. He could not have been more wrong. He felt himself stirring at the sight of her. She was undeniably attractive, but there was something else about her. An allure. A seductiveness. Something few women possess naturally. In some ways it was a curse. So often such women unwittingly became prey for men like him. Life could be so unfair.

"Well, what say you, Dame?"

He smiled broadly, showing her his full set of white teeth. He had always been proud of his smile, and he had found that many an evil thought and deed could be successfully hidden behind a nice smile.

CHAPTER 23

Cecily hesitated at the door to Isabella's chamber when she heard the low murmur of voices from within. She could hear Isabella's voice distinctly but could not tell for certain who was with her. Cecily wondered whether she should leave and return later but quickly decided against such a course. If she left now, she might not come back at all. So, Cecily armed herself with her most charming smile, knocked, and entered.

Isabella was sitting in front of the grotesque mirror in her nightdress, brushing her hair. She liked doing that, even though she had a perfectly good maid.

Cecily looked about the room in confusion. "Oh, pardon me, Isabella. I had thought I heard someone else in here with you."

Isabella barely inclined her head by way of recognition. "Oh, that. No, I was just praying. That must have been what you heard."

Cecily thought it a little ironic that Isabella chose to pray in front of her mirror while grooming herself, rather than using the prie-dieu of which she and Justus had made such a big fuss—so much for her liking to spend time on her knees. She was almost certain that she had heard two people, though, and might even have suspected Isabella of having been engaged in a vigorous conversation with herself, were the notion not quite so absurd and more than a little disturbing.

Reminding herself firmly of why she had come, Cecily bit down on her cynicism and resumed her now slightly forced, but she hoped still ingratiating, smile.

"You look lovely tonight, Isabella. Your hair shines like spun gold."

It was a specious compliment, but the kind of thing Isabella liked to hear, and she did indeed pause her brushing long enough to smile into the mirror at Cecily, even if the smile was distant and never reached her eyes. Still, it was a start, and Cecily was reasonably encouraged.

"I could brush it for you if you liked."

Cecily almost gagged. She could not believe she had offered to do such a thing. Thankfully, Isabella gave Cecily another hollow smile and shook her head.

"I just wanted to thank you, Isabella, for your discretion when we met with the Dominican. It might have become awkward for me were you to have mentioned certain things."

Isabella rounded on Cecily, her face a mask of anger.

"Don't thank me so soon!" she hissed.

Cecily was taken completely by surprise and took a step back, finding herself actually a little frightened by Isabella's vehemence.

"I know you hate me, Cecily. I have known it since the day I arrived. You were jealous that another woman might take your place in this house. That she might share a place in your father's heart."

"That's not true!" exclaimed Cecily loudly, though inwardly she had to admit that she was not overly fond of her father's wife. She thought her a silly and vapid creature who was never likely to prove a good companion for him. To begin with, she was far too young, and she was more than a little peculiar, what with her imagined illnesses and her vagaries. Not to mention the strange fascination with personal grooming.

"It *is* true and you know it. You have made it very clear, always acting as if you are better than me. You think you are so smart, with all your silly books and papers. Don't think I don't notice how you are always trying to use big words around me, and how you just *have* to speak in French or Latin every now and then to make me look foolish."

There was something to that also, Cecily had to admit.

"Not once did you think how difficult it might be for me in a strange household, or that I might be lonely so far from my own family."

Isabella was spitting venom. Her face was all screwed up, and she clutched the hairbrush in a white-knuckled fist like she might use it as a weapon.

"No, Isabella," protested Cecily, "I have always wanted you to feel welcome."

That too was a bit of a stretch. Actually, it was a blatant lie.

Isabella's eyes narrowed accusingly. "Is that so? Is that why you still hold the keys to my own house, the stores, and the chambers? Keys that should rightly be mine to keep. It is I, and not you, who is lady of this house. The keys and everything they unlock belong to me by my right as a wife."

Cecily blinked in surprise, once more taken aback by Isabella's anger.

"But . . . but, Isabella," she spluttered. "We had supposed— no, we *believed*—that you did not wish to manage the household." Cecily searched her mind for a polite way to say what she was thinking. "That you preferred to have somebody else deal with those details . . . under your supervision of course."

Isabella's eyes flicked to the side, unconsciously conceding the point.

"Should you wish to have the keys, I would of course yield them to you. I shall fetch them at once."

"Well, that is not really the meat of the problem," demurred

Isabella in a decidedly more conciliatory tone, evading what had become a difficult subject.

Cecily decided to seize the olive branch. "If I have appeared unwelcoming to you, that is entirely my fault, and I am truly sorry. Perhaps we can try anew. Could we do that, Isabella? We could be friends, like sisters."

Cecily's attempt at reconciliation had quite the opposite effect to that which she had intended, and Isabella's face contorted with rage.

"Friends? Why on earth would I want to be friends with you? You who begrudge my son his inheritance, who plot against him? Your own brother."

Cecily was almost at a loss for words. "But . . . that is ridiculous. It is simply not true," she finally managed to say. And this time she spoke the truth.

"It is too!" Isabella snapped back. "He is your brother, and yet you plot against him. I see you with his father, huddled in secret discussions. Whispering all the time. Don't think I don't know what you are up to. You smile and you simper, but I know what you are, Cecily." Isabella turned to face the mirror and resumed brushing her hair, tugging angrily at it. "And what is it exactly that you are doing with the young man from Lincoln, Cecily? I see the way you look at him, with shameful eyes. I know what you want from him. What you imagine him doing to you. It's not fair that you should get him when I am stuck with that flatulent old boor."

"Isabella, you are imaging things."

"Oh really? I don't think so. I see you making eyes at him. I'll wager you think about him at night, don't you, when you are alone in your bed? That you think of him touching you . . . Don't try to deny it. I know it is true. Well, you cannot trust him. He will betray you. All men betray you in the end."

Cecily was becoming mad herself at all the accusations

being tossed her way. "And yet you trust the friar, Isabella. Isn't he a man?"

Isabella paused her brushing and looked at her reflection thoughtfully.

"He is different," she eventually concluded.

"Different? The man's a fanatic. He's as mad as—"

Cecily bit down on her words, but not quickly enough. Isabella whirled around. "As mad as whom, Cecily?" she hissed.

Cecily did not answer.

"As mad as whom?"

Cecily shook her head. "Isabella—" she began, but got no further.

"And what is it that you and your maid get up to so secretly at night anyway? Where is it that you go, Cecily? Where is it that you send her?"

Cecily gasped and then went on the offensive herself.

"I am not the only one with secrets, am I, Isabella? What secrets are you keeping pray tell? Why did your family's old steward come here? What did he say to you? What is it that you know?" It was Isabella's turn to be shocked. "And what was all that mummery with the friar, Isabella? Playing the helpless girl and batting your eyelids at him. Perhaps you think of him at night, in your bed, touching you."

Isabella gaped. "How dare you! He is my confessor! And he is very interested in your midnight frolics, I can tell you."

A sudden chill swept through Cecily's body. It was a long moment before she could speak.

"What have you said to him, Isabella?"

Isabella turned back to her mirror and began brushing her hair again.

"Isabella? What have you told him?"

"Friar Justus was kind enough to hear my confession," she replied in a much calmer tone, "and he asked whether I had seen anything wicked. I could scarce lie to him now, could I? Not in confession." Her eyes became wide and round, all doe-like innocence. "Why? Is there something he should not know about? Are you doing something wicked, Cecily?"

Cecily's voice came out in a hoarse whisper: "You have no idea what you have done, Isabella."

Isabella glanced at Cecily in her mirror. "Do I not? Perhaps I am not as simple as you think. It is not *I* who is stealing about at night. It is not *I* who am plotting to steal my brother's inheritance."

Cecily stood motionless for a long time, the horrifying ramifications of what Isabella had done flooding through her mind, and then she walked from the chamber on unsteady legs, leaving Isabella staring calmly at her reflection.

Chapter 24

Thomas had still not been able to speak with Isabella, but since his discussion with Alice, he had been turning her strange behavior over and over again in his mind. How she avoided him. How she refused to answer his questions. Her mysterious relationship with Roger Lacy. And he had become more convinced than ever that she was in some way at the heart of this mystery. He recalled vividly now the first time he had met her in the little stone chapel and how she had emerged so furtively from Elyas's private cell, a guilty look on her face, almost as if Thomas had caught her in the midst of some indiscretion. At the time he had attributed Isabella's conduct to whimsy, but the inconsistencies in her explanation were now all too apparent to him. Why would she wait for the chaplain in his cell? Why would she not simply have summoned the man to her chambers or even to the private chapel in the manor house? For such a lady to be waiting for the chaplain in his personal quarters seemed to Thomas unseemly and unlikely. It had been pricking at him and had brought him back to the chapel, to where he had seen her that day.

"A bird does not shit in its own nest." Wasn't that what Alice had said to him?

Thomas pushed the door to the small room ajar, letting it

swing slowly inward, the light from the chapel spilling in to illuminate the inner gloom of the chaplain's cell.

The chaplain's quarters were meager indeed, as austere as the chapel itself. There were few furnishings inside: a cot with a thin mattress, covered in blankets that were neatly tucked and stretched firm; a shelf and a humble wooden cross on the wall; a traveling trunk; a milking stool with a bible sat atop; and a small rush mat covering the floor by the side of the bed. The walls were whitewashed plaster and the floor flagged stone. It had to be a cold and uncomfortable room come winter.

There was only one thing here he saw that could be of interest. He eased open the lid of the trunk. There was not much to see in there either: spare bedding, changes of clothes, a book or two. He lowered the lid and looked about him. He had heard the distinct scraping of furniture over wood before he had run into Isabella. She could have been sitting on the stool, he supposed, and have risen when she heard him. No, that would not have made such a sound. He tried the trunk. It was heavier than he had expected, much heavier, and when he dragged it to the side, it made the same scraping sound he had heard.

Kneeling down Thomas could see that one of the stone flags had been disturbed. He traced the edges with his fingertip and reached into his boot for the small knife he carried there. It was not much more than a fletching knife, really, but the blade was tempered steel and slid nicely into the crack. With it he was able to raise the flag just enough to reach beneath with the tips of his fingers and lift it up.

A small compartment had been carved out beneath the stone. The sides and floor were perfectly square and level, betraying an obsessive mind. Inside was a knife, much larger and much uglier than his own. There were also two small sacks, one filled to bursting with coin, the other with jewelry—brooches, rings, buckles, and one very ugly necklace. Neither interested him so much as the leather pouch. He picked it up, unstrung the tie and unfolded the pouch on the floor. Secured to the leather by strips of thread were a dozen neatly arranged locks of hair. The last one caught Thomas's eyes at once. Red. The same red as that of Margareta, the girl he had found in the woods. Next to it was a lock of almost golden hair. Another rare shade, and one he had only recently seen.

Twelve locks of hair. Twelve mementos for the sick man that left them here.

Thomas suddenly felt ill. He had been completely fooled, completely taken in. How could he have been so blind? He recalled the simpering face, the feigned humility, the pretense of horror and distress at the miller's death. How Elyas must have laughed at them all, even the miller's wife as he pretended to comfort her. Here was the monster of which Alice had spoken, hidden in plain sight exactly as she had said he would be.

Thomas's stomach lurched, and he covered his mouth with the back of his hand until the feeling of nausea passed.

He closed the pouch and replaced it. Then he reached for the only other thing in the compartment—several sheaves of neatly folded parchment tied with a slender blue ribbon. He unfolded the papers, drew them closer to the light from the door, and began reading the words scrawled across the vellum in an almost childlike script. And everything became clear. Everything fell into place.

He replaced the stone flag and trunk as he had found them and walked out of the chapel, across the courtyard, and into the Great Hall. Cecily came running up to him in a flurry of green skirts held up in her hands to reveal the white stockings and velvet shoes beneath. He could tell from her face that she was frantic.

"Thomas, I am in trouble! We are all in trouble!" she said breathlessly.

Thomas gripped Cecily's shoulders as she tried to catch her breath.

"Tell me. It cannot be more shocking than what I have to tell you."

"Isabella has told the Dominican about Alice. Well, not about her, I think, but enough. He knows that Hunydd visits the forest at night, and I am sure he will have followed her. I sent her out again earlier. You were right—I should not have done so, and now I have put us all in danger."

The words tumbled out in a rush, chasing one another so as to be almost insensible. Cecily grasped his hand. "Do you not understand, Thomas? I sent Hunydd to Alice, and I believe the Dominican will have followed. Isabella has told him all she knows—all she suspects. What if he has found Alice? What if Hunydd tells him?"

Thomas passed his hand across his brow. Things were coming together quickly. Strangely enough, even though disaster was in the air, he felt calm, perhaps even calmer now that the crisis had finally arrived.

Thomas briefly explained what he had uncovered in the chaplain's cell, only leaving out the details about the letters now tucked into his breast pocket. Cecily did not need to know about those. In truth, he did not know himself what to do with them, but he could figure that mess out after they had dealt with this one.

Cecily looked at him aghast but then, to her credit, took it in stride. "I shall have the guards seize him at once. He cannot be far."

As Thomas turned to leave, she caught his arm. "Thomas, be careful. I do not like the look of the man the Dominican has with him. That Guy de Hokenham, I think he calls himself. There is something . . . not right about him. He looks dangerous."

Thomas nodded and then he was running out the door, calling back over his shoulder for her to send for the constable.

Thomas was afraid, and fear gave energy to his actions. As he ran for his horse, his mind was already racing ahead. What if he were too late? And even if he were not, what could he hope to achieve? He doubted the night could end well.

★ ★ ★

Guy of Hokenham smiled. It was a wide smile, and even by the dirty light from the saucer lamp, Hunydd could see all his cracked and yellowed teeth.

"I cannot understand why all those fools moon about over your mistress. If they'd only open their eyes, they'd see there's a far tastier morsel right under their noses."

The tip of Guy's tongue darted out over his lips. It reminded Hunydd of a snake she had once seen slithering through the grass.

"Yes," he said, his eyes sliding over her from head to toe, "a much sweeter dish by far."

Hunydd was sitting on a crude bench in the abandoned hut at the edge of the forest that she passed by each night on her way to visit Alice. She thought about making a dash for the door, but Guy would catch her easily, and then he would hurt her. He'd already hurt her. When he had snatched her outside the village, he'd been really rough. His hands had pinched and groped. And he had deliberately torn her dress. That made her mad. It was her best kirtle, the one she liked to wear when she visited Dame Alice. She didn't even know what they had done with the pretty cloak her mistress had given her. Lady Cecily was sure to be angry with her for losing it. A tear trickled down Hunydd's cheek.

Guy dragged a stool over and sat down in front of her, close enough for Hunydd to smell his fetid breath.

"You like that Lester, don't you?"

Hunydd clutched the torn kirtle to her chest.

"Don't go fooling yourself, girl. He's not interested in some cottar's daughter. He'll be wanting to find himself a rich wife with a nice fat dowry, not a simple maid without a penny to her name."

His tongue flicked out again, licking his already wet lips.

"Why'd you want a pretty boy like that anyway? What you need is a real man. Someone who'd appreciate you and treat you right."

His voice was thick and raspy.

"That old friar is going to try you for a witch, you know."

"A–A witch. Why would he say I am a witch?"

"Silly girl," chuckled Guy, genuinely amused at her naivety. "Don't you even know who it is you've been visiting with? And by the time he's done with you, you'll confess to whatever he wants. I'm no angel, but the friar, he likes to hurt people. I've seen it in his eyes."

Guy leaned forward on his stool.

"Oh, he'll start nice enough. He'll ask you questions and be all friendly like. But then, even if you tell him what he wants to hear, he'll get nasty. He'll tie your hands together behind your back and haul them up in the air above your head. I've seen them do it. It'll hurt like a bastard and near pull your arms out of their sockets. And he'll just leave you hanging like that for a while. Give you a little time to yourself to think on things.

"Then he'll come back and strip you naked as the day you was born. And he'll ask you more questions. And it won't matter none to him what you say, he'll take the lash to you anyway. He'll lash you six times, and you'll think he's done. But then he'll give you six more, and then six more, till your back's all cut up and sliced.

"That's about the time when you'll tell him how you and that witch cavorted about naked with each other, how you pissed on the cross, and how you summoned demons so you could both lie with them. You might not think you'll say those things, but you will. Just like Kyteler's maid told that bishop in Ireland exactly what he wanted to hear. You'll even tell him how you poisoned the old vicar and killed Roger Lacy, leaving him lying across the altar to show how much you hate God."

"I won't tell him that," she half-shouted, half-sobbed. "I won't, because I didn't do any of that."

Guy shrugged.

"Maybe you did and maybe you didn't. It don't matter none. He'll whip the story out of you either way. Then he'll take you down, and you'll think he's done with you, and you'll be so happy you'll cry. But he isn't done with you. No, not nearly. Next, he'll straddle you over a wooden plank with bags of flour tied to your ankles and your hands still bound behind your back, and he'll leave you like that. After a while, it'll hurt so much you'll think you're going to split in two. You'll be screaming for him to come back, and when he does, he'll make you tell him everything all over again. And you will. Only you won't be able to remember all the lies you told him last time, so you'll make up some new ones. You'll tell him about even more wicked things you did, because you think that's what he wants to hear. And you'll tell him how you repent of all you've done and beg for forgiveness.

"But he's still not done. You'll think it can't hurt any worse, but you'd be wrong. Because next, he'll heat up some irons in the fire till they glow a nice cherry-red, and he'll place them on your back, on your legs, on your stomach. Aye, he'll even put them on your tits. And he's got other toys he'll want to use on you as well. I've seen them in his baggage. And they'll hurt even more than what he's already done.

"By now all you'll want is for it to end. You'll say anything he tells you to, and put your mark on anything he gives you.

"And then they'll tie you to a stake and you'll burn. But before you do, the old friar will be sure to tell you how he's saved your soul. And tell you how you ought to be grateful to him.

"You might not believe what I'm telling you, girl, but that's exactly what happened to Kyteler's maid. The one she left behind to die in her place. She'll leave you behind too; you see if she don't."

Hunydd was staring at him, her eyes round and wet. She knew what he was saying was a lie. It *had* to be. But all of a sudden she was terrified, and she felt very alone.

"Of course, it doesn't have to be like that for you. If you were to be nice to me, I could speak to the friar. We're close, you see, him and me. He *needs* me. If I were to ask him, he'd go easy on you. I could tell him as how you'd cooperate. And you could tell him about all the wicked things that Irish woman and your mistress have got up to in the forest. You might have to lay it on a little thick, but it's your mistress he really wants, and better her than you, I say. Maybe we could give him another name or two, just to be safe. Someone you're none too fond of, or some daft old bat from the village nobody would miss much.

"Who knows, with me speaking up for you, he might let you go. He might even give you a reward."

Guy leaned even closer and winked. "And all you got to do is be nice to me. Just do what I tell you. So, what do you say, my pretty, are you going to play nice?"

And that's when Hunydd spat full in his face.

For a moment he was too stunned to move. Then he grabbed Hunydd's arm and pulled her roughly to her feet. She tried to pull away from him, but his hand gripped her wrist tightly, crushing and painful.

"Let me go," she squealed, pushing at him with one hand and holding up her kirtle with the other.

"I'm going to forget you did that, seeing as how you've had a rough night. But you won't be doing it again."

He pinned her arms to her side and pulled her close so she could hardly move at all.

"There's no need for this to be unpleasant. If you do right by me, I'll make sure you like it. And once you've seen what I have to offer, you'll come around to my way of thinking soon enough. You'll forget all about your pretty boy."

She squealed through pursed lips as his tongue slithered out over her mouth and then licked her slowly from jaw to ear, leaving a sticky mess of saliva wherever it touched.

Guy laughed out loud. "That's the spirit, little one. I think we've had enough petting now, though. You'll bend to me girl, one way or another. I'll break your will, or I'll break you in half."

★   ★   ★

Thomas had just hobbled his horse near the old assart where he, John, and Will had held their strange midnight vigil, and was about to launch into the trees to find the track that would take him to Alice's cottage when he heard a muffled cry of anguish and fear from inside the hut. He did not stop to think, but ran toward it and burst through the door, hard enough that it bounced off the wall and slammed shut behind him.

Hunydd was on the floor, her kirtle torn halfway down her back. She scuttled into a corner, where she huddled like a beaten animal, clutching her ragged clothes about her.

Guy whirled around, hunched over and snarling like a wolf defending its kill. When he saw Thomas was alone, he uncoiled his body and drew himself up to his full lanky height.

"Where's the big man, then?"

When Thomas did not answer, Guy flashed a broad, crack-toothed grin. He was calm, unconcerned, his thumb idly rubbing the hilt of his knife.

"All alone tonight, eh? Best be on your way, cully. I've cut down men twice your size."

Thomas did not doubt it. The man was not large, but wiry, all sinew and muscle. He was likely quick and knew how to kill. Killing for most men did not come naturally. To this one it did. It did not matter how big you were, a knife across a tendon would cripple you, and a sharp blade to a vital point would end you. Being larger just meant you fell heavier in the end.

Guy slipped the knife halfway from its sheath, letting the blade rasp against the leather. "You'd be wise to bugger off now while you still can. This here's none of your business. Playing the hero will only get you dead."

Thomas was breathing heavily. He glanced at Hunydd, saw the frightened expression on her face, and set his feet.

Guy's laugh was full of scorn. "Think you can match with me, boy? That's funny."

He drew his knife slowly, menacingly. It was a wicked blade, a huntsman's knife. Guy tested the edge with his thumb and looked up at Thomas from the narrowed slits of his eyes.

"This here's the knife I use for nights like this. On other nights I have a nice thin rodello. *Sticker,* I call it. That one's good for when you come up behind a fellow. Nice and clean. Just a quick thrust to the heart or liver."

He jabbed forward, pantomiming a back stab.

"It's over real quick. No mess, no fuss. No cleaning up afterward. This one, though," he said, holding his knife up to the light, "this one I call *Slasher.* It makes a real mess when it cuts. The blade slices through a man's skin and muscle like it isn't even there. I keep the edge real sharp, too sharp to shave with. Just a touch and you'll bleed like a butchered swine."

Thomas edged to the side, trying to draw Guy farther away from Hunydd.

"*Sticker. Slasher,*" he mocked. "Those are names a child would come up with. What do you call yourself? *Gabbler?*"

"Oh, so you're a funny man, Lester. You won't be so funny when you're bleeding all over the floor. Maybe I'll give you a nice smile, though, all the way from one ear to the other."

Guy dropped low into a knife fighter's stance. "Last chance, boy."

Hunydd's eyes widened, and she flung herself at him.

"No, don't hurt him," she shrieked, clutching at the hand that held the knife. "Please!"

Guy was fast. He spun around, backhanded her, and shoved her hard against the wall, where she crumpled to the ground in a heap.

Thomas could feel the old anger welling up inside him. He'd kept a lid on it for a long time. No longer.

Had Guy not been the victor of so many back-alley brawls and knife fights, he might have been a little less confident. He might then have wondered why Thomas was unafraid. He might have noticed that he stood perfectly balanced, his muscles relaxed, his feet spread to bear his weight evenly so that he could easily spring in any direction. And he might even have realized he was not facing a drunken lout this time, or some unsuspecting victim, but a trained fighter.

Thomas was no farmer. Truly he was poor at it. Things did not seem to want to grow for him. Bishop Henry had once jokingly told him that he had what some folk called a brown thumb. No, Thomas was no farmer; he was and always had been a soldier. At times he had fooled himself into believing he could be something else and that perhaps the darkness would not follow him if he were a man of peace, surrounded by nature, making things grow. Or even a man of business, growing a nice healthy profit. But now that he stood facing Guy, all the things he thought to have forgotten came back to him.

As it happens, the fight did not last long at all. Guy came on in a rush. He knew that speed was the key to victory. The first cut was often the decisive one. He lunged and slashed, sweeping the knife from left to right, using short, wicked strokes as experienced knife fighters do. Just one cut, that was all he needed. Blue light flashed along the blade as it sliced and danced back and forth. Thomas backed away slowly, ducking from side to side, letting Guy advance toward him, and then, seeing his moment, with instinct more than thought, he sprang, caught Guy's wrist, and wrenched it forward.

The knifeman lurched off balance, caught by the surprising move. Guy recovered his feet quickly, but Thomas too was aware of the need to be decisive and smashed his palm upward under Guy's chin. Not too hard, but enough to rock Guy's head back. It was a stunning blow, and Thomas knew then that the fight was already won. He twisted Guy's wrist sharply, and the knife tumbled from numb fingers and clattered to the floor. Thomas was on him before the blade even struck dirt. Holding him steady by his twisted arm, he punched Guy hard in the face. Once. Twice. He heard the crack as Guy's nose broke, spraying a gout of blood over them both. But Thomas hit him again and again, Guy's head rebounding wickedly from each blow. There was no light in the man's eyes now, and he sagged limply, held up only by Thomas's grip.

Thomas drew back his fist to strike him again; a knuckled blow to the temple this time—a killing blow. But he happened to glance across and see Hunydd's expression. She was staring up at him in shock, her eyes big and round, and her hand pressed over her gaping mouth. Thomas froze in place. His chest was heaving, and his hair had fallen across his eyes. He probably looked half-crazed. The mist parted, and he could suddenly see Guy's ruined face, the blood smearing his fist and clothes, the way he must look to Hunydd, and he let Guy fall to the ground, dropping him like a sack of flour.

Thomas was filled with shame. He knew Hunydd would never look at him the same way again. They never did.

Hunydd clambered slowly to her feet. When Thomas reached out to help her, she brushed his arm aside, barely looking at him, and limped over to Guy. Holding her torn kirtle to her body, she delivered a vicious kick to his ribs with the toe of her neat little ankle boot. And another. And another. Drawing her leg back each time and grunting with effort. Guy's body jerked spasmodically, and Thomas heard the distinct cracking of a rib bone, maybe two, before he managed to rouse himself and haul her off.

It was then that the cottage door shuddered under a sudden, tremendous impact and burst inward, the frame shattering with a great crack, the door splintering almost down its entire length.

"I'll have you, you bastard!" yelled Constable John, his face a livid mask of fury.

When he saw the ruined body slumped on the floor, and the two of them standing over it, John unbunched his fists and hitched his belt up about his belly. "Well, I guess that's taken care of then. And there was me looking forward to a bit of a scrap. Especially with that bastard."

Hunydd gasped out loud. "Oh, God, Dame Alice! Thomas, they made me tell. I am so sorry. They said they would hurt me. They said—"

Thomas grasped her shoulders and looked her in the eyes. "All will be well, Hunydd, you'll see. And none of this is your fault." She looked down, and he tipped her chin up so she looked back at him. "Whatever happens, it's not your fault. Do you believe me?"

She nodded once, and he glanced from her to the body and then to the constable. The big man read his thoughts.

"Don't you worry; I'll take care of them both. Go and do what needs to be done, and be right quick about it."

Thomas nodded his thanks and was off, leaving the constable holding Hunydd gently to his chest. He did not look back. Had he done so, he might have seen that the black eyes following him bore not a trace of worry, and that her mouth twitched just slightly at the corner.

Deep down Hunydd had known that Thomas would save her in the end, and he had been so brave, like a knight from some old ballad riding to save his one true love. It was so romantic. Dawn was coming soon, and with it a new day. Everything was as it should be, just as she had imagined. And Hunydd was not afraid anymore.

CHAPTER 25

*There shall not be found with thee any one that maketh his son
or his daughter to pass through the fire, one that useth divination, one that practiseth augury, or an enchanter, or a sorcerer, or
a charmer, or a consulter with a familiar spirit, or a wizard, or a
necromancer. For whosoever doeth these things is an abomination
unto Jehovah; and because of these abominations Jehovah thy
God doth drive them out from before thee.*

—Deuteronomy 18:10–12

Friar Justus could scarcely believe his good fortune. *A witch.*
He had uncovered an honest to goodness witch. And not
just some mad old dabbler in the dark arts, but the Kilkenny
Sorceress herself! Hers was a capture sure to excite the whole of
Christendom.

His staff squelched and sucked at the mud of the leaf-strewn
forest path as he thumped it down excitedly in rhythm to his
stride.

God had finally seen fit to reward his faith. At long last he
was about to face a true diabolist. A woman known to be a necromancer and an invoker of demons, armed with spells, incantations, and God only knew what other unholy powers.

The Dominican's pace slowed to an amble. It was said Dame Alice Kyteler had killed at least three men. That she had summoned a powerful incubus to do her bidding. That she drank blood from the skulls of her victims. Justus now stood motionless in the middle of the path, gnawing his lip, his confidence slowly but surely ebbing away.

He had been so anxious to confront Kyteler before she could manage an escape that he had left Guy behind with strict instructions to follow along only after he had secured the maid for future examination. In hindsight that seemed a little rash. Perhaps he should have waited for Guy. Perhaps he should even turn back.

The Dominican huffed angrily. That was the Devil speaking, trying to sow seeds of doubt in his mind and deter him from his path. He would not listen to him. Besides, it was not as if he was unprepared. Justus patted the satchel hanging at his hip and felt the comfortable heft of his Bible and the irons with which he intended to shackle her. He had his cross. And he had his staff, hewn from solid English oak and weighted with a heavy brass tip. It had served before to deliver a beating or two to those he found wanting in grace, and it would more than suffice if Kyteler needed to be disciplined. Most importantly, he reminded himself, he would be shielded by his faith in the Lord. What greater protection could there possibly be against evil?

Justus stabbed his staff into the ground and strode ahead, ashamed of his momentary weakness. His pace quickened, and in his excitement he had to hold himself back from breaking into an unseemly shuffling run.

Once he had secured the witch, he would be able to bring the full weight of the Inquisition to bear upon Bottesford. Naturally, he would be the lead inquisitor. And there would need to be a second, someone who would defer to his experience, who would let him take the lead in the interrogations. A Franciscan would be perfect for the task—they tended to be meek and snivelly.

And there would be trials. The witch. The maid. And Lady Cecily would soon find out what it meant to harbor a known heretic. De Bray too. And even Lady Isabella. It was true that Isabella had helped him, and Justus would remember that in the final accounting, but there was something very disturbing about her, and he could not get the image of that unholy mirror out of his mind. No, she would have to be tried as well.

But he was getting ahead of himself. First, let him bring home his prize.

The little cottage squatted in the clearing, dark and foreboding, its thatched roof spilling out over the walls like a ragged mop of hair over a glowering brow. As Justus approached, the very air about him grew stale. He could sense the corruption and smell the sweet, cloying scent of death and decay. It was a fitting nest for one who communed with the dead.

Candlelight flared behind the shutters and winked at him accusingly through the cracks. Somehow she knew he was there. She had sensed his presence. Good. It was for the best. It is not for the servant of God to creep about in the darkness like a common sneak thief, and Justus was keen to confront his nemesis. He strode purposefully toward the cottage, trampling the Michaelmas daisies underfoot, and burst through the door, sending it shuddering against the wattle wall with a gratifying crash.

And there she was, in the center of the room, dressed only in her shift, a shocked expression on her face, a smoky candle almost falling from the hand that held it.

Justus shook his hand loose from his sleeve and pointed a bony finger at her. "Stand fast thou foul demon lover. I am come to visit upon you the wrath of the Lord God Almighty."

He had thought long and hard about what to say as he had walked through the forest. The words did not come out quite as he had planned, though they were good enough, and he could always work on them a little before recounting the tale. His pose, at least, was suitably heroic. He stood tall and erect, chest puffed out, legs spread wide, feet and staff planted firmly on the ground, head held aloft, eyes blazing with righteous fury, and his finger pointing accusingly at her as he pronounced God's judgment.

The impression was rather spoiled though when the door rebounded back sharply from the wall, striking him painfully on the shoulder and rear, causing him to take a staggering step or two to the side. A small detail, he thought, that could reasonably be omitted from the final telling.

Justus glanced about the room, lit only by the sputtering light from her candle, and found himself quite disappointed with what he saw. It was, in fact, a rather ordinary little cottage, with crumbling wattle walls, a mud-packed floor presently scattered with rushes in an attempt at homeliness, and a central stone hearth over which was suspended an ancient bronze cooking pot. Other than a slightly dank and musty odor, the only thing remarkable about it was the large, wonky table occupying fully one side of the room. There was no mirror, no diabolical statue, no heathen shrine or defaced crucifix. At least not that he could see. Nor was Dame Alice at all what he had imagined.

He lowered his arm and felt the tension draining out of him.

"I must say you do not look much like a murderess."

"Perhaps that is because I am not."

Justus harrumphed. "In truth, I was expecting something a little more . . . sinister."

Justus was not quite sure what he had imaged such a famous sorceress would look like. In his mind he supposed he had pictured her as an old hag crouched over a pagan altar, sacrificing a goat; or perhaps sprawled on the floor, naked limbs entwined in a lascivious embrace with her demon lover. As it was, she stood barefoot, dressed in the kind of long white shift any elegant lady might wear to bed, her hair uncovered and hanging down over her left shoulder in a tight braid secured with what looked to be twists of damascene lace. To all intents and purposes she looked rather more like a common fleece merchant's wife than a witch. Quite ordinary. And she was hardly threatening, standing there half-naked with her trembling hand clutching her smoky candle. How foolish he had been, allowing his fears to get the better of him. This one would give him no trouble, no trouble at all.

"Did I not know any better, I might take you for some wealthy burgher's wife."

"I *was* a wealthy burgher's wife."

Justus harrumphed again. She had probably cast a glamor to hide her true form. She had also likely hidden away the tokens of her devilry. No matter. He was sure a diligent inquiry would reveal more than enough iniquity here to condemn her.

"Perhaps you were a once a burgher's wife, but we both know what you have become."

Justus smiled smugly, his confidence growing by the second. "I am sorry to have disturbed your rest, but I could not risk you fleeing again."

She licked her lips and Justus's smile widened. She was actually afraid of him. That was good. Very good and very reassuring.

"You are Friar Justus?"

Justus could hear the soft Irish brogue. Some people found it charming. To his ear it was grating and common, even more so than the guttural tones of the Northerners.

"Ah, I see my fame goes before me. Then you must know why I am here. Did you really think you could escape God's judgment?"

"You wrong me, sir. I have done nothing of which I should be ashamed or for which God would judge me."

Justus hooted derisorily. First would come the denials. It was always the same.

"You say that you are innocent, madam, and yet you flee from justice."

Alice grimaced as though she had tasted something very bitter. "Justice. Is that what you call it? What *justice* could I expect at the hands of Richard Ledrede. He had already decided my fate. I would receive no justice there. I am an innocent woman who has been terribly wronged. Cast out of her home and forced to flee for her life."

"Yet your accomplices all confessed freely to your crimes."

"They confessed under torture." The hand holding the candle was shaking noticeably now, spilling its flickering, smoky light hither and thither. Were she any more afraid, she might drop it altogether.

"You appear to be afraid of me, dear. Am I so fearsome a sight?"

She smiled weakly. "Who would not be afraid when faced with an inquisitor such as yourself?"

Justus knew she was doing her best to be agreeable, but he enjoyed the compliment nevertheless. In truth, he supposed he had been fishing for it. He reminded himself that pride was a sin. Whatever fame or glory he would receive for tonight's work belonged to God. Justus was but a humble instrument of His power.

"I am sure if we sit down like reasonable people, I can explain everything to you." Alice gestured to the table. "I have some wine. Perhaps we might share a cup. It is from the vineyards of Gascony. I am sure you will find it to your liking."

"Oh, that's rich, madam," he sneered. "Do you take me for a fool that I would accept a cup of wine from the hands of a woman known to have poisoned her husbands. I think not."

"Then I could offer you money. I do not have much, but

what little I managed to bring with me is yours if you just let me go. I shall never return. You have my word."

First come the denials, and now the bribes. Again, how terribly predictable she was. And how prophetic had been his words at that first audience before the lord of the manor when he had declared that Alice Kyteler would not escape God's judgment. He had not known then that the very woman of whom he spoke was within arm's reach, and he could not have imagined that it would be he, Friar Justus, who delivered her unto that judgment. Surely God's grace had filled him that day. He had always known God was saving him for something special and was ashamed now at his moments of weakness when he had begun to despair.

When he responded, it was with smug satisfaction: "You mistake me. I have given myself to God's service. Man can have but one master. He cannot serve God and mammon both. No, lady, money is nothing to me."

This felt right. Rebuffing her with the word of God. Justus could almost see himself in the chapter house before his brethren describing the scene. He could also see himself summoned to recount events before the archbishop, or even to Avignon to appear before the pope. Yes, why not the pontiff? He made a mental note to scour his bible before then for verses that might further augment the story. That might flesh it out, so to speak. But so far, he had to say he was quite pleased with his performance.

Alice was casting about nervously.

"Oh, there is no escape for you, witch, and I am much stronger than I look."

And in that moment he felt strong. He felt young, tall, and powerful. There were no more aching bones. Even the persistent catch and scratch at the back of his throat seemed no longer to be such an irritant. What would they say now in Avignon?

What would they say at the Dominican house in London? Justus, the one who battled against an invoker of demons and cast her down. The one who matched wits with the Devil's disciple and overcame her.

"And, besides," he added, "my man will be here soon. Rather you deal with me than him. He is a bit of a brute and is unlikely to be as gentle with you as I."

Where was that villain anyway? He really ought to have been there by now. Perhaps it was a mistake to leave him with the girl. He was so easily tempted by the lures of the flesh. If Guy had laid his hands on her . . . well, there was nothing Justus could do about it now.

Alice lowered the candle and looked up coyly from under her lashes. Her eyes were a remarkable violet, and when she spoke, it was with a low, honeyed voice as smoky as the candle she was tipping about.

"Must we really be enemies, Justus? I assure you that I am quite innocent of the charges leveled against me. And perhaps there is something else I have to offer that would be more to your liking. Something that might appeal to a strong, powerful man such as yourself."

The light threw into relief the swell of her bosom against the thin linen fabric, and she lifted her chemise with her free hand, showing first a calf, then a knee, and then a flash of pale thigh.

"I feel sure we could come to some mutually agreeable arrangement, something that might prove pleasing to both of us. I know what men like, and I am sure that you will not be disappointed. If you allow me, if you permit me, I can show you a heaven right here on earth, and in return you can fill me with your . . . grace. I would be willing to do anything to convince you of my innocence. Truly, . . . anything."

She gave him another sultry look and lifted her skirts

just a little higher, giving him a glimpse of the pleasure that awaited him.

Justus had to grudgingly admit that she was attractive, beautiful even, and for a moment he actually found himself intrigued by the possibilities. He could have her now. She would let him do what he wanted with her. She would even let him beat her if he wished. His eyes wandered slowly up her leg, to her tits, to her mouth, to her eyes, and then he remembered what she was. And he remembered that a beautiful woman in want of discretion was as a gold ring in a pig's snout.

"Do not try to tempt me, harlot. I have given myself to God's service. Your arts and allures have no power over me."

"I have no arts, I tell you," she insisted angrily, letting the chemise fall back to the floor, almost stamping her foot in annoyance. "And any allure I have is only what the good Lord gave to me the day I was born."

This was just as Justus had imagined. It was too perfect. It was as though the Devil himself were testing him through this woman, just as he had tested Jesus in the garden of Gethsemane. First greed. Then avarice. Now lust. It mattered not to what sin she appealed, however; Justus was not one to be turned from his task. He was as the rock, impervious to her charms.

"No, you shall not tempt me."

He coughed. She was burning something foul in her cheap candle. The smoke was filthy and acrid, stinging his eyes, cloying in his throat. He wiped his eyes with the back of his hand. *Some witch,* he thought. She could not even trim a candle properly.

"Let me go, I beg you. I shall leave and not return."

Pleading. After denials and bribes it always came to pleading. Why, he should write his own treatise on interviewing heretics. Something that would put De Gui's nonsensical scribbles to shame. How his wisdom would be revered.

Alice hung her head. "What . . . what will happen to me now?"

And there it was. The final phase: resignation and fear, and so quickly arrived at.

"Will you turn me over to the bishop?"

"That fat Irish fool. Hmm, perhaps, but I shall have a few questions for you myself first."

Yes, she would face questioning from a real inquisitor. No doubt she would lie and he would be forced to employ harsher measures. Slowly the lies would give way to half-truths, and then the sweet moment would arrive when she would tell him everything: all her filthy secrets; the names of all her acolytes, all her accomplices, and all those who had offered her succor and comfort. Anything he wanted.

"If you cooperate fully and throw yourself on God's mercy, there may yet be redemption, even for one such as you."

Her redemption would be the fire. She would burn when he was done with her. He had no doubt of that. But let her nurse some slim hope. She would be far more malleable and willing to confess to her crimes if she thought that she might thereby receive mercy.

Justus coughed again, a dry hacking cough that almost bent him over. His eyes were tearing up from that foul smoke. As much as he was enjoying himself, it was time to end this exchange and take her somewhere where the examination might be more intimate and where there would be no damned untrimmed smoky candles. There was no ventilation at all in this miserable squat hole.

Justus reached into his bag. He would shackle her hand and foot and parade her through the village like the wicked temptress she was.

"Come now, matham, ith time for uth to go."

The friar was appalled to find that his words had come out slurred, almost like those of a drunken sot. He coughed again.

The smoke was becoming unbearable, choking almost, and it was burning his eyes. He scrubbed angrily at them to clear his vision. The light from the candle seemed to be getting blurry. He wiped the back of his hand across his eyes again. But it was not just the light that was blurry. Her face was blurry too, and the room was beginning to spin. Justus shook his head, trying to clear his thoughts.

The hand that held the candle was no longer trembling, and Alice smiled slowly—an unpleasant, knowing smile that chilled the Dominican's blood.

"I am sorry, is my candle bothering you, priest? I made it myself, you know. It is somewhat acrid I must admit, but I have become used to it. To others the smoke can be irritating, though—deadly even."

She had such bright teeth. Her eyes seemed to change color, and they were so large, the pupils huge, the entire eye almost black. Justus was entranced by her, spellbound, and could not look away.

"You see the irritation from the smoke encourages the rubbing of eyes, allowing the poison to seep deeper into the body. It is quite a clever trick, really. I actually got the idea from the common nettle. Who would have thought it? Scratching at the nettle rash only makes it worse, you see."

She laughed out loud. The sound was tinny in his ears.

"And you thought I would poison you with wine. How crude, when there are so many more effective methods. The poison enters the body so much more quickly, so much more effectively, through the eyes. But then, as an experienced herbalist, you would understand this."

She was mocking him, but the Dominican found that he scarcely cared. He was coughing harder now, his breath wheezing in his chest. It was becoming difficult to inhale, and he was dragging air into his lungs.

Alice jutted out her lower lip and pouted at him. "But, Friar, you do not seem interested in my candle at all, and after I spent so much time in its crafting. I am quite hurt. Was this not precisely the sort of thing that you came here to find?"

Her face was swimming before him now. If he did not leave at once, he was sure he would faint.

"No!" he exclaimed loudly, tearing his eyes away from her. He stumbled backward, tore open the door, and lurched out into the night, sucking in great lungfuls of air. He had dropped his staff somewhere. He did not remember having done so. And that scent—he could not get it out of his nostrils. It was making it difficult for him to concentrate. Difficult to breathe.

Justus staggered away from the hut on unsteady legs, walking like a drunken man. He could sense her behind him and hear the drag-thump of his satchel as she trailed it along the floor. He had dropped that as well, it would seem.

The Dominican took a few more stiff steps and fell to his knees. He turned to see her close behind him. Her eyes were full black now, her face pale like that of a corpse, all except her lips, which were blood-red and peeled back to reveal such bright, white teeth.

Justus threw his hands into the air and lifted his face to the heavens: "Oh, Lord, send fire, send lightning, let the earth open and swallow her."

Alice paused and looked about, turning her face first to one side and then the other.

"Shall we give Him a moment or two?" she asked in a perversely reasonable manner.

She lifted the hem of her shift and stamped on the ground. "No, nothing, I'm afraid."

"O Lord," he wailed, "burn the foul mocking words in her mouth; set her tongue on fire that she might not pollute this world with her filthy sacrilege. Let her taste naught but the ashes of her corruption."

Alice smiled and licked her lips slowly, lasciviously, the pink tongue circling her mouth fully. "Still nothing? Well, I imagine He is terribly busy, what with all the wailing and fawning that goes on in church these days. There is so much for Him to listen to. So many favors asked. So many sinners who wish to unburden their souls. You should not take it personally."

She stepped closer, and Justus shrank away from her, falling over backward, bumping his backside hard on the ground and sending a jarring pain up through his spine.

"God shall smite you," he tossed over his shoulder as he crawled away. "He shall burn you in the fires of hell. He shall—"

His latest outburst was greeted by gales of mocking laughter. "Oh, you men and your hellfire. I know, I know, Eve's daughter and all that." She wiped a tear from her eye. "You are such a silly old goat, but I must confess I have not had as good a laugh in some time. Well, I would hate to disappoint you, and we really must be moving along. I have things to do and places to go—a ship to catch before the next tide turns. I have so very little time for this sort of thing. I am sure that you understand."

"You would not dare to touch a servant of the Lord. Stay back, you whore of Satan. Beelzebub's bitch!"

Justus fumbled at his chest for the cross that hung there. He thrust it out at her and turned his head aside, his eyes screwed firmly shut.

And suddenly, something wonderful happened. Something miraculous. She stopped, rooted to the spot. The Dominican opened first one eye, then the other, and was surprised to see her standing dumbfounded, a startled expression on her face. A surge of triumph flowed though him. God had answered his pleas and confounded her. He had given his servant power over the witch.

His lips curled in triumph, and grasping the cross more tightly, he staggered to his knees, thrusting it toward her, feeling its power, God's own grace working through him. The witch was confused. Dazed. Paralyzed. It was as though God had turned her into a pillar of salt as he did with Lot's wife.

"Yes, yes, feel the might of the Lord," he sneered. "Feel him acting through his loyal servant. How great Thou art, Lord," he proclaimed loudly, casting a tear-streaked face upward. "Thou hast blessed thy servant indeed this night!"

Alice's face suffused with delight, and she clapped her hands together in glee.

"Oh, that's wonderful, Father. I shall have to remember that. I have been called so many things, but never that. *Beelzebub's bitch*," she repeated, rolling the words around appreciatively in her mouth. "It has a certain . . . cadence to it. You really are so very clever."

She reached down, plucked the cross from his nerveless fingers, and gave his nose a playful little tweak. The Dominican blinked once in shock, then let out a piteous howl.

Justus was sobbing as he half-stumbled, half-crawled toward a small byre where he imagined the cottage's inhabitants must have kept their animals when the living still claimed this unholy place. His left leg seemed to have stopped working altogether, and he dragged it along behind him. *Scrape, thump. Scrape, thump.* It was almost too much effort to move anymore, and he barely made it into the little shed before collapsing onto his face, tasting dirt and aged, rotten straw in his mouth, no longer able to move any of his limbs, as helpless as a landed fish. He could hear a strange keening whine and realized it was coming from him. Drool was dribbling down his chin, and he feared he might just have emptied his bladder.

He could only move his head now, and so he did, and then wished he hadn't as he saw a madman stripped to his waist and lashed to a post, his bulging eyes rolling white, and his mouth twisted and frothy with spittle. The madman looked remarkably like De Bray's chaplain. Or how the man might appear if beggared and reduced to imbecility. On seeing Justus, he began a strange ululating laughter that ended in something Justus could only describe as a maniacal cackle; a cackle that itself ended in a sob and then pathetic little whimpering sounds once Alice stepped over the threshold.

"Ah, I see you have found my other guest. You may remember Father Elyas. Well, at least that was what he called himself for a while. He came here thinking to extort from me. Imagine, trying to take advantage of a poor defenseless woman. And such things he suggested. Why, it would make you blush. I truly doubt there will be any place for him in God's kingdom. Your visit, by contrast, has been quite amusing."

Justus wanted to curse her again, but his tongue was numb, and he could only manage to utter small half sounds from his throat.

"Wi'ed, wi'ed, mmppff—"

She stuffed a smelly, greasy rag into his mouth, wadding it inside until his cheeks bulged.

"That's quite enough now. I am starting to get offended. You shall soon be completely unable to move, though I am afraid you will feel all."

A muffled moan escaped from somewhere deep in his throat.

"Now what comes first in your torture—ah, sorry, your interview? Oh yes, I have it. Women always need to have their clothes removed, don't they? It makes them more compliant, I understand. But that is of no great moment to me. I have been removing my clothes for men since I was a slip of a girl. I imagine it might make you a little uncomfortable, however. But you should remember we are all the same before God. And besides, I have seen it all before."

Justus looked up at her helplessly. Her hair had become disheveled and hung loosely about her like a mane. The lines of her face had hardened, and her eyes glinted with crazed malice. Her voice was no longer soft and honeyed, but as hard as flint, as cold as ice, filled with bitterness and fury.

"Did you truly imagine you could challenge me? That you could gainsay and humiliate me? A pathetic creature such as you, who comes here with your cheap bag of tricks and lies? I shall show you terror from which no cross nor monkish robe can protect you. I shall bring you to your knees in horror, little man."

Justus mewled in terror, and the thing that had once called itself Elyas looked on with goggling eyes, cackling wildly, drool dribbling down from a crooked, sagging mouth.

CHAPTER 26

Friar Justus had seen his victory crumble and turn to ash in his hands. In the end, it was Thomas who found him. He had been stripped naked and was shackled with his own irons. His elbows were trussed to his knees. His bony backside, blackened with pitch and covered with feathers, was thrust up in the air. Strips of his own robes had been stuffed deep into his mouth. On hearing someone approach, he began squirming about frantically, uttering a tirade of muffled squeals.

The memory brought a smile to Thomas's face even now.

As for Alice, she had completely disappeared with all her belongings. How she had contrived to do so, he could not say. And yet there could be no doubt that she was gone. Seeing what she had wrought, Thomas felt no need to follow and make sure of her safety. Rather, he pitied those who crossed her path.

Thomas stood by the rood screen of Saint Mary's Church. He had found his murderer there, knelt before the very altar he had desecrated, staring about him wildly, the altar cloth gripped tightly in his fist as though it was the last stick of a capsized ship. There appeared to be little left of the man he had been. His face was drawn and pale, the cheeks hollow, his hair bristling this way and that as though he had been dragged backward more than once through a hedge. His tattered robe did little to cover his dignity and looked to be stained with what Thomas suspected was his own night soil.

"I seen it, I tell you," he wailed. "Those eyes. It's the Devil I seen. The Devil! It's coming for me. For what I done."

It had been like that all morning. Every now and then he would scream and flap his arms in front of his face like he was warding off a swarm of stinging flies. Sometimes he would curl up into a tight ball, rocking backward and forward with his arms wrapped protectively around his head. And sometimes he would just stare vacantly, drool dribbling down his chin.

"Oh, Jesu miserere. Domine ne in furore," he pleaded, tears streaming down his face.

Thomas heard the sound of sandaled feet, and the young Dominican friar walked up next to him. For a moment he stood watching the babbling remnant of De Bray's chaplain in silence.

"His mind has completely gone. There is nothing left of the man." Thomas could not recall having heard the young friar speak before. "I wonder what she did to him."

"I don't know," replied Thomas, "but he will not leave the altar. He screams if anyone tries to pull him from it. Brother Eustace said to leave him there until he exhausts himself."

"Did he really do all of those terrible things?"

Thomas nodded. "Those things and many more, I suspect."

The madman's eyes fell on the friar. "Oh, Father in heaven, bless me, please. Bless me, for I am in hell!"

He started to crawl toward Dominic but then hesitated and scuttled back to the altar, wiping his grimy cheek against the cloth still clutched in his fist.

It would have been easy for Dominic to go to him, to bless him as he asked. But he was apparently disinclined to do so. "Who is he?"

Thomas shook his head. "I do not know. But he is not Father Elyas. I suspect that poor man lies in a ditch or marsh somewhere between here and Oxford. I do not know who he truly is or where he is from. Or what drove him to this."

"Do you think we shall ever know?"

"I doubt it. As you said, his wits are gone."

"Look at the way his eyes roll, Thomas. The way he flaps his arms before him. What is it that he sees? Of what is he afraid?"

"I don't know. I don't *want* to know."

That was not entirely true. Thomas did know of hexes like this one, and what visions they could conjure, but he had never seen one so powerful or one that worked so fast.

Dominic shrugged. "Well, God has surely punished him for his sins now. Who is to say this fate is not worse than others that might await him. The sheriff may still choose to hang him, of course."

A mad cackle erupted from the creature, followed by another look of mortal terror.

"Though a noose may be a kindness to him now. I do wonder what could have happened to him. I suppose we will never know. And why did he kill the old man, Lacy, in the first place? A harmless beggar?"

"Some mad reason of his own, I suppose," Thomas answered evasively. He was not about to betray what he knew. The letters he had taken from the chaplain's hidey-hole were still stuffed inside the breast of his tunic, and they would remain there until he could return them to their author.

Dominic looked at Thomas for a long while without saying anything, until the madman began wailing again.

"I didn't see. I didn't see. Not at first. How could I? Oh, God, please help me. She says he'll come for me. That he'll drag me down to hell, where I shall roast in hellfire, where I shall be tormented without end. That demons will feast upon my very soul!"

Having seen enough, Thomas and the friar walked outside,

where they saw Justus sitting astride a mule, looking at Thomas with hate-filled eyes.

"Thomas," began Dominic, "my brother asked that I speak with you on his behalf. It is our desire that this matter be considered concluded. You have your murderer. There is no need for any more to be said."

"And what of blasphemy? What of heresy?"

"As far as I can tell the priest died of a heart condition; three others died at the hands of a madman. What need is there to discuss blasphemy?"

Thomas jerked his chin at Justus. "And he is alright with that?"

Dominic shrugged. "He wants nothing said. His pride would be crushed were it to be known that he had Kyteler in his grasp and lost her through his own arrogance. That and the things she did to him. He will take that to the grave, I think. In some ways she broke him as surely as she did the fool at the altar. No, as far as anybody but we few know, Dame Alice was never here. There was no heresy. There was no witch. Soon the Church shall forget about this place, and its people can all go back to the quietude and anonymity they enjoyed before ever any of us arrived. I think that is best for all concerned."

"And what of you? What of your abbot?"

"My brother's conduct does not reflect well on our order. We are all too aware of his . . . tendencies. We are also aware of the unfortunate reputation we have garnered in recent years thanks to a few misguided men like Justus. That is why I was asked to accompany him in the first place. I think I can speak for the abbot in saying that silence on this matter suits us as much as it does everyone else. Nor will the archbishop be disappointed to hear nothing has come of this little escapade. His assistance was reluctant at best."

"And Despenser?"

"I fear dark times are coming, Thomas. Rebellion is in the

wind again, and the war with France goes poorly. The king and Despenser will have little time to be concerned with the comings and goings in a little provincial village."

Thomas nodded and grasped Dominic's arm, feeling the pressure returned. "Then I think we have an understanding." He spoke a little louder for the benefit of their audience. "Please thank Friar Justus for his visit and wish him a comfortable journey back to London."

The Dominican huffed loudly and shifted uncomfortably on his mule, his rear end doubtless still tender from the vigorous scrubbing it had needed—a scrubbing Thomas had made sure was performed by several women from the village who had laughed giddily throughout the entire process.

Constable John lumbered up, casting a sullen gaze at the friars as they headed down to the village main street.

"Well it's good riddance to them two I say."

"Friar Dominic is not like his master."

"I guess there's hope then." John spat to the side to ward off evil. "Is he still in there?"

"Yes, he won't be coming out soon, John. Eustace will come for him when he has spent his strength and has no choice but to sleep."

John spat again. "I always knew there was something fishy about him. I said as much to Dotty more than once. It don't surprise me none that he's the one that did it. I had it in my mind all along it might be him."

"Not demons? Not witches then?"

"Like I said, I keep an open mind."

"Did you find anything, John?"

Thomas had dispatched the constable with a few other men to search for signs of Alice's passing in the woods.

"Maybe," he answered. "We found some track at the edge of the forest leading to the Melton road. Way I figure it, she'll be making her way to Hull and catching a ship from there. You want that we should follow?"

Thomas shook his head, and the constable nodded in both agreement and relief, and then flinched as a loud wail echoed from the church.

"You don't suppose she was, well, that she was really, you know . . ." John left his fear unspoken lest it bring down bad fortune upon them.

"I don't know for sure, John."

Ah, but Thomas did know. He wondered whether he had always known from the first time they met. He thought that maybe he had.

"But I do know that she was not the woman our madman thought her to be. I suspect he came to extort her wealth. Perhaps on seeing her, he wanted more. He imagined that he was the monster, not she."

John puffed out his cheeks. "And to think we sat down at her table." His shook his head in disbelief. "Will you be on your way now?"

"I have to visit the manor first."

"Oh, aye." The constable raised his eyebrows and smirked. "Left something there did you?"

Thomas laughed, touched the bulge at the breast of his tunic, and slapped John on one of his massive arms. "I have some letters to deliver, and then I shall head back to Lincoln."

"Well, I suppose this is it then?" John in his turn clapped Thomas on the shoulder. "I shall speak with the reeve, and we'll work something out for your place, make sure it's ready for you when you return. You'll be welcome here, by more than just the manor."

Thomas smiled his gratitude. The big oaf had grown on him, and he proceeded to crush Thomas in a monstrous embrace that left him almost as breathless as Cecily's kiss.

★ ★ ★

A short while later Thomas stood in Isabella's parlor. They were alone, and she had listened as he recounted the events of the night.

"I believe these are yours, my lady. You wrote them long ago, when you were very young."

He held the bundle of letters out to her.

She reached out to take them but hesitated, looking up at him suspiciously. "You give them to me freely?"

"They are not mine to keep. They belong to the one who wrote them in the first place."

Isabella gasped out the breath she had been holding and snatched them from his hand. She held them quickly to the candle's flame before he could change his mind and, once they were well alight, tossed them into the brazier and stood silently watching them burn.

Hers was a sad tale. She had written the letters to another man not long before she had married De Bray. To an uncle, Thomas believed. She had pleaded for him to fetch her away, her and the child she feared that she carried for him, each letter scrawled in its childlike hand more desperate than the last. But he never came. The letters had gone unanswered. They had been entrusted to the steward, Roger Lacy. Thomas wondered whether the old man had ever thought to deliver them or whether he had somehow learned their content at the time and simply squirreled them away for future use. Her family must have married Isabella hurriedly, before she showed. The story, and Isabella's . . . oddities explained how a gruff old soldier like De Bray was able to secure such a seemingly advantageous match to the beautiful young daughter of a powerful family. A match that, unbeknownst to him, had also brought with it a bastard child who by rights would stand to inherit nothing but shame.

"You will not mention this?" she asked over her shoulder,

still watching the smoldering ash. "Even to Cecily . . . *especially* to Cecily?"

"I will not."

She sighed with relief, and then turned to him, looked down and swallowed thickly. "And, . . . and in return?"

"And in return I only ask that you live a happy life. The life you were meant to live. And that you raise your son to be a good man who will one day be a good lord to the people here."

"You ask nothing of me? Even though I treated you ill?"

Thomas shook his head.

"Do you judge me?"

"Not I."

She averted her eyes. "He made me do things, Thomas." It was the first time he remembered her using his name. "Terrible things."

"I think I know the kind of man he was. He shall never trouble you again."

At that moment the door banged open, and Isabella's son came running in and hurled himself at his mother, burying his face in her skirts. She put her arm around him and looked up at Thomas with tear-filled eyes.

"And, my lady," he added as an afterthought, "might I suggest you rid yourself of that mirror?"

Isabella knotted her brows together, looking from him to the mirror and then back again, giving him a bewildered look that suggested she suspected him to be half mad.

★   ★   ★

Cecily was waiting for him at the entrance to the Great Hall. Thomas realized that by keeping Isabella's secret, he might be depriving her of a valuable inheritance, but he had chosen what he thought to be the lesser evil, and Cecily had made clear that she had no wish to be a wealthy heiress, vulnerable to unscrupulous men who would only seek to use her for her birthright. In all, he thought she would approve of his decision. Either way, the decision was made.

"What will you do now, Thomas?" she asked.

"I must report to Bishop Henry, though I doubt he will believe what I tell him."

Thomas would have to be fairly circumspect with the truth. The tale Dominic suggested would serve best.

"And after. Will you return?"

"I think I must, my lady." He smiled at her. "Did you forget that I have land here? A hundred acres or so, I believe."

She laughed. "So you do, and I am glad. It would please me for you to return soon."

She looked down shyly and touched him lightly on his arm. He covered her hand with his own.

"It would please me too, Cecily."

No further words were necessary.

De Bray limped out to join them and put an arm around his daughter's shoulder. He looked better. There was a healthy flush of color in his cheeks, and he looked younger, less fragile, like he was regaining his strength.

Thomas said his farewells, and they both stood at the top of the steps, watching him ride away.

"He will come back, won't he?" Cecily asked.

"Do you like him so much, then?"

She ignored the question, knowing her father already knew the answer. "He will come back. I know he will. He has a reason to do so. And he is a knight's son, is he not?"

De Bray squeezed her shoulder, and she snuggled against him. "Yes, he is. And I have already written to Henry. He will make sure your young man is back here soon enough. Now, come inside. You and I have some things to discuss."

CHAPTER 27

Thomas was harnessing his horse when he heard her running through the mud, the little ankle boots sucking and squelching against the wet ground. She stopped a few paces away, breathing heavily, one hand clapped to her linen cap, a small sack dangling from the other.

Thomas barely looked up from his task. "You have come a long way, Hunydd." The walk from the manor to his little cottage was well over a mile, and it looked as though she had covered the distance in some haste. "Won't Lady Cecily miss you?"

She ignored his question.

"She said you are leaving?"

"I am. I must make my report to the Bishop of Lincoln."

Hunydd chewed her lip in thought. "I have never seen Lincoln. They say the cathedral sits high on top of the hill so that it can be seen for miles all around. They say it is the finest church in all of England."

"It is one of the finest, to be sure," he allowed.

"I should like very much to see Lincoln, Thomas. I should like to see the imp you told me about. The one the angel trapped up on the stone pillar after he had spanked the other one. I should like you to tell me the story again."

Thomas nodded to the sack she held dangling from her hand. "What's that you have there?"

"Only what I need to bring with me."

He tightened the cinches on his horse's saddle. "You would be a runaway, Hunydd."

The lord of a manor had a year to hunt down any villein of his that left the estate, in which time he could drag them back to be branded and to face justice.

"I don't care. And in any case, they won't call me a runaway. You see, I am—" She paused awkwardly, her face flushing even more. "I am—"

"De Bray's bastard child?"

"Yes," she replied emphatically. "It does not make me dirty, does it, to be a bastard? My mother said it was not my sin. That it was my father's sin. You don't think less of me now, do you?"

"Why would I?"

He nodded again to the sack she now clutched to her chest. "You travel light."

"I don't need much. It's not fair that they took me from my mother, Thomas, that they brought me here and made me their servant. But if I must serve them, then I would see some of the world first. I should like to see it with you. To travel as you have done, even if only for a little while. And . . . and I would not be any bother to you. I can take care of myself. I can take care of you as well. You would not regret it if you were to take me with you."

Thomas turned to face her. "You should know I was married once and that I loved my wife"

Hunydd looked at him, completely unmoved, as if he had said nothing. She had sensed it on him of course. The sadness of a love cut short, of a great loss. But there was more. She had noticed the pendant he wore the first time she saw him. He probably didn't even know it was a charm. But she knew, and she knew it meant he had once been claimed by another—one like her, who must have felt the same attraction to him that she did.

"You should also know that whatever is left of my heart to give is now pledged to another, should she wish it. If I were to take you with me, it would only be to see you settled in a respectable home, and I would tell your father of your whereabouts. He may insist that I bring you back, and I would have little choice but to do so. Howsoever you believe he has wronged you, he is still your father, and he has that right. I can promise you no more than this, Hunydd."

She bit her lip and nodded her understanding.

Without another word, he took her little sack and she watched as he secured it to the sumpter pony.

"I'll make you a pillion seat so you can ride behind me," he said over his shoulder.

Hunydd grinned. The Dominican had been such a fool. What had he been thinking? A sacrifice in a church—that was not how magic was woven. Not the kind of powerful magic that had brought Thomas to her. No, that required other kinds of sacrifices, more personal sacrifices that had nothing to do with Christians, or with their churches, or their ceremonies.

"Will we be able to gallop again, please?" she asked excitedly. "I liked that."

Thomas laughed. It was a wonderful sound to Hunydd's ears, and she could not keep the foolish grin off her face as he lifted her to the pillion seat and climbed up in front of her. She gripped him around the waist and felt a thrill in her stomach. She had never been to a city like Lincoln. There must be wonderful things to see, and she would be with Thomas. Hunydd squeezed hard, scarce believing her good fortune. She was almost bursting with happiness.

A part of her even regretted having ever poisoned her father, feeding him dose after dose of the poison, small measures that would condemn him to a slow, debilitating death. She had hated him, she supposed. He had ravished her mother, and even if he had not, even if her mother had lied and had given herself to him willingly, he had deserted them both, which to Hunydd's mind was just as bad, maybe even worse. And then he had dragged her from her home to serve her own sister. A sister who lived in luxury while he would not even acknowledge Hunydd to the world, just as much his own flesh and blood as Cecily.

But none of that mattered to her anymore. He had been punished enough, and she would allow him to recover and live out the rest of his life in loneliness with his arrogant daughter. Hunydd had what she wanted.

The horse was moving under them in a steady rolling gait, and Hunydd clung on to Thomas tighter, her stomach trembling.

She did not at all regret killing the vicar. He was a hypocrite, preaching righteousness, punishing others for their sins while his own eyes wandered. Hunydd had not liked the way he touched her, the way his soft hands lingered when she had gone to him for confession. Nor the things he had suggested she ought to do for penance. She had tipped a concoction of her own making into his wine one evening. A heady brew sure to set the old man's pulse racing and speed him on his journey to the next life. Perhaps it had been unnecessary, but at the time she had thought it for the best.

Thomas felt warm and strong, and she felt safe with him. She pressed her cheek against his back. True he had promised her nothing. For the moment his head was still too full of Cecily, but that would soon change. There were many ways to bind a man. Ways her mother had taught her. Old ways. Ways that her people had used before the Church. Ways of which perhaps even Alice did not know and of which she would certainly not approve. The spell Hunydd had wrought with the little wax poppet, now hidden safely away among the clothes in her sack, was but one of them, and she could tell it was working. Otherwise he would not have agreed to take her with him. Not without first speaking to her father, or to her sister.

She snuggled closer against him. He belonged to her now.

"Will you show me the imp?"

Thomas nodded.

It was not an imp. She already knew that. It was the green man. Christians were so silly sometimes. They thought the old beliefs were dead, when instead they were just carried forward in their own symbols, like the Celtic cross that hung around Thomas's neck. Like their Holy Days that just happened to fall on the same days as the ancient festivals. And like the green man, who sat high on the pillar of their cathedral, watching over them in their house of worship, laughing at them while they prayed to their God. Hunydd would be sure to say a prayer in the cathedral as well. But she would pray to her own Gods: to Beltane, to Diana, to Hecate, to Eostre, and to the spirits of her ancestors.

"Shall we gallop soon?"

Thomas laughed and Hunydd felt her stomach tremble again. She was finally doing it. She was leaving to start her own life. For the first time, she was sure that she was truly happy. And she would make Thomas happy as well. She just knew it.

CHAPTER 28

This businesse about these witches troubled all the state of Ireland the more, for that the ladie was supported by certeine of the nobilitie, and lastlie conveied over into England, since which time it could never be understood what became of hir.
—The Lady Alice Kettle,
Holinshed's Chronicle of Ireland (sub anno 1323)

Alice Kyteler stood on the prow of the ship swathed in a dark hooded cloak, watching the Calais harbor slide ever closer. It was a French port, and not ideal, but it was the only destination she could reach in such haste.

A man stepped up beside her. He was tall and powerfully built. Shrewd, black eyes looked out from a handsome face, burnished a deep bronze by the sun of some distant Southern clime. Alice did not turn to him. Instead, she drew the cloak closer against the sea breeze that whipped and flapped the hem around her legs.

"Now you choose to turn up," she said.

The man rested his hands on the rail and looked out over the harbor. "You made quite a mess back there, Alice." His deep voice was heavily accented, as exotic as his complexion. "I thought you were going to be discreetly from now on?"

"It was not my doing this time," she snapped. "They left me no choice. Am I not to defend myself now?"

"Oh, Alice. It never is your doing, is it?" He sighed deeply. "No matter. Another life lies ahead of us now. And I am sure there is more than enough here in France to keep us amused for the time being."

He paused to study her face awhile. "You should be happy, Alice, to finally be free of those men and all their lies and zealous bigotry, and yet I sense that you are not. Are you worried . . . perhaps about your niece?"

"I am."

"You fear some blame will attach to her for what has transpired?"

Alice shook her head. "No, it is not that. The Dominican has suffered a terrible humiliation and no doubt will now slink back from whence he came with his tail tucked firmly between his legs. I do worry that Cecily has inherited my outspokenness and with it my knack for getting into trouble. But it is more than that also . . . I think it entirely possible that she is in love."

"But that is wonderful news, Alice! From what you told me, Thomas Lester is a good man, and love is one of the greatest gifts, is it not?"

"Perhaps. But theirs will not be an easy path. There will be many difficulties for them to overcome, many challenges to their affection for each other, and I see them both being hurt."

The man stroked his finely groomed beard and looked to the horizon, considering her words carefully before responding. He knew by now that when Alice Kyteler foresaw trouble, it was well to take note.

"You may be right, Alice. But when has love ever been easy? You must allow your niece to live her life as she sees fit, and I sense that all will be well in the end. Now, set aside your worries. Let us rather enjoy this moment while we may. We are in France. You are free. And we are together. Is that not enough for now?"

She nodded distractedly, then touched his hand lightly with the tips of her fingers, and they both smiled as they looked out over the beckoning lights of Calais.

ACKNOWLEDGMENTS

I would like to acknowledge the support of my lovely wife, Kathy, and our two children, Graham and Sophie, who have all been kind enough to read or listen to countless drafts and redrafts. It has been a long journey, but I could not have done it without you. And finally, my agent Mitchell Waters, for believing in a writer and turning him into an author.

AUTHOR'S NOTE

Growing up in the small market town of Grantham, I was always fascinated by the historic Vale of Belvoir, situated only a few miles down the road from where I lived. The vale is a beautiful part of England, comprising low-lying pastures, farmlands, and quaint villages, all dominated by Belvoir Castle, sitting up high on its hill, erected on the site of an old Norman stronghold built in the eleventh century by one of William the Conqueror's knights as part of ongoing efforts to pacify the newly conquered kingdom. There is a Bottesford village in the vale, although I have imbued it with a life and characters it most certainly did not have, and at the time it would have been part of the Belvoir estate, ruled over by Baron William de Ross.

Thomas's story is set against the backdrop of the fascinating dynastic struggle that was going on in England during the early fourteenth century. Edward II was not a particularly good king, and for much of his reign was beset by unrest fueled in part by the failure of his Scottish wars and the excesses of his court favorites. Edward survived one rebellion led by his cousin, the Earl of Lancaster, only to then be deposed by his wife, Queen Isabella, and her reputed lover, Sir Roger Mortimer, following which he suffered a brutal death, supposedly involving the use of a red-hot poker.

Queen Isabella's regency did not last long. As it turns out, the two usurpers weren't much better than what had come before, and they were in turn overthrown by Edward's son, King Edward III, who went on to become one of England's most powerful monarchs, fighting a successful war in France and shattering the flower of French nobility at the historic battle of Crecy.

Although this is very much a work of fiction, several of the characters Thomas mentions are based on historical figures: Henry Burghersh was indeed the Bishop of Lincoln; the likely mad John Deydras really did claim to be the true King of England and was promptly hanged for sedition (as was his supposedly diabolical cat); and John of Nottingham was accused of conspiring with twenty-seven of Coventry's leading citizens to assassinate various members of the king's inner circle by magical means.

The king's favorite, Hugh Despenser the younger, appears to have been a particularly despicable individual, rightly earning Cecily's opprobrium. The degree to which he was reviled at the time is probably best understood by the nature of his execution, in which he was publicly flogged, hanged, and then released before full asphyxiation only so that he might be castrated and burned alive. For whatever reason, Queen Isabella particularly hated Despenser and is said to have presided over the entire spectacle, gorging herself on food and wine as she did, fully living up to her nickname as the *She-Wolf of France*.

As for Alice Kyteler, she was real enough, and so notorious did she become that her story warranted a fairly sizeable entry in Holinshed's authoritative sixteenth-century *Chronicles of England, Scotland and Ireland*. For purposes of this story, I have chosen to make Alice somewhat younger than she would have been in real life, but that seemed only fair. After all, any witch worth her salt would surely have been more than capable of casting a good old-fashioned glamor to hide her age, and let us not forget, wicked witch or no, Alice was captivating enough to lead four of Ireland's most prominent men to the altar.

Whatever happened to Alice? To this day nobody knows for sure. Was she truly a witch? Did she really poison her husbands? Or was she just a successful and powerful woman who made enemies? We shall leave that to the historians.

REFERENCES

The quotation at the beginning of this novel is from St. Thomas, Aquinas, The Summa Theologica, Supplement to the Third Part, Question 58, Art. 2, as literally translated by the Fathers of the English Dominican Province, first published in 1911 and 1920 by Burns, Oates and Washbourne Ltd. in London, and then republished by Benziger Bros. in 1947 in the United States.

Portions of the papal bull, Super Illius Specula, quoted in chapters 3 and 14 are from: James J. Walsh, The Supposed Warfare Between Medical Science and Theology, published in the Medical Library and Historical Journal, Vol IV (1906), p.263 at p.281.

The quotations in chapters 20 and 28 are entries from the sixteenth century Holinshed's Chronicle of Ireland as quoted in: Thomas Wright (ed.), A Contemporary Narrative of the Proceedings Against Dame Alice Kyteler, Prosecuted for Sorcery in 1324, printed for the Camden Society, London, 1842-43, p. 45-46.

Quotations from the Bible are taken from the American Standard Version which has passed into public domain and can be found at several places online.